# CHRISTINE HART

# Terra Nova

## The Variant Conspiracy, Book 3

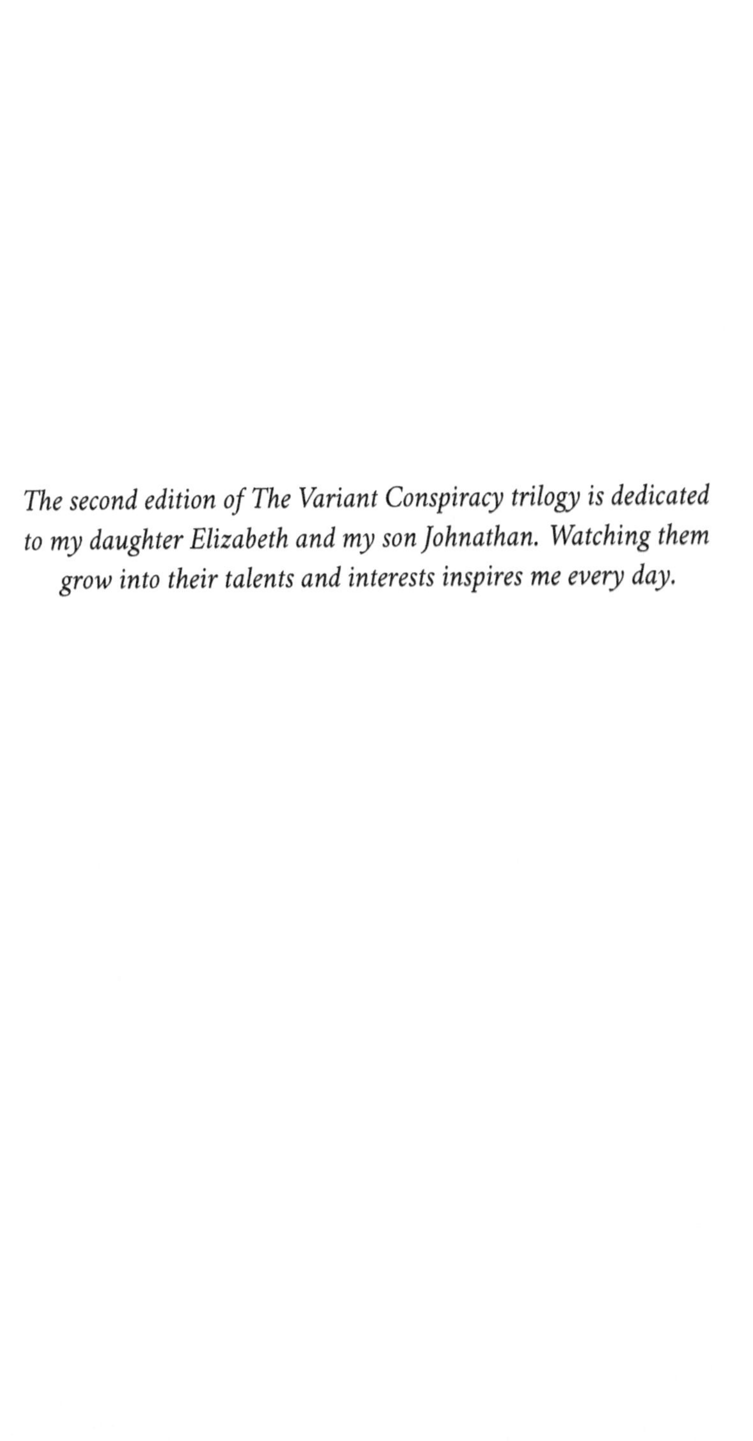

*The second edition of The Variant Conspiracy trilogy is dedicated to my daughter Elizabeth and my son Johnathan. Watching them grow into their talents and interests inspires me every day.*

# Acknowledgments

The Variant Conspiracy trilogy was originally published in 2016 by Soul Mate Publishing. Thank you to my publisher Debby Gilbert and editor Samantha McMahon for helping me bring these books to life.

# Chapter 1

I surveyed the dark London alley, its air heavy with odors of fat and fuel. Go-go boys gyrated in the window of a dance club across the adjacent street. Club music reverberated off the buildings around me while I pulled my boyfriend Jonah through an interspatial portal.

"Welcome to Soho," I said.

Our former co-worker Melissa gave him a half smile.

Jonah rubbed his arctic blue eyes. In the dark alley, his black hair glistened like wet ink. He stood tall beside me, gripping my shoulders protectively as though he didn't trust our surroundings. I still smelled the dust of the Mojave Desert and the soot from the trailer fire on his damp T-shirt.

"Wild. We're really in London." He smiled down at me. "What is Soho?"

"It used to be the red-light district." Melissa unzipped and stepped out of her dusty dirt-biking pants. She discarded them in the back corner of the alley. Her remaining clothes were a simple white waffle shirt and denim shorts. She unraveled her disheveled hair and re-wound her bun carefully. "That's why Evonatura chose it. You can have an interesting cast of characters like variants and all their weird and wonderful talents in this neighborhood without standing out too much."

My friend Faith stepped through the portal and nearly bumped into Jonah. She stumbled forward. Her purple dreadlocks picked up a shaft of electric blue from a black light across the street. Her steel nose stud and eyebrow ring glinted with neon light.

"Yeah, you'll want to move away from the portal until everyone is here." Melissa waved us away from the floating silver oval. "I hope they don't dawdle. It gives me a headache keeping a gateway open for too long."

I guided Jonah to the graffiti-coated brick wall on the other side of the alley. Faith dusted off her charred cargo pants and grimy black tank top as she followed us. My twin brother Ilya resembled a discarded rag doll in his ripped jeans and tangled mop of cinnamon hair as he stepped through the portal. Next came Jonah's best friend Cole and then our resident bodyguard Josh. Those two carried themselves like weathered soldiers, both muscular, dirty, and wearing week-old beard stubble.

"So where exactly do we go from here?" said Jonah.

Melissa closed her portal and then stretched her arms and neck. "We don't want to get too close to Evonatura right now. We should lay low until we can figure out the best plan of attack."

"We'll need rooms. Anything rent by the hour around here?" said Faith.

"What did you have in mind?" Ilya playfully elbowed his

girlfriend.

"Be serious," Faith answered with a frown.

"I'm pretty sure there's a place around the corner above a pub that should work. It's not rent by the hour, but it's seedy enough that Ivan wouldn't go near it," said Melissa.

"How well do you know the neighborhood?" I asked.

"Think of it this way. When *I* was in charge of Ivan's travel arrangements, *I* frequently scouted locations in person," said Melissa.

It suddenly occurred to me how and why Melissa had been a better assistant to Ivan than I ever could have been. I stared back at her as I tried to form the right response.

Faith elbowed past Melissa and me, making her way to the street. "Speaking of you working for Ivan, how do we know you're not still on the payroll? How do we know we can trust you?"

"Babe, when I read her mind back in the desert, I got enough to know she's on our side." Ilya calmed Faith by putting his hand on her arm.

"Wait, I'll go first just in case. We don't know where Ivan and Tatiana are. Or Ralph and Adelaide for that matter." Josh jogged forward, his vest flapping against his chest. His mention of my estranged father and aunt only sparked an image of my sister, brainwashed and following them into god-knows-what.

Josh glanced up and down the street. He nodded for us to join him. The nightlife bopped on the busy club and pub-filled road. Nobody matched the exotic flair of the window dancers, but most had dressed to impress while we resembled failed wilderness trekkers. The pedestrian traffic felt like a festival; a summer weekend in the city at a bare minimum.

And then I realized that I no longer knew the night of the week. I pulled my phone out of my bag and checked, 10:16 PM on Thursday, September third. My phone had already picked up local time. I caught my reflection in a dark shop window. Soot and dust covered me like everyone else. Since I was much shorter than my companions, I looked exceptionally waif-like in my fitted three-quarter shirt, sporting wild hair in desperate need of a brush.

We followed Melissa to a façade coated in flat black paint. Round red light bulbs spelled the word, Incinerator above the door. Melissa passed the bouncer and stopped at a glass-shielded wicket below a sign for Berwick Hostel. The wicket was set inside a stairwell beside the bar's entrance. She pulled a wallet out of her shoulder bag.

"Four double rooms please," said Melissa.

"How do you figure four?" said Josh, startling Melissa.

"Ilya and Faith, Irina and Jonah, you and Cole, and another for me," she said as though the assignments were obvious.

"You're not bunking on your own. Not until I can vouch for you myself. For all I know you can fool mind-readers and psychics." Josh stood the tallest among us by far. His spiky hair was full of debris. His bare arms shone with sweat under his military vest and cutoff shirt.

"I thought we covered this already. Either way, I'm not shacking up with some guy I hardly know. These are tiny rooms," said Melissa flatly.

"You know us. Why don't you humor Josh for one night? We'll be on our best behavior if you stay with us. I'll even take the floor." Cole's tanned skin and coffee-brown eyes warmed his square jaw. In the light from the stairwell, I could see dirt and charred fragments in his sandy hair.

"He takes the floor." Melissa pointed at Josh.

"Fine," said Josh.

"I've got five singles and one double, love. Take your pick," said the round bald man behind the glass.

"Two singles and one double then." Melissa passed the man a credit card.

"That'll be seventy-five quid for the double and fifty each for the singles. Two pounds fifty per towel,"

"Good thing we are bunking together. How much is that in dollars?" said Cole.

"Way too much for this place," said Faith.

"It's over three hundred dollars!" Josh tapped on his phone.

"Why are towels extra?" said Jonah.

"Can't you do better since we're paying together, like a group rate or something?" said Melissa.

"Where do you think this is? That's the last-minute price. Take it or leave it. I'll fill up before the night's out with our without your lot," said the man.

"I guess you win. Six towels too please," said Melissa.

"You're on the tenth and twelfth floors. Rooms ten-o-nine, ten-o-eight and twelve-ten. Loo's at the end of the hall on both." He passed a trio of grungy tags with patina-coated keys to Melissa.

We followed her up the narrow stairwell that allowed single-file movement with little elbow room. The stairs went upward in a square spiral for several stories. The first door we passed was an exit for the third floor. My legs ached and my lungs burned by the time we reached the tenth where Melissa passed the keys to Faith and me.

"I don't know about you guys, but I'm going to wash my hair and hit this club for a few drinks. We just jumped ahead seven hours and I need a little sedative to help me get some sleep," said Melissa.

"Works for me." Faith pushed open the fire door to the main hallway.

"Yeah, what the hell? It's not like we go out very often," said Ilya.

"See you downstairs then." Melissa continued up the stairs. Josh and Cole kept walking behind her. I could have sworn I saw Josh eyeing Melissa's shorts.

"We're not supposed to be partying. We're supposed to …" I said, pausing to think of the right way to phrase 'save the world' without sounding melodramatic.

"Get the bad guys?" Faith arched her eyebrows. We arrived at rooms 1008 and 1009.

"Save the human race?" said Ilya.

"Well, yes," I said.

"Nevermind stoic inclinations. Shouldn't we worry about being seen?" In the dim hallway, Jonah's eyes glowed with a neon-like intensity.

"Depends on how weird this neighborhood is," said Ilya.

"Let's hope that London has a high variant population. And with Evonatura a few blocks over, we might even see some tonight." Jonah took the room key from my hand and unlocked our door.

"Will they know who – or what – we are if they notice us?" I said to Ilya and Faith. Ilya spoke, but I didn't hear him.

Instead, my first night at The Looking Glass in Victoria popped into my mind. Rubin had taken me to meet Jonah and Cole. Casey had been guarding the door. The day before, I had seen Cole and Casey fighting in the street. It had been almost six months ago, but it felt like the distant past.

"Hey, Irina, are you going first in the shower or am I?" Faith waved her hand in front of my face. I couldn't break my train of thought to answer her. I kept puzzling over why the image of Casey guarding a club door was so prominent.

"We don't need to worry about being seen downstairs. I doubt Ivan will let his people out to party, in Soho or anywhere else. He'll have everyone with him in lockdown if I know anything about how his mind works," said Ilya.

"If we do see any variants, Ilya can listen in and see if any of them work for Evonatura or even know Ivan. And since you're in la-la land, I'm getting the first shower," said Faith.

It reassured me that we would be on guard, possibly gathering useful information. The last time I'd been in a club with Jonah, I'd made an ass out of myself. Tonight promised a different experience.

My turn in the shower came quickly even though I'd waited until last. And then I learned why everyone else had only taken a few minutes each. The entire bathroom had not been cleaned in a very long time. The shower stall smelled of mildew and the water wouldn't go above lukewarm with hot turned on full.

I cursed the indifferent clerk until I thought about warming up with a cocktail. And after that, Jonah. I studied the hostel's scratched-up bathroom mirror and smiled on my way out the door.

The tiny closet-sized hostel room felt even smaller with Jonah and me inside it. He sat on the edge of the bed in the corner of the room while I pulled on a white blouse usually reserved for work. It wasn't something I'd wear to a club, but I had limited options in my old canvas backpack. With my black pants, the outfit gave me an edgy femininity.

I brushed my towel-dried, dye-darkened hair and slipped a hoop earring into each ear. I drew dark lines along my eyelashes and dusted on my favorite metallic rust eyeshadow. I finished with pink lip gloss and stepped back to let Jonah evaluate the results. He grinned at me and I felt pretty. I wanted the moment to last forever.

Jonah looked downright dapper with his gelled black wavy hair, his preppy baby blue collared shirt, and dark blue denim pants. I suppressed the urge to kiss him. If I touched him, I knew we would never get back out of our tiny room.

The bouncer at the Incinerator looked nothing like Casey. Instead, he was a short, bony man with thinning gray hair and a baggy black leather coat. He sneered at us as he stepped aside to let us enter.

Faith wore a fitted v-neck T-shirt with her old roller derby team's logo on the front. With her camouflage print pants, she parodied an off-duty soldier. Like Cole, Faith was muscular and built for battle. The T-shirt showed it off tonight more than usual.

Ilya was slender like me. He blended into the walls with his shaggy hair and faded black clothes.

Only Jonah truly stood out. I briefly considered asking him to go back upstairs and find something more fitting for a gothic club, but combined with his eyes, the blue-on-blue effect was too attractive to undo.

Inside the club, an open-air courtyard-style structure contained three levels of writhing bodies. The scene emulated a medieval painting depicting the evils of excess. Beautiful gothic women swayed disdainfully alongside unimpressed black-clad men. Green and purple lights flashed overhead. A UV black light gave bits of white and light fabric an unmistakable bright icy glow. Dry ice fog billowed through the lower level.

"Let's go check out the basement. That'll be a better place to lay low," said Jonah.

"I'll do a pass through the upstairs and see if Cole, Josh, and Melissa are here yet. It'll give me a chance to scan for variants too," said Ilya.

"Then I guess I'll get the drinks." Faith pulled a large flat hair elastic from her pocket and tied back her long dreads. Faith was ready to rumble. I felt grateful she and Cole were on our side.

Jonah and I descended the open-frame wrought iron stairwell. I felt like a lamb among wolves as I held Jonah's hand, following him down the metal spiral.

We reached the floor and encountered a room shrouded by the artificial dusty mist I'd seen drifting through the air from above.

"We won't find them in this," I said.

Jonah turned to the back wall stairwell and I followed him.

"Then they won't see us either," Jonah pulled me towards him and spun me around so my back faced the wall.

He leaned in and kissed me softly, at first. I kissed back and he went deeper, as he ran his hand up the side of my body, behind me, and down to my rear. He grabbed it firmly and pulled my pelvis into his. I stretched up so he could stand straight. I returned his gesture and slipped my hands into his back pockets.

"Dude, you can't do that to my sister when I'm nearby. I can hear her brain. It's NOT cool," said Ilya, suddenly next to us.

"Get lost. Go find Faith," I said.

"You were the one who wanted to stay on-mission tonight,"

said Ilya.

"Did you find Cole and the others?" Jonah appeared completely unruffled despite our brief moment.

"No, they haven't come down yet, but I did find a handful of variants. They're either Evonatura employees or some other sort of professionals. No thoughts about food or bathing or where to sleep. If London has street variants, they're not here," said Ilya.

"What kind of variations? Or could you tell?" I asked.

"I know a variant mind when I hear one because we all think about hiding or blending. It's not an exact science, but sometimes I do hear a thought related to a variation. There's a guy upstairs who will shatter glass and eardrums if he speaks out loud. He's considering having his vocal cords cut for good. He already knows sign language and is passing himself off as a mute," said Ilya.

"That's awful. Does he hurt variants too?" I asked.

"Hard to say without asking him," said Ilya.

"He's the sort of variant that would interest Ivan. If he can't function around regular humans, he'd be easy to sell on a post-Compendium world," said Jonah.

"Should we talk to him? We could use everyone we can get." I blinked expectantly at my boyfriend and then my brother.

"I don't think we should risk it. What if he already works for our father? We'd give ourselves up and have to run again with no fresh leads," said Ilya.

Faith returned with four glowing green drinks in a cup holder tray. Clear plastic cups, lids, and straws let the liquid inside glow through. It smacked of something that would spawn ninja turtles. "These are the Incinerator's toxic spills. They're just vodka and lemon-lime soda with something that glows. The bartender said it's non-toxic, kinda like glow stick stuff, but not. Some shit that glows, but you can still drink."

Jonah reluctantly took a plastic cup. "Are you sure we *should* drink it?"

"It's not going to kill us. No more so than the alcohol." Ilya picked up a cup and took a long generous pull on his straw.

I took an experimental sip. It tasted like vodka and soda. There was a mildly synthetic aftertaste. I took another, much larger sip. Aha – the warmth I'd been craving since my shower. I might stand a chance of sleeping tonight after all.

Jonah took a slurp on his straw, pausing to let the liquid do its work. He leered at me with a devilish grin and grabbed my hand, pulling me off to the dance floor. His touch radiated energy into me, right through my skin waking up every cell in my body.

He leaned down and kissed me, running his hands through my hair. His powerful grip felt restrained like his mind fought to control his body. The intensity surpassed our first night together. After we had spent so long hobbled by his unstable mutation, first hurting me and then nearly killing him, we were both finally stronger than ever.

"I can't help myself. I *need* to touch you. I don't ever want to let you go. We're going to make up for some lost time tonight." His lips brushed my ear as he spoke. His fingers traced the line of my neck, sending shivers down my spine. So much for sleep!

<h1 style="text-align:center">Chapter 2</h1>

We danced and drank in the basement of the Incinerator until my mouth hurt from smiling. Even Melissa had fun. She'd changed into an uncharacteristic black dress. I couldn't imagine where she'd gotten it. Josh and Cole were back to their regular athletic and skater selves respectively. We didn't fit together visually, but our emotional bonds were now as palpable as steel cable. I briefly forgot that we weren't just a pack of twenty-somethings in a club blowing off steam.

Cole crushed a metal napkin dispenser against Josh's chest and they roared with laughter. Faith juggled a single flame between three candles on three sconces overhead. Jonah turned our drinks into whirlpools. I lifted each friend a few inches off the ground as they danced. Nobody paid attention to us, but Ilya threw up a curtain of fog blending in with the dry ice and enclosing our corner just in case.

I felt sleepy when Jonah took my hand and waved goodbye to our friends. A nervous giddiness mingled with my fatigue.

Then I pictured taking Jonah home to meet my family and the thought made me sad. He would have to settle for meeting Gemma – if we found her. I felt worse still. Tears leaked from my eyes as I climbed the stairs behind Jonah. I wiped my eyes carefully before we reached the tenth floor.

Jonah unlocked our room and gestured for me to go in first. He sat on our bed and motioned for me to do the same. "What's wrong? You're upset."

"I was thinking about you meeting my parents. If I'd been a normal girl, then Rubin wouldn't have murdered them. You'd just come over one day and my mom would make dinner. They wouldn't impress you, but you'd be *their* idea of a great catch. You'd be all handsome, wearing a polo shirt and telling Darryl about your science degree. Gemma wouldn't be the center of attention for once." I blew out a sigh that I hadn't noticed I was holding.

"I'm sorry your parents were taken from you. When this is all over, we'll meet my cold, clinical doctor parents and you'll see the whole family meet-and-greet is overrated," said Jonah, holding my hand.

"We have to get Gemma back before Ivan finds someone else to tamper with her memory or worse. I know what he's capable of and he has my sister. I can't shake the feeling that something awful is going to happen to her." Desperation seized my heart and I felt my lungs constricting.

"We'll get her back. Don't forget that together, our little crew is a force of nature. We were goofing off tonight, but we're *all* at peak strength now."

"All of us?" I asked with wide eyes.

"I took my first maintenance shot while you were in the shower. The volume of serum I have will last for a month.

We'll get to Ivan within a week, two tops. And - if this course of treatment doesn't reverse my symptoms - I'll get back to a lab and perfect the synthesis of more serum. Ilya can help me find a mass spectrometer – assuming we'll need to break in somewhere to use one. From there, I'll take it on my own. You don't need to worry about me ever again." Jonah leaned over and kissed me.

I kissed him back softly. I wanted to savor him this time before that biological energy returned and blotted out my thoughts. We had a whole night alone together and didn't know when it would happen again.

I stopped to take off my shirt and Jonah unbuttoned his, never taking his eyes off me. His smooth white chest had a sprinkling of fine black hair. I hadn't looked closely before now. I ran my hand across his pecs feeling the contrast of taut muscles, soft skin, and smooth wiry hair.

"Not as nice as yours, is it?" said Jonah with a wry smile.

"Just different," I smiled back at him.

Jonah reached behind my back and unhooked my bra with a snap. He kissed me again before I could ask how many bras he'd unhooked before he learned to do it with a quick flick. That primal power he infused me with in the club returned with a vengeance and I let go of everything.

* * *

Breakfast was more like brunch by the time we got organized the next morning. Melissa stopped at the Berwick Hostel's office to book our rooms for another night and got directions to a nearby pub called The Lazy Toad.

My stomach had not thanked me for the four over-priced

Toxic Spills I'd consumed. Our hostel's room had two teabags, a teapot, and a hotplate. We hadn't bothered to try brewing a pot.

The Lazy Toad had the accessories and smells I'd expected from a British pub. A red phone booth occupied the far corner. Old deep frying permeated the air. The walls were a warm cream color, covered in pastoral paintings and portraits of contemporary royalty including Princess Diana and Queen Elizabeth II. It occurred to me that the owners catered to tourists more than locals. Did British people crave images of the countryside and pseudo-stars from their aristocracy? I figured it was still a mixed bag or the local tabloids would be out of business.

Customers occupied most of the tables. A harried young woman cleared and wiped down a large booth for us. It took nearly half an hour, but she eventually served us the breakfast special, eggs over-easy, back bacon, sausage, beans in red sauce, and fried tomatoes. She left two bottles on the table, malt vinegar and something she called brown sauce.

"Now that we're all good and hung over, who wants to plan a trip to Evonatura?" said Josh as we ate slowly.

"They have a regular alarm system, I know that much. Assume this office is operating as normal. Their CEO Claude Mueller is a complete hard-ass in his own right. He's unlikely to shut down or even close temporarily on Ivan or Tatiana's say-so," said Melissa.

Josh and Cole frowned as they ate. Jonah and I had stopped to listen, while Faith seemed completely content to savor her meal.

Ilya contemplated the scenario pensively. "I can listen in from a distance. And we can watch who comes and goes. We'll establish who's working there and when we're ready, we can corner them one by one on the street outside."

"Corner them and what?" I poked at my cold leftover beans.

"Incapacitate them." Cole nodded at Josh who appeared to agree.

"Exactly how do we do that?" I said.

"How far are you prepared to go?" Melissa regarded Josh and Cole with a look that implied violence was required. "I mean, we. How far are *we* prepared to go? Public exposure? Or something more permanent?"

"We're trying to disrupt their operations, exposing them if necessary." Jonah's tone suggested caution.

"We tried exposing them the 'right' way and we failed miserably, getting a journalist killed. Maybe coming out is inevitable for variants," said Ilya flatly. He gave Faith a 'Why not?' expression. Faith's frown reassured me.

"It's not fair to make that decision for every variant on the planet. We could call the local cops and report Evonatura for creating a dangerous illegal substance. If we can get them shut down, we might buy some time. We can pool our photos, knowledge, and evidence. We'll start tweeting it or publishing it ourselves somehow," I said.

"What hard evidence do we have that a plot called *The Compendium Transmuto* is being carried out? Nothing that would inspire the police or government to act quickly. Nothing that would go viral on any form of social media. Our documents read like conspiracy theories. All we can do is prove that mutants from comic books are real. Which could distract the world from the existential threat some of us pose. You might find it necessary to take harsher measures than a little embarrassing publicity. Bloodier measures. Convincing people will take time, time we don't have. Even so, if everyone knew about us and accepted us, that knowledge and resulting warm fuzzies won't immunize them to Terra Nova." Melissa's intense expression unnerved me.

The image of the coyote's gruesome death in the Mojave leaped straight into my mind's eye. I shuddered. I wondered how long Melissa had wanted to get away from Ivan. Either way, she was ready to go to war now.

"So, you want us to start assassinating people?" Faith made a stabbing gesture with her fork.

"I'm saying it might be necessary. Our first goal is to get Terra Nova out of Ivan's hands, for good. But after that, if we don't have all the information, we can't be confident we're stopping everything." Melissa glanced at each of us earnestly.

"We've talked about using force before, but in self-defense. Not like a preventative measure," said Jonah.

I believed Melissa and her words sank to the bottom of my stomach like a stone. Jonah's dejected expression matched mine.

"Isn't that what *The Compendium* is supposed to cover? We'll use it to make a checklist. We go one by one. Bam. Bam." Cole pounded his solid left palm with a meaty right fist.

Ilya ran a hand through his hair to steady himself. "She's worried that any or all of the companies and people involved have projects on the side, initiatives inspired by *The Compendium*, but not tracked by it. Even a little homemade contagion or mutant pet is a problem." Ilya looked at Melissa, still reading her mind.

"True, but we're talking about catastrophes here. I say we comb through *The Compendium* and come up with a list of threats. From there, we can categorize the level of severity, location, and strategies for stopping each," said Cole.

I saw the wheels of his analytical mind turning behind his eyes. He hadn't humanized the problem yet.

"That's all fine and good, but while you're creating a spreadsheet and an action plan, Ivan will head off to wherever the hell he plans to release Terra Nova. He's scrapped his original timeline now that he knows we're trying to stop him." Melissa leaned forward as her voice gained volume.

"We all agree Terra Nova is our first target, right? The single Compendium project that can kickstart a human extinction," I said.

Everyone nodded.

"All right," I said. "We can morally take whatever measures are needed to put a stop to it, a certain and final stop. We'll have to see how things unfold and respond accordingly."

Jonah fixated on the wall ahead with grim determination. "It does simplify things for now. We can move on to a more systematic approach to *The Compendium* after we eliminate Terra Nova."

I pored over the table, pausing at each pair of eyes. "Don't forget about my sister. We need her back. That's not optional."

"Of course not," said Jonah.

"How brainwashed is Gemma? On a scale of zero to ten, zero being not at all and ten being irreversible," I asked Melissa. I hoped like hell she was going to throw me a bone and say something mildly comforting.

"I can't know what she's thinking. She might just be playing along with them. But maybe she drank the Kool-Aid," said Melissa, shaking her head.

"Make an educated guess," I said sternly.

"She seems dedicated. I'd say seven, maybe eight." Melissa's features conveyed sympathy, but I still felt a swell of anger in my heart.

Faith leaned back with her hands behind her head. "Shit, that's not good. Should we risk adding this girl to our list if she'll fight us?"

"We'll give her the benefit of the doubt." Cole glared at his insensitive sister.

"Are we ready to go to Evonatura now?" Josh checked something in his vest.

I realized with sudden panic that Josh still had his gun. Before I said anything, Ilya nudged me.

"I think I can manage a little camouflage once I get the rest of this food into me," said Ilya.

We finished our breakfast quickly and Cole paid for everyone. I wondered briefly what his credit card balance had climbed to in the past few weeks. How much cash did we have collectively? We'd have to find out soon.

Ilya led us to an alley down the street from The Lazy Toad. It was a grimy alley much like where we'd arrived. The smell threatened to destabilize my breakfast.

"Okay folks, hang on to your hats." Ilya closed his eyes. I waited for a tingling sensation, but nothing came. Slowly my friends became blurry and I blinked my eyes again and again. The air around me felt thick, like a familiar moist fog. I blinked and blinked until I stared at six strangers.

A businessman with cropped blond hair, wearing an unremarkable charcoal suit, stood where Jonah had. In Cole's place was a similar young businessman in a gray suit and tie, bulky like Cole, with similar dark brown eyes. The dark slicked back hair shone in sharp contrast to his regular ultra-short cut.

Faith had become a clean-cut teenager in a school uniform. Only the girl's dreadlocks, now jet black, hinted at her real identity.

Josh was an older man in heavy canvas pants and a plain T-shirt. His tool belt suggested trades of some sort.

Melissa was a young mom. She had brown hair in a ponytail and wore a pink jogging suit. Her face was bare of makeup.

Ilya himself had transformed into a street punk, a decades-old stereotype of what you might expect to see in a rough London neighborhood.

I walked around the corner to the glass window of a laundromat to see my reflection. I had messy blonde hair and a stretchy sweater with rips throughout over skin-tight faded blue jeans. It wasn't my style, but the girl in the window looked interesting.

"When we get there, we'll have to split up to avoid drawing suspicion." Ilya stepped to the window beside me. His voice hadn't changed and the effect was unnerving.

Our group all looked at our reflections. We stood for a long moment gawking at our new selves.

"Irina, you stay with me. Jonah and Cole can stick together, like businessmen on a break. Then maybe Melissa and Josh as a couple with Faith on her own, like she's waiting for a parent to pick her up. Remember guys, we're not a group and we don't know each other. You're playing a character, someone who happens to be near this office," said Ilya.

"Follow me," said Melissa.

# Chapter 3

Evonatura's office turned out to be a trendy narrow building made of clean brown brick. I'd expected a slice of Frankenstein's castle, but this building looked like a townhouse brochure.

We followed Melissa past the entrance. Ilya pulled me into an alcove two doors down and gestured at everyone else to keep moving.

"So what do we do now?" I asked Ilya.

His punk disguise frowned at me with an unsettling intensity. "Pretend you're trying to find something in your bag. We'll look natural while stopped and I can listen to the building. It's that or start making out," Ilya teased.

"Gross. That's not even funny."

"Yes it is. Learn to handle a joke."

"I'm telling Faith you said it."

"Go for it. Because she's never shot a messenger," said Ilya. I wondered why he was acting like a jerk. I decided it had to be stress, and maybe guilt.

"There's only so long I can keep digging through my bag," I said as a young hipster couple walked past us.

"Shhhhh. More digging, less talking. Stop worrying about me. It's distracting."

Jonah and Cole appeared next to a phone repair shop across the street. Their young business personas blended right in as they waited in front of the cement wall, alternating between chatting and tapping on phones.

Faith had taken a post at a bus stop. Melissa and Josh were nowhere in sight, but I hoped they had good views of Evonatura.

I glanced up from my bag as Rose and Sage walked past our alcove wearing full-length beige trench coats. I gasped and their heads snapped in my direction in unison. They peeked at Ilya and me only for a second, not breaking stride as they did so. Our disguises did their jobs.

The harpy twins were as striking as ever. They had brushed and ironed their long platinum hair. The pair looked like incognito brides who hadn't seen the sun in years. Nobody in Soho seemed to mind, so Evonatura's CEO had been right about the neighborhood. Not that I'd doubted a peer of Ivan's.

My pulse raced as Casey lumbered behind them moments later. I had gained control of myself and didn't gasp. I only stole one quick glimpse of him, flicking my gaze up from my bag as I intently stirred its contents.

I waited several minutes before I dared to speak. "Have you heard anyone else we know in the building?"

"I think Gemma is there, but so are our father and Aunt Tat."

"You can't read Ivan, but what about Tatiana? Now that she's a variant," I said as quietly as possible.

"Aunt Tat is different, wilder, but I can still hear her in words. She's angry that Evonatura hasn't torn down this office. She thinks they're ready to launch Terra Nova and the rest of *The Compendium*. They're pretty sure Melissa came to us. Rose and Sage are ready to rip Melissa in half if they find her." Ilya's punk persona concentrated on the wall next to him.

"What about the Evonatura staff? How many are there?" I leaned towards my brother, barely breathing.

"Casey has a counterpart. His name is Gregory. I can't quite make out his variation. I think he's a shifter of some sort. Maybe he has an exoskeleton like Josh. He keeps visualizing his skin transforming to brick." Ilya squinted as he listened harder.

"There has to be more. Are there office workers?" I saw a brief flash of a girl like me, answering a phone, not remotely aware of the malice all around her. I had come to know the difference between a vision and my imagination. It was only speculation, but it frightened me all the same.

"I don't think Claude is there yet. They're waiting for him. Two men are thinking about the rabbits they've been testing. They've been recording how long it takes animal after animal to die from Terra Nova. They think it's too fast for the contagion to spread at maximum velocity. They cremate the animals afterward for safety. When they're done with the rabbits, they're moving on to some stray dogs Casey grabbed off the street. Every other Evonatura project is on hold until Terra Nova is perfected."

"That's horrible! Those poor animals. If I had any doubts about violence on these assholes, it's gone now."

"Yes, it's awful but stay focused," Ilya said. "We can't run right in there and start yelling and tearing the place to pieces."

"Wait a second." My voice rose. "If they're still testing the virus, they're not ready to release it right now."

Ilya nodded. "Correct. Now, shhh. I need to concentrate."

I took a deep breath and let it out slowly while I waited, feeling helpless and useless as Ilya listened to the air.

"There's also a young girl, very young, like seven or eight years old. She can transform organic matter into crystals. Aunt Tat cultivated some vines for the girl to practice on one leaf at a time. They might let her go home, but they might keep her. Aunt Tat isn't sure yet."

Despite his artificially rough exterior, I could see that everything my brother heard bothered him. My stomach turned over too. "Are there other tenants in the building? Something we could use as a way in? Maybe we could save the girl."

"Wait. Aunt Tat just took a call. Claude isn't coming in today! Shit, she's furious! They're getting ready to leave. At least she's taking that girl home now. Let's get out of here before they walk past us. I'm not taking any chances that Ivan will recognize us. For all we know, he can smell us."

I followed my brother back the way we had come. It occurred to me that the moment before was the first time Ilya had called our father by his name, completing the detachment of their relationship. I shot an urgent glare at Jonah and Cole, beckoning to them subtly, yet still noticeable from across the street. Faith saw me instantly and rose to follow.

"Don't worry about Josh and Melissa. They're right behind us. Keep staring ahead. You're only with me. We'll regroup at the hostel."

We were a group again as we marched up the Berwick Hostel stairs. I glimpsed behind me and saw my friends back to normal since Ilya had lifted their disguises.

"Josh, Cole, Melissa, can we use your room? It's the only one that isn't a closet," said Ilya.

I pictured getting Jonah back to our closet-sized room and a smile crossed my lips. I forced it away. We all had to focus.

"Of course. What did you find out?" Cole's tense form emitted a hunger for action.

"I think I know how to get us in," said Ilya after we had filed into the small double bedroom.

"What do we need to do?" said Faith.

"My idea could work as early as tomorrow if you guys can help me find the missing pieces of the puzzle," said Ilya.

"What's your plan?" said Cole.

"If we can capture Rose and Sage, I can send in Melissa and Irina disguised as the harpy twins, provided they don't have to take off their coats. I don't think I've ever studied those wings enough to make convincing copies. And they damn sure wouldn't actually fly." Ilya sounded disappointed in the limitations of his illusory abilities. He tapped his puckered mouth, deep in thought.

"How the hell are we supposed to grab the harpy sisters?" Faith demanded, glaring impatiently at her boyfriend.

"I told you there was a missing piece," said Ilya.

"It's too bad that Ralph is gone. One bite each is all it would take," said Jonah.

I shook my head. If he'd personally seen Ralph and Adelaide meeting with that monstrous thug Thorn, forming an alliance that got innocent students killed, he wouldn't want Ralph back.

"That reminds me, I heard no sign of Adelaide or Ralph at Evonatura," said Ilya.

"We should assume they're in the city and still working for *The Compendium*." Cole drove his thumb into his other palm and alternated occasionally, as though the muscles in his hands needed preparation.

"Agreed, but all we can do is keep our eyes and ears – and whatever else – on alert. For the harpy twins, I think we should try something a bit more traditional. If we steal a tranquilizer gun from whatever animal control they have here in London, all we need to do is follow the girls home. We can knock them out and bind them. After that, it's straightforward. Melissa and Irina sneak into Evonatura the next day and destroy the Terra Nova experiments. They might find Gemma too and convince her to leave with them." Josh's mention of stealing and using a tranquilizer gun sparked a wave of nervous energy. But the prospect of getting Gemma back motivated me.

"We need a plan that includes stealing every last vial of Terra Nova. We need to be sure that every sample created is destroyed. And that every scrap of data they have is wiped out," said Jonah. He watched Josh and Cole with a steady eye.

"Then Melissa and I take the tranquilizer gun with us. We hit everyone we see. We take everything we can. And if we can't talk my sister into coming with us, we'll dart her and pack her on our backs." I sat a little straighter.

Jonah put his hand on my shoulder. "You won't be fast enough. You'll need more than just the two of you. Signal me when you're ready and I'll come in."

"No, it should be me and Cole," said Josh.

"Someone needs to help me go over all this Compendium stuff in the netbook. It's loaded with docs and data, right?" Faith nodded her dreads at the innocuous black plastic case on the tiny dresser.

"There's more stuff in there than I know. And you'll have to crack it. The folders were password protected when I had access to the network." Melissa crossed her arms.

"This plan needs work, guys," Josh said urgently. "We don't know who will be where. There are some dangerous people in there. Strategy and assault tactics are my business. It's why you came to me in the first place."

Faith glared at Josh, her fists balled at her sides. "So you're thinking of stealing some surveillance tech too? Won't it take for-ev-er to create a picture of *exactly* how things are laid out inside?"

"That's not what I'm saying. If we had the time, I'd love to get the layout before we enter. But I'm thinking of getting Ilya and Irina to interrogate Rose and Sage. They'll give up what they know whether they like it or not. And it'll give Irina and Melissa a chance to familiarize themselves with the girls they need to impersonate," said Josh, satisfied his expertise had won.

"Couldn't we just get Jonah to cook up some knockout gas and take them all out that way?" Faith relaxed again, leaning back on the dresser.

"Even if I could make something like that, it's hard to get the dosage right for variants. Most formulas have humans in mind and most variants are more robust. For Rose and Sage, a tranquilizer dart is probably still a better plan." Jonah cast Josh a gaze of confident support.

"It's settled then. We'll tranquilize Rose and Sage, mine them for info, and then disguise Irina and Melissa. It's not my best work, but it'll have to do." Josh squeezed his fists, ready to act.

Faith's research quickly uncovered that London required very little wild animal control and that aggressive wildlife attacks were rare in the United Kingdom. The London Zoo, on the other hand, possessed some large and dangerous animals, therefore making the likelihood of tranquilizer guns and darts a possibility.

While Melissa and Faith stayed behind to work on cracking and reviewing our precious Compendium files, the rest of us headed downstairs. I asked the apathetic plum-haired employee of the Berwick Hostel how to get to the London Zoo.

"That's in Regent's Park. Got to take the Tube." The woman furnished us with a pamphlet on the London Underground and a map of Regent's Park before she resumed her disinterested assessment of her newspaper.

Josh and Cole took turns examining the snarl of rainbow pipes on the London Underground route map. Back home, we'd only had to contend with Vancouver's three train lines which barely intersected. Anxiety bubbled in my stomach as the guys argued about where to go from our current location. Ilya busied himself by restoring our disguises.

Cole concluded we needed to take the Bakerloo Line from a station a few blocks away. It would be one stop on the train, but then a long walk on foot.

The station on Oxford Street was easy to spot amid the throngs shuffling through the streets. A large blue sign with Oxford Circus Station crowned a stairwell that plunged under the pavement. I had always pictured my first subterranean train ride taking place in New York, but I had also watched too much television as a child. We fell in with the stream of human traffic filing down to the Underground.

We plugged some change into the turnstiles and pushed into the barriers. When we reached the platform, I finally understood why people casually referred to the Underground as the Tube. We were in a cylindrical cavity filled with curved ad posters fitted to the concave stone walls.

I had time to read ads for a European airline, a local shoe store, and a new nature show on the BBC before a sleek white train with red doors and blue trim slid onto the track in front of us.

"Mind the gap. Mind the gap," said a melodic British woman's voice as we boarded a car.

The train rocketed forward and click-clacked along the tracks for several minutes until our announcer said, "Next stop, Regent's Park."

I stole a glance at the dark glass across from where we sat. My reflection of messy blonde hair and that baggy sweater unsettled me. I did not look like the sort of person who would discreetly steal a gun, even a mere dart gun. *If I looked the part, wouldn't that end badly?* I shrugged. My regular reflection wouldn't have inspired my confidence either.

The train slowed to a stop and released us along with a small surge of other people. We went with the flow of bodies up the stairs and out onto the street where we came face to face with trees bursting out over a cement wall.

I placed my hand on the back of a metal bench around the corner from the Tube exit. London disappeared. I stood in a modern white and steel apartment with Tatiana and Ivan.

"I don't want to be in this city one day longer than necessary!" Tatiana's green-tinged skin and hair stood out against the stark décor.

Ivan turned from the bar with a glass of gold liquid in his

hand. "At the rate this hotel charges, I can't agree more." He swirled the drink and took a sip. His face had completely healed, back to his normally pale and ginger complexion.

"I don't give a shit about human money! That's the whole fucking point! Let's rid ourselves of this circus!" Tatiana waved around the room as though it represented the world.

"How about we save the tirade for another day." Ivan eyed the main door and pointed. On cue, Gemma entered the room, smiling. Her bright green eyes and full lips were pretty as ever. Her long sandy hair was tied back behind her neck, simple but elegant.

A jolt from behind broke my contact with the bench and knocked me out of my vision. I landed back on the street across from an urban park. I whirled around to see what had hit me, angry that I didn't get more information.

Jonah in his businessman disguise held my arm. Concern animated the unfamiliar face. "What happened when that guy bumped you? Are you all right?"

My other stranger companions stared at me with matching furrowed brows.

"Damn busy city. I was in the middle of a vision. I saw Ivan and Tatiana in a hotel room. Then Gemma joined them. That's all I got!" I glared at the pedestrian traffic flowing beside me.

"A vision? From what, the bench?" Jonah looked at the simple seat in disbelief.

"They might be nearby then. One of them must have sat there." Cole eyed the bench like a crime scene.

I contemplated touching it again for another attempt. I willed the vision to return. I tried to center myself, thinking frantically about how I had tapped into visions without an object before.

"Guys, I know this is thrilling, but we're on the street in broad daylight. Not exactly a slow part of the city either," said Ilya's punk façade.

"At least I saw that Gemma is safe. Let's go get some dart guns," I said reluctantly.

# Chapter 4

Regent's Park lived up to its name. Beyond the cement wall along the tube station entrance, an elegant black metal fence stretched around green space in both directions. Across the street from the park, terraced houses gleamed with opulence. The whole neighborhood emanated a regal vibe.

Cole led us along the black fence and into the park past a small green sign for the London Zoo. The sign's arrow pointed down a wide pedestrian road lined with huge trees and wrought iron benches. Tourists milled about on the manicured path ahead which stretched into the horizon.

"How far does this thing go?" I said.

"We just keep walking straight until we hit the zoo," said Cole.

"Is this going to take all day?" I took a deep breath trying to center myself.

"Calm down. It's not that far," said Josh.

"We've got the rest of the day anyway. We can't risk hitting

Rose and Sage until nighttime." Jonah's voice coming from a guy in a strange suit did not calm me.

"Businessmen don't hang out with punks, so you two should fall behind us a bit. As soon as I catch sight of a zoo employee, I can change us again," Ilya said to Jonah and Cole.

"I'll take point." Dressed for construction work, Josh appeared very sure of himself.

"What?" I said.

"I'll go first." Josh jogged ahead into the park while Jonah and Cole stopped to play with their phones.

"If I could somehow have a vision of where Rose and Sage are staying, we might not have to wait for a chance to follow them home. If everyone bailed on Evonatura this morning, there's no point in going back this afternoon. And we'll lose a whole extra day waiting for them to lead us to where they're crashing," I said to Ilya as we walked.

I felt myself adjusting to the strange person next to me. Watching my own fake blond hair flow around me in the breeze amused me.

We reached rows of red, white, and yellow flowers sculpted into oval beds. Paths led off to more gardens on our right, but we couldn't wander. We came to a beautiful stone three-tiered fountain and I paused, only for a moment.

"We'll travel properly someday. You and Jonah, me and Faith. We'll come back and see all the European cities the way they're meant to be seen." Ilya pulled gently on my arm and we resumed our brisk walk.

"What about Cole? And Gemma? We should bring them too." Worry for Gemma's safety quickly replaced the stab of guilt I felt when I pictured Cole's endearing smile. I hadn't seen him smile in weeks.

"Sure, why not? The more the merrier," said Ilya.

"Once we get this dart gun, how are we going to get it back to the hostel?" I asked quietly.

"I'll disguise it somehow. Depends on what we find. I think some of these things are like rifles and some are like handguns. I'm hoping for the latter, since this a zoo and not a game reserve." My brother's comfort with the topic of stealing a tranquilizer gun reminded me that he was more at home on the fringe of society.

We reached the London Zoo's entrance gate. Josh was already inside and gave a quick wave from his seat on a cement barrier.

"Two please," Ilya said politely to the grandmotherly ticket agent. She glowered at us as she passed our tickets back to us.

"Thank you!" I said cheerfully as I turned my back on her.

"Have you seen what you need of their uniforms?" said Josh.

I stole a glance back and saw Cole and Jonah at a ticket window.

"Oh yeah. Once we find a quiet corner to 'change' we're good to go," said Ilya.

Josh glanced at the people around us. "I'm more concerned about finding the 'equipment' we need and making sure we're undisturbed."

"You're only changing our clothes, right? We could say we're new and that we got lost." I rolled back on my heels, uncomfortable down to my bones at the prospect of being caught.

"That won't buy us any time alone in their vet wing," said Josh.

"I'll hit on someone." I flipped my hair playfully.

Jonah lifted his eyebrows. "Really?"

"What? It could work!" I said.

"No, it won't. Have you met yourself? You're an introvert with the social confidence of a bookkeeper. Let Josh handle it," said Ilya.

"You could have just said no," I glowered at my brother. He ignored me.

"First thing, we need uniforms. That alcove with the washrooms. Follow me." Ilya beckoned us.

We followed him to the men's side and found the room empty. He wasted no time and I felt the misty fog around me once more. In the washroom mirror, I saw my blonde self upgraded to a uniform. My hair was tied back much more neatly. *Impressive*, I thought.

"Let's go find a map," said the middle-aged tradesman-turned-naturalist Josh.

We followed him single file out of the bathroom and to an illustrated map poster on a nearby metal stand.

"Look for a building that says 'hospital' or something unmarked altogether. They don't want people in the vet space, so it will be labeled discreetly or not at all," said Josh.

We scanned the poster as a group.

"Hey, they're building a lion exhibit," Ilya said conversationally.

"Focus!" blurted Josh.

"Just trying to lighten the mood." Ilya lifted the air in front of him.

"What about this? An education center." Cole put his finger on the map.

"These buildings down here are unmarked." Jonah peered more closely.

"No, it's this one. Like a church, but there's a plus sign on it.

Doesn't that mean medicine?" I said.

"It's a place to start," said Josh.

"And it's just over there," said Cole, pointing ahead.

We followed his line of sight across the courtyard to where a steeple peeked out over a bank of palm trees. Josh set off and we followed him.

Sure enough, a sign over the door read ZSL Resident Care in large red letters. Another placard hung from a plastic chain across the entrance. 'No Entry. Sick animals are healing. Please don't disturb them.'

"Let's hope they've got more than meds in here," said Jonah as he unhooked and lifted the plastic chain so we could all pass. Josh ran ahead to the glass window down the hall.

"Excuse me, hello?" he called out.

Adrenaline surged inside me, but I trusted Josh and kept silent. I peered into the room on the other side of the glass. The white room had a counter bordering the wall everywhere I could see with closed cabinet doors. In the middle of the room, a stainless steel island displayed a monkey-like animal tied down with an IV in its back.

"Yes, how may I help you?" said a man with large yellow rubber gloves.

"We're part of the American exchange program completing our orientation. I was told we would have a guide for the hospital," said Josh confidently.

"I'm sorry. I have no idea what you mean. What exchange program?" The man's eyebrows formed a confused V shape.

"We're due in the aviary in half an hour. Do you mind taking some time now?" said Josh.

"Listen, mate, I'm in the middle of hydration therapy for a lemur. I don't have time to show you 'round the vet's quarters."

"Not a problem, we'll take a quick peek and get out of your hair." Josh didn't wait for the man to respond but marched ahead to the rooms at the back.

"We need to move quickly now. Ilya, once we find a tranquilizer, you're going to have to think fast to turn it into something else as we leave." Josh spoke just loudly enough for us to hear.

He opened the first door he found. The room was full of empty wire frame cages. The next room was a broom closet. The last door opened on a small room full of closed white cabinets. We filed inside and each of us started opening cupboard doors.

"It's this one." Josh rattled the handle on a door locked with a small deadbolt.

"I'll get that." Cole stepped between Josh and the cabinet, bending down to grab the door from a lip at the bottom. Cole gave a sharp tug on the door. A loud snap startled everyone but him.

The door swung open and a rack of rifles stared back at us. On a shelf above the rifles rested a stand with two handgun-style weapons alongside several trays of darts.

"Find a bag," said Josh.

I ran back to the room of cages and grabbed a canvas tote bag I'd seen crumpled on a stack of crates.

"Here," I thrust the bag at Josh. He transferred the handguns to the bag and emptied the trays of darts.

"Anyone want some takeout?" said Ilya as the bag blurred and resolved as a brown paper bag stamped with Salty's Fish and Chips over the Union Jack flag.

"We go straight back to the bathroom. New disguises, and then directly back to the train station. Everyone clear?" said

Josh.

"Yup." Ilya led the way back through the animal hospital.

I glanced over at the genuine zoo employee as we passed. He intently prodded the lemur's back.

Back in the zoo bathroom, Ilya transformed us again. I became a curvy redhead in a white dress with blue flowers and a lavender cardigan. I'd impersonated a girl from the Little House on the Prairie.

Josh had become a grizzly man with silver beard stubble and a leather jacket. Cole, Jonah, and Ilya all became thirty-something hipsters in stovepipe jeans. The hipsters left first, then Josh nodded at me and I fell in a few paces behind him.

We marched back to the train station without breaking stride, keeping our formation until we reunited in the stairwell of the Berwick Hostel. Relief washed over me as Ilya lifted our disguises.

"Knock, knock," said Ilya as he opened the door to the double room where Faith and Melissa had been trying to crack *The Compendium* files.

"Any luck so far?" said Cole.

Melissa glanced up, steel blue eyes intent. "The drive I downloaded contained exactly what I'd thought. The folders are meticulously organized into work sites, research projects, and personnel files."

"We found a floor plan, project summary, and physiological projections for Terra Nova. It's not happening here in London. Soho is just an office, a glorified filing cabinet. The real work is being done at a large lab under a lavish estate called Chatham Park," said Faith.

"The estate's administrator is a variant aligned with Claude Mueller. If these docs are up-to-date, Chatham Park is where the biological oil is being manufactured. That place has the supply Ivan needs to start a global pandemic. But there's no way of knowing if Chatham is the only location," said Melissa.

"Are you sure about this? An old world estate isn't the kind of place you'd expect to find a lab," said Cole.

"If the original owner was an eccentric cult member, you'd be surprised what kind of underground levels the place could have." Melissa re-clipped her glossy dark hair into her signature twist.

"What now?" I said.

"She's not kidding. I saw the floor plan. There's a memo here from Tatiana to Ivan that says, and I quote, '*The proprietor assures me the main house's underground levels are intact and suitable for our purposes. Access can be gained from the property of a church in the nearby town to ensure we are not discovered. We may encounter fumes due to additional excavation attempted by the original owner. We should pursue extensive site testing before we commit to manufacturing Terra Nova at this location,*'" read Faith.

"We don't need to break into the Soho office at all then," said Cole.

"What about their animal testing? We still need Gemma back!" I rubbed my face after I noticed the volume in my voice.

"Sorry, yes, of course we do." Cole put his hand on my shoulder and took it away again quickly.

"I'll go by myself if necessary. I'm not leaving her." I swallowed hard, feeling hot tears welling in my eyes.

"No, we'll stick to the plan. Starting with getting Rose and Sage alone. Why don't you try for that vision now?" said Jonah.

I blinked up at him. My boyfriend's sympathy made me angry for some reason. "I'll get my cards," I grumbled.

I went straight to my room. I found my cards and sat down on the bed to shuffle them. I peeked out our tiny window at the fire escape outside and the brick wall across the alley. Were Rose and Sage in a room just like this one? Somewhere nearby? Or the fancy hotel where I'd seen the Krylovs?

I concentrated on their faces as I shuffled the cards. The glasses and the hotplate on the side table started to rattle as I focused harder.

The room around me grew dim and my eyes fluttered. When I could focus again, I wasn't in my hotel room. I was in the rafters of a building with huge stained glass flower windows, like a church. I willed my perspective down to the wood plank floor of the room and squinted back up to see Rose and Sage hanging down, their wings wrapped around them like cloak-cocoons as they slept.

I nudged my viewpoint through one of the glass flowers and looked back to the building. It was a huge Gothic cathedral with two rectangular towers stretching into the sky. I closed my eyes and pictured my hotel room. When I opened my eyes, I was sitting on my bed again. I took a deep breath. It wouldn't take long to find out how many large Gothic cathedrals were in the London core.

Jonah opened the door and shut it carefully. "Did you see anything?"

"They're in a cathedral. I think we can assume it's nearby. I'll recognize the building when I see it."

Jonah sat next to me on the bed and his scent caught me. The dirt of our trip still lingered without access to laundry. But his well-groomed body smelled luscious. I leaned in instinctively.

He needed no other encouragement to meet my lips with his. The magnetic draw of his new energized aura drew me against his body.

"Irina!" yelled Ilya from outside our door. "Knock it off! Faith needs you to browse photos of cathedrals."

Embarrassment flooded my chest and I stood up abruptly, blushing.

Jonah smirked at me. "Is he going to listen at the door every night?"

"Not if I levitate him onto a nearby roof." I rolled my eyes, pushed my humiliation away, and reached for the door.

# Chapter 5

U nfortunately for Rose and Sage, they had chosen to squat in the single most popular Gothic cathedral in London, Westminster Abbey. Faith found photos of the building from my vision online in less than a minute.

Two of the cathedral's galleries had been opened up for renovations and conversion to museum space. Which made the rafters of the galleries a perfect hiding space at night – if you were the sort of person who could get comfortable there.

"So who's going to go?" Cole massaged his palms again, still ready for action.

"I'm the best shot, so I'll take one tranquilizer. Who else can shoot? We've got two targets and two dart guns, so we should try to hit them simultaneously." Josh surveyed each of us.

"I can shoot," said Melissa. We all gaped at her in amazement. "What? I can," she added bluntly.

"I'll come.  I can pinpoint their location, even if they're asleep."  Ilya tapped his temple as though we needed a reminder of his abilities.

"Irina should come too. She's seen the inside of the cathedral," said Josh.

Fear crept up my spine, followed by shame, as I visualized the harpy twins waking and attacking faster than I could fight them off while an alarm blared in the background. Heat flooded my face. I pushed the feeling aside.

"If Rose and Sage wake up, I can try to hold them telekinetically. But how do we get into the cathedral? I'm sure it'll be locked and armed by the time Rose and Sage are sleeping up in the rafters." I mimed a hanging gesture in a feeble attempt to communicate what I'd seen.

"I'll short the alarm. Nellie would have done a better job, but I can manage." Faith glowered at the ground.

"I can probably pull the doors open, but Cole is stronger than I am, so he should come too." Josh nodded at Cole.

"I'm not staying here by myself. I'm as strong as the rest of you now." Jonah stood tall next to me.

"So we're all going?" Faith pulled out her dreadlock hair tie and fixed it in place.

"We'll leave at midnight." Cole glanced at his watch.

* * *

Ilya disguised us once more before we exited the stairwell of the Berwick Hostel. London was quiet and dark by the middle of the night, except for clubs like The Incinerator. We hailed a cab on the street.

"Westminster Abbey please." I took the front seat. My friends filed into the bench seats behind me.

"Abbey'll be closed for the night, Miss," said the driver.

"We're just meeting some friends on the corner. Hard to

mistake Westminster Abbey for somewhere else, right?" I said in my perkiest voice.

"Too true, Miss. The Abbey it shall be." The driver pulled out onto the street.

Twenty minutes later I tipped him generously – or what I hoped was generous after the currency conversion – and we scanned the lawn in front of the Abbey.

Rose and Sage could be awake, peering out the window directly at us and they wouldn't know who stood in front of them because of our disguises. We clustered around a tree in the adjacent yard and watched the Abbey for a few minutes.

"The harpy twins are definitely up in the rafters. I'm pretty sure they're asleep. That, or they're meditating." Ilya stepped out from under the cover of leaves for a better line of sight.

"What about security? Can you hear anyone?" said Josh.

"One guard for sure," said Ilya. "Wait, hang on … It is just one. He's grouchy about being on his own since peak season isn't quite finished."

We stood silent until a man in a white shirt and black pants sauntered to the Abbey's front door and stopped.

"Can you hit him with the dart from here?" I asked.

"Give me a uniform like his," Josh said to Ilya.

Josh's clothes blurred and resolved again into a uniform exactly like the guard's across the street.

"Make sure you guys look like you're hanging out or waiting for someone. Don't stare at the guard. Once I catch his attention, he'll be on alert," said Josh.

The older tradesman version of Josh, now a security guard, crossed the street and greeted the real guard with a handshake. Josh had the tranquilizer gun tucked into the back of his pants. We could see it, but the guard couldn't. Josh said something as he shook the guard's hand, distracting the man as he pulled the loaded tranquilizer gun from his back and fired.

The guard frowned with confusion. His face melted into sleep as he dropped. Josh caught him and placed him gently in a seated position, tucked into a shadow cast by a ridge on the wall. He beckoned at us to come to him. "Faith, find the alarm. Hurry! We can't risk someone finding us with an unconscious guard."

Faith lifted her hand to the door and hovered around the edge until she found something. Her hand followed an unseen line. She slapped the wall and concentrated. A loud POP exploded inside the wall. "It should be good now," she said confidently.

Cole reached out to the huge oak French doors. He pushed them open with ease. Josh lifted the guard by his arms and dragged him. When the doors were shut again and my eyes adjusted, I saw the towering ornate beauty of the cathedral. But like the park, there wasn't time to linger.

"Head to the left." Ilya led the way and we followed down a corridor to a stairwell which wound upward.

"Is this the right room?" said Josh as we emerged in an oversized attic. I squinted up into the rafters praying I would see two hanging humanoid bat shapes. It was too dark. I couldn't see. I glanced over at the flower windows. They were the same as my vision.

"Yes, but I can't see them. They're not here," I said desperately.

"I can't see them either," said Melissa. Her voice sounded tense.

"Ilya, are you sure this is the tower?" said Josh.

SCREEEEEEE pierced our ears as the whooshing sound of

flapping wings exploded over our heads.

Josh fired a dart into the flurry of leathery cloaks beating above us.

"NOOOOooooooo!" screamed one sister as the other fell.

Melissa whipped her head up and made eye contact with the harpy still in the air. She raised her gun and fired, hitting the winged woman squarely in the chest. She went limp and fell to the ground a few feet from her twin.

We stood in shock for a moment, each catching our breath. Cole snapped out of it first and picked up a sleeping harpy, carefully folding up one wing after the other, tucking her leather appendages up against her back. With his left arm around the girl, Cole plucked a long copper pipe off a nearby pile. He wound the pipe around the winged woman forming a spiral around her body. Cole placed her on the ground, asleep and trapped. Josh lifted and presented the other sister to Cole, who wrapped another pipe into a matching coil.

"Well, what now?" Jonah perused the restrained women.

"For Irina and Ilya to interrogate them, we need them awake. And we need privacy." Melissa nudged one of the harpies with the toe of her shoe.

"How about the roof of the hostel? We can leave them up there and tranquilize them again after the interrogation is over," said Josh, peering upward as though we were already back in our rooms.

"How do we get them to the roof?" I asked.

"I can handle that." Melissa swooped her arm and opened a portal.

"If you can do that, then why let us go through the production of breaking in here?" said Jonah motioning at the space around us.

"I can't open a portal to somewhere I've never been. It won't work if I can't visualize the space," said Melissa.

"And you were up on the roof of the hostel?" said Cole.

"Actually, yes, I went up there when I couldn't sleep last night. You never know when you need to make a speedy exit, so I always make a point of familiarizing myself with my surroundings. You want to discuss this further or do you want to get the hell out of here?"

An alarm WAAAaaaiiiled from the floor below us.

"The guard must have woken up," said Jonah.

"Not possible. More likely another guard just discovered him," said Josh.

"All the more reason to get going," said Cole.

He picked up one of the winged women and marched into Melissa's portal. Josh followed Cole with our other prisoner. The rest of my friends followed until just Melissa and I remained.

"Do you think we can impersonate Rose and Sage well enough to fool Ivan and Tatiana?" I said.

"I think it's our best option if you badly need to separate your sister from the Krylovs," Melissa answered hurriedly. She gestured for me to walk through her portal.

"Then tell me you're ready to risk *your* safety to free *my* sister." I held her gaze for a beat.

"You don't trust me, do you?" Melissa glared at me.

"I trust most people to put their personal quality of life before the lives of strangers. Do you see value in reuniting two sisters? And adding a healer to our group?"

"The latter, for sure. As for sisters, I wouldn't know. I'll make you this deal – if I can help get your sister back, I will. But if she fights us? If she's truly committed to Ivan, I will let her go. She may have chosen him with her eyes wide open, fully informed.  Unlikely, but possible," said Melissa.  She pointed at her portal again.

"I know, but she's my sister," I said, holding on until I knew she understood me.

"And I swear, I'll try to help." Melissa's face seemed sincere as I stepped through her liquid window.

# Chapter 6

"Traitor!" snarled Rose. The harpy twins were propped up against the wall, bound by pipes, sitting on Cole's bed in their double room at the Berwick Hostel.

If the twins were awake, it was easier to tell them apart since Rose's eyes were a darker gray. Sage slumbered away, propped next to her sister.

"I think you'd better look in the mirror before you call *us* traitors," I said.

"I'm talking to her!" Rose violently whipped her head at Melissa.

"That's rich!" blurted Melissa. "What convinced you to side with Ivan? You were ready to fight him, in Victoria, when you learned about less-than-painless medical tests. When I stayed on after I learned about *The Compendium*, I thought I was being loyal," Melissa said. "But, you two ran off to Ilya's beach. And I said, 'Hey, I can sympathize,' knowing that your alternative was living in a sewer. But then you ran to Ivan and Tatiana with arms wide open. Why? Ruining the planet for billions so that *you* can have your pick of habitats sounds fair?"

We watched Rose's angry face intently, crowded on what little floor space surrounded the bed. It felt claustrophobic to be penned in so close to a pair of angry and powerful variants who wanted to kill us.

"You lied to us!" Rose yelled at Ilya.

"What?" Surprise filled my brother's face.

"You told us it would never get better, that Ivan would keep us in the sewer, testing, and dawdling, letting us waste away. I would have waited it out if I knew the real plan," Rose said bitterly.

"I told you what I believed to be true. I didn't know his whole agenda. Now that I do, I'm trying to stop him. And I'm his son!" shouted Ilya.

I looked at the hostel room door, hoping no one was in the hallway outside.

"How can you possibly think *The Compendium* is an acceptable plan?" Jonah said to Rose.

"How can you expect us to keep hiding when there's a chance to live out in the open, celebrated and admired?" said Rose.

"Is that what he promised you? Celebrity status?" said Faith. She crossed her arms and glared at Rose.

"There's every chance that if variants came out, people would accept us. Especially in this day and age," I said.

"Easy for you to say. You've never seen the expression on someone's face when they see who you are for the first time. People gawk at me like I'm deformed. Then they want to know how my wings are attached. Where does that lead?" Rose's pale face melted into a plaintive expression. Nobody moved and her features animated with rage again as she fought helplessly within her pipe prison.

"This is pointless. We're not going to convince each other of anything," said Josh.

"Then why not just kill us?" said Rose. Sage began to stir.

"We're not killing anyone. Unless it's self-defense. We're not like you. We don't want to watch the world burn," said Cole.

"You're going to have to kill Ivan to stop him. And good luck with that," said Rose.

"What are we doing here?" said Sage as she regained consciousness.

"Ilya, you go first. What have you got?" said Josh, ignoring Sage.

"Rose wants to get to a phone to call someplace called The Belgravia Park Hotel. That's where everyone who doesn't need to sleep upside down is staying. Except Casey. He's sleeping on the Evonatura office couch," said Ilya.

"What's our best way in?" Faith stared hard at Rose.

"Get him out of my head!" snapped Rose.

"You guys are going to be so sorry. You've finally crossed the line with the Krylovs," said Sage groggily, her head lolling forward.

"And the rest of *The Compendium* team." Rose resumed trying to break free, only bouncing on the bed.

"How do we get inside Evonatura?" shouted Cole. He glared at Rose with raw hatred as he leaned forward and gripped the side of her pipe restraint. The metal creaked under his fist.

"Easy, man. We don't want anyone complaining to the hostel," said Jonah.

"They've been working security with Casey and Evonatura's guy, Gregory. Aside from their CEO Mueller, only those men have keys and the alarm code. The harpy twins here are assigned to the roof, to watch for us." Ilya couldn't repress a grin.

"Did a pretty shitty job of being lookouts, didn't you?" Faith smiled, but her face had a mix of satisfaction and disgust.

"Hey, my illusions are bulletproof. We would have fooled anyone." Ilya raised a hand in mock submission.

"Should we go in at night? Or stick to the infiltration plan? How much will they expect the girls to interact at Evonatura? A bunch of chitchat is risky," said Josh.

"Tatiana's going to get her way soon. Claude is closing the Evonatura London office," said Ilya, ignoring Josh and curiously peering at Sage. "Any day now? Really?"

Rose glowered at her groggy sister and wriggled helplessly inside her copper coil.

"Tatiana is an expert in getting what she wants. And she thinks we're a threat," I said.

"She's right this time." Anger washed over Jonah's face.

"We don't need the alarm code. I can short it like any other and Cole can pop the door." Faith shrugged and shoved her hands in her pockets.

"No, that's not going to work." Ilya shook his head.

"These two don't need to hear this." Josh pulled out his tranquilizer gun and shot Rose in the chest.

"Asssss…" her head dropped before she could finish the word.

"He's right. You don't stand a chance," said Sage.

Josh shot Sage next and held his arm up for silence until her head dropped again. "Okay, continue."

"If the sisters' thoughts are accurate, any interruption in the alarm's circuit and Claude Mueller is personally notified.

He'll contact Casey and Gregory immediately. Gregory lives across the street. All Casey has to do is wake up. They won't call the cops. They won't slow down. They'll start firing. And throwing punches, which for them is pretty deadly too."

"What if Gemma isn't there when we break in?" I asked without trying to mask my fear.

"A break-in is our backup plan. For now, we stick to plan A, disguises, and infiltration." Josh made a chopping gesture with one hand onto the other, decisive as always.

"How long should we hang on to these two?" Faith nodded in the sisters' direction with disdain.

"Are you ready to replicate them?" Melissa asked Ilya.

"Yeah, I can swing it." Ilya inspected them carefully nevertheless.

"Assuming we do this tomorrow morning, we could just leave them here when we check out," said Cole.

"Irina, it's your turn. See what they saw," said Jonah, gently touching the small of my back.

I stepped forward and leaned onto the bed to reach Sage's foot. She seemed like the safer target, closer to me. I put my hand on her calf. She jerked her leg in her sleep, but I held her. Trying to pinpoint my vision, I pictured Rose and Sage walking past me on the sidewalk outside the Evonatura façade and closed my eyes.

I was pulled onto the sidewalk behind Rose and Sage. Ahead, Casey turned into the brown brick and cream stucco building. Rose and Sage quickly closed the distance and followed him up the stairs. Casey punched a code into a keypad on the wall inside the main door. We got to him just as he'd finished. The door remained armed during the day.

Rose and Sage followed Casey up the stairs and into a sitting room where Ivan read a magazine. Two men in lab coats were also in the sitting room reading, but they had clipboards and frowns on their faces.  Casey and Ivan exchanged a brisk greeting. Casey passed through into a kitchen and continued to a dark hallway. The harpy twins remained in the kitchen. I paused with them.

Tatiana's green hue had not faded as she stood over a small pot of something steaming inside the office's kitchenette. My sister Gemma sat at a small round dining table picking at a plate of buttered toast. She wore a knit tank top and looked comfortable despite being out of place in an office. She wasn't smiling this time though.

"You need your strength, sweetie.  The hot chocolate is almost ready. I know it sounds strange, but try dunking your toast in the cocoa.  It has to be white toast and real butter. You'll be surprised how comforting it tastes.  My mother taught us that when we were children," said Tatiana.

Gemma gazed up at Tatiana and managed a small smile. Tatiana posed as the caring aunt she never had been to me. Then again, she hadn't been kind to a single person in my presence.  This behavior was part of some game with my sister. Tatiana crossed the kitchenette with her steaming pot and poured hot chocolate into Gemma's waiting mug, then smoothed the hair on my sister's head with obvious fondness.

"What a nice little family we're becoming," said Rose as Tatiana and Gemma noticed the sisters' entrance.

A tall redheaded woman in a beige pantsuit entered the kitchen from the hallway Casey had gone down.

"We've nearly completed packing. It'll be a tight squeeze at Chatham, but the lads are ready to shift gears and work on-site for a while," said the redhead. Her refined accent, perfect skin, and sculpted French roll were intimidating. She looked like an ideal counterpart for my aunt.

"Excellent. I would please me if today was the last operational day here," said Tatiana.

"We're not ready to move out just yet. We have a bit of admin to sort. I've had trouble hiring a van. We should finish tomorrow. Monday at the latest," said the redhead.

"Helen, I realize you don't have to follow my recommendations, but I suggest you come in on Saturday to wrap up if you don't finish tomorrow," said Tatiana.

Gemma thoughtfully dunked a chunk of toast in her hot chocolate as Tatiana gave Helen a sweet smirk that chilled me. Helen looked concerned too as she returned Tatiana's smile. Helen smiled again in my direction as a greeting to Rose and Sage before she bowed back out of the room.

"Rose, Sage, don't you two need to be on duty up top?" said Tatiana once the click-clack of Helen's heels had faded. She didn't wait for a reply from either sister.

"Don't underestimate my niece and nephew or their friends. I'd like to leave London with all loose ends tied - properly. Wouldn't you two like to earn that service bonus Ivan is offering? I'd hate to see it go to this Gregory fellow, keen as he is," said Tatiana.

Gemma lifted her head and stared right at me. Her inquisitive eyebrows signaled interest, but her mouth rested peacefully, void of the concern I would have expected while someone discussed my assassination in front of her. What had they done to her?

I released Sage's leg. I was back in the crowded hostel room with my friends staring desperately at my face.

"What did you see?" said Jonah.

"Ilya's right, they're on lookout duty at Evonatura. I saw what happened after they passed us on the street this morning. Ivan wants us dead. Tatiana is pushing hard to get them moved to Chatham Park. Tomorrow might be their last day in Soho," I said.

"What about your sister?" said Faith.

"She's safe. But, she's totally out of the loop. I need to get some sleep myself." I rubbed my eyes and then my temples before I left the room. I heard footsteps behind me and knew it was Jonah.

My head swam as I walked methodically back to our room. I still had to come up with a convincing reason to get Gemma to leave the Evonatura office with me. I would be disguised as one of the harpy sisters, but they didn't seem to have the bond with her that Tatiana did. Even if I got Gemma away from Tatiana and Ivan, how could I be sure she would stay with me and my friends?

Should I bring a tranquilizer gun and hope Melissa could help me carry her off? Maybe I could shove her through a portal if Melissa could create a safe escape. Had Gemma been sincerely comfortable with Ivan putting a hit out on me? Didn't she understand Tatiana's instructions? I had to believe that my naive little sister was blissfully ignorant. Or brainwashed. Or drugged.

"What are you thinking about?" Jonah closed the door as I sat down on our bed.

"Don't overreact, but I'm not one hundred percent sure my sister will side with us," I said, physically hurting in my chest as I spoke.

"But, you said she doesn't understand. Once you explain it properly, I'm sure she'll see it our way." Jonah sounded certain.

"I don't think she does understand, but I'm mostly giving her the benefit of the doubt. I can't hear her thoughts. I can't help but think she's been conned, or drugged," I said. I swallowed hard and drew a deep breath.

"Well, as soon as Ilya gets near her, we will know how she feels. You know her better than any Innoviro or Evonatura people do. I'm sure you can help her see the light," Jonah put his hand on my shoulder. I didn't need my brother's gift to sense my boyfriend's need to comfort me.

I frowned, deep in thought. Jonah leaned in and kissed me. I didn't think it possible, but the urge to connect with him grew stronger daily. His touch sent waves of energy through me as he pinned me to the wall. I worried something was going wrong again, but it felt too good to stop.

"Can you feel that?" I asked breathlessly.

"What?" Jonah broke away from my neck.

"Something is coming from you into me. It's like you're infusing energy into my body. It's electric," I said.

"It's both of us. I can feel a rush, like a surge of power when I touch you." Jonah kissed me and pulled back to meet my gaze. His aqua eyes gleamed as he caught his breath. "We're not normal. I think this is what it's like to be with another variant, a healthy one. There's nothing wrong with us. You have to trust me. Trust us," he said.

# Chapter 7

We returned to The Lazy Toad pub for breakfast, but I wasn't myself. Melissa and I had already been transformed into Rose and Sage. We'd left the twins freshly tranquilized and planned to head directly to Evonatura once we had food in our bellies.

"Melissa and I will leave first, but you should all keep close tabs on us." Hearing Rose's voice come from my mouth unnerved me. Ilya had to concentrate hard to change our voices. I had been skeptical, but I had to concede that his skills were flawless and effective.

"Don't be afraid to take off your jackets, since you're wearing their originals. If you don't act naturally, you might give yourselves away. I took my time to study the twins' wings, so yours will look pretty near perfect. Do not, under any circumstances, try to fly. I'll give the rest of us new disguises." Ilya's scowl rattled me, ramping up my adrenaline.

"After we have Irina's sister, we should be on the next train to Chester. It's the town closest to Chatham Park," said Cole.

"Between the Berwick staff finding the harpy twins and the potential release of Terra Nova, there's no time to waste." Josh checked his vest, bulkier now with his second weapon.

"Leave your bags with us. You can't risk having any possessions that Rose or Sage might not carry." Jonah reached out to take my backpack.

"I'm nervous. Is that weird?" An awkward laugh popped out of my mouth.

"If you weren't a bit freaked out, I'd say you're not paying attention. Speaking of risk, Josh, be sure you're in the alley next to the Evonatura entrance. I'll grab you if we need you." Melissa looked exactly like Sage in appearance and voice.

"I guess there's no point in dawdling any longer." I stood up and stretched tall. The extra height was still weird.

"We'll be in and out as fast as we can. And I've still got my tranquilizer gun." Melissa stood and patted where the gun lay concealed under her coat.

The two of us walked side-by-side down the street and I marveled at how we effortlessly mirrored each other. Ilya and I were twins, but different genders and features left us feeling distinctly unique despite our connection. Today, I felt close to Melissa although I didn't much like her when we worked at Innoviro.

At the Evonatura building, we approached smoothly and confidently. I felt proud of my acting ability even though I hadn't yet said a word to anyone.

I pressed the call button on the intercom and we waited. And waited. I pressed the button again with dread closing cold fingers around my heart. We waited, probing for some sign of life in the building. I peered through the glass door, eyeing the stairwell and surrounding lobby. I tried the door.

"They must have already left," said Melissa.

"Or nobody's here yet. Maybe we should wait here a while."

"You can wait here, but now that I've seen the stairwell, I can get us into that lobby." Melissa swooped her arm in front of her as discretely as possible and her silver oval appeared.

I whipped around to see if we were being watched, by civilians more than anyone else. So far we hadn't drawn any attention. I turned my focus back to the hallway and another oval hung in the air just ten feet ahead into the lobby.

"Easy peasy," said Melissa as she entered.

I followed and she closed her portal. "What about the alarm? Will it go off if we move around?"

"We'll just have to find out the hard way." Melissa set off up the stairs and I ran to catch her. We passed through the sitting room where I'd seen Ivan and the lab techs lounging. Nobody was in the room, but I felt tense anyway, waiting for someone to appear and attack at any moment. I relaxed as I remembered how easily Melissa could get us out of a tight spot. Our Rose and Sage disguise held perfectly.

We entered the kitchen and found it empty too. I removed my trench coat and saw wings unfold in both directions in my peripheral vision. The illusion tricked me enough that I was surprised when no sensation accompanied my extra appendages.

"I can't feel my wings. Can you feel yours?" I asked Melissa.

"Focus, Irina," said Melissa in a hushed voice.

"Focus on what. They're not here. We missed them." My heart sank as I accepted that we were too late.

Melissa continued down the hallway where Casey and the Evonatura administrator Helen had been. I sat down at the small dining table where Gemma had been sipping

Tatiana's hot chocolate. I blinked and blinked, fighting tears. I swallowed and took a deep breath. Gemma was just at Chatham Park, not lost to me forever. I had to stay strong, to get my sister back and stop *The Compendium* crew from launching Terra Nova.

"I'm going to bring Josh in for a second opinion. Sit tight." Melissa opened a portal and popped through it.

The gateway stayed open until a tall dark stranger in a black trench coat stepped out followed by Melissa.

"You both stay here until I've done a full sweep of the entire office," said Josh, dressed as though he'd just left The Matrix. His unchanged voice gave him away.

Josh explored the far hallway as Melissa had done. I had no interest in their empty offices anyway. Only my sister and the virus mattered to me.

"He's not going to find anything, but he is the expert," said Melissa.

"I vote we go straight to Chatham Park. We've still got plenty of darts for the tranquilizer guns. If we can't convince them we're Rose and Sage, we can zap Gemma, grab her, and fight our way out." My fake wings flapped as my animated arms flailed.

"Remember what I told you about putting Compendium defeat before recovering your sister?" said Melissa.

"I know, I know. Just let me hope, will you?" I said earnestly.

"I can't say that I know how you feel. I don't have any brothers or sisters. But I can empathize all the same." Melissa's head snapped to the side as footsteps came down the hall.

"I'll clear the rest of the space, but I'm pretty sure you're right," said Josh. He stepped towards the sitting room and froze as we all heard a chime and a door close in the distance.

A metal-on-metal sound followed. I couldn't place what it was.

"Was that the front door?" Melissa clamped her hand over her mouth.

"Hide!" I blurted to Josh.

He darted back around the corner of the hallway past the kitchen.

Footsteps thudded along the floor and as we stood frozen to the ground in fear, Ralph and Adelaide appeared in the kitchen doorway. A huge green humanoid reptile and half supermodel-half octopus woman glowered at me. I had forgotten how frightening they were as a pair.

"What are you two doing here?" Instinctively, Adelaide lifted several tentacles in surprise. She used a tentacle to push a glossy ringlet of hair out of her beautiful face.

"We … uh …," I said desperately trying to think of an explanation, or something, anything, that would convince Adelaide I was Rose.

"We thought there was more clean-up to do today," said Melissa, doing her best to act natural as Sage.

"Tatiana is ready to tear you both in half." Ralph's words dripped with irritation, but his reptile face remained expressionless. A crisp new Union Jack shirt and dark denim pants would have screamed tourist on anyone other than Ralph.

"Doesn't that tell you what kind of a woman she is?" I blurted angrily, still sizing up the reptile man formerly my ally.

Adelaide's eyes narrowed and she shuffled forward to examine me.

"Does it matter what kind of person she is, as long as she gets the job done?" Ralph came closer.

"Since when did you start caring about Tatiana's personality?" Adelaide cocked her head to the side.

"I don't care. I just want this all to go smoothly, with Terra Nova I mean." I heard the anxiety rippling through my voice.

"Well then, you better not pull stunts like not showing up for work. You know you're supposed to be at Chatham already. You were there at the last staff meeting." Adelaide didn't take her eyes off either of us.

"Nobody knew where you both were. It looked like bad news for a while there. I'll text Casey and let him know we found you and that you didn't make the trip last night," said Ralph.

I watched with wonder as Ralph operated his phone with clawed fingers. I hadn't known that he was capable of the dexterity required. His fingertips, such as they were, moved deftly on the surface of the small glass screen.

"Just think, after Terra Nova is released, you won't have to wait for the completion of *The Compendium* to start flying during the day, out in the open. And my days of wheeling around town will be over." Adelaide poured herself into a loveseat at the side of the room.

"We're all anticipating a lot more freedom." Ralph put his phone back in his pocket.

"Well, I guess we should get going." I clamped my hands together as though the useless gesture might spur us onward.

"Where to? You got someplace better to be?" Adelaide moved over to the kitchenette fridge, opened the door, and browsed with two tentacles while a third held the door handle.

"Rose and I were just going to grab some lunch." Melissa's delivery was much more believable than mine.

"Would you mind bringing it back here? We'd like some

of whatever you're getting. Ivan hooked me up with a new van so we could do the door-to-door thing. Ralph can get me out of the van and into a building, but that's about all we can manage without making a scene. I never thought I'd say this, but I miss American drive-through windows. It made life so much easier." Adelaide closed the fridge, dejected.

We all perked up as the alarm's door chime sounded again.

"Did you leave the door unlocked?" Adelaide asked Ralph.

"No, of course not," said Ralph.

Adelaide rolled her lovely eyes.

Footsteps filled the hall again. It was far too much noise for one or even two people. Ilya, Faith, Cole, and Jonah spilled into the kitchen completely undisguised. Ilya looked positively sick. They all stopped short as they saw the four of us, fake Rose, fake Sage, Ralph, and Adelaide.

"What the hell is this now?" Adelaide slammed the fridge door shut.

"Sorry ... I-" Ilya dropped to his knees clutching his stomach. He retched and then threw up the disgusting remains of his breakfast.

"He ate a chocolate bar that had nuts in it or something," Cole explained, ignoring Ralph and Adelaide.

"He's allergic to cashews!" shouted Faith, glaring at her brother.

"He dropped our disguises to keep yours going." Jonah regarded me apologetically. His eyes darted to Ralph and Adelaide, watching them as they gawked at us.

"So why are you here?" Melissa took a step backward, preparing for the obvious.

"We couldn't be sure Ilya was holding your illusions in place." Jonah stepped between me and Ralph.

Ilya groaned and I felt the familiar mist of his illusion fading away.

"I knew it!" Adelaide glared at me, then Melissa.

"You brats are a day late and a dollar short," said Ralph.

"I think you'd better turn around and go back to wherever you came from. You made a go of saving all those stupid grubby humans. And you failed. You'll live," said Adelaide.

"And nobody else will." Pipes in the wall groaned as Jonah's temper rose.

"You're such a self-centered bitch!" Faith's words oozed with hatred.

"Watch it, punkette. I'm in a good mood today, but you're changing that." Adelaide smoothed her hair back with a tentacle.

"That beak in your throat isn't enough to save you now," Faith took a wider stance to brace herself.

Adelaide's face lit with shock as Josh jumped out from the back hallway knocking Ralph to the floor. She reared up and opened her mouth wide. Her hooked throat tendril shot out at Josh, but I was ready. I held my arm out, willing a hard grip on Adelaide's hook. Josh and Ralph wrestled on the ground.

Adelaide gave a confused grunt and I lifted my other hand, holding her steady remotely. I could feel her strength while she struggled to break free. "I can't hold her for long. Somebody better do something!"

Faith reached out and shot a stream of fire at Adelaide's hooked tendril which floated in mid-air, held by my sheer willpower. The fire connected with the tendril and ignited with a bright flare. Fire slid along the tendril and down Adelaide's throat where it whooshed to life, engulfing Adelaide in a flash. Faith watched with wide eyes and a dropped jaw.

"Noooooooooooo!" Ralph broke free from Josh. Cole stepped forward and landed a right hook on Ralph's jaw.

Ralph flew high in the air and hit the ceiling with a loud SLAP before he crashed back down to the floor. His long forked tongue slid out of his mouth while his broken body lay motionless. Blood flowed from behind his cracked skull and I knew he was dead.

Adelaide's charred body lay in a sprawl of black tentacles. The smoke detector beeped shrilly in our ears.

"I didn't mean to kill her. I just tried to burn her beak thing off!" shouted Faith over the alarm.

"Yeah, well I didn't mean to kill Ralph either. But it was us or them," Cole grabbed his sister's arm. I stared at the bodies, my feet glued to the floor.

"It's time to go." Jonah closed the distance between us and grabbed my hand, pulling me back out of the kitchen.

"Walk, don't run!" Josh called, while we fled from the building. "We don't want civilian attention."

# Chapter 8

We hailed a large black passenger cab on the street outside Evonatura. Melissa slipped into the alley to open a portal to the hostel. My heartbeat pounded in my ears as the others debated in hissing whispers. Should we hide nearby? When would Ilya be well enough for more disguises? Could the police connect anything at that office to any of us? What would happen to Rose and Sage when the hostel staff discovered them? Should we leave them on the roof to fend for themselves? The cab pulled over and everyone shut up. Melissa reappeared loaded up with our luggage. Cole and the driver transferred the bags into the cab.

"Euston Station, please." Melissa shut the cab's front passenger door.

The air in the cab filled with tension as the vehicle wove through traffic.

"How much of a lead do we figure Ivan's got?" Cole sat across from me in the back of the cab, his warm complexion undisturbed.

"Based on the fact that they didn't have much more than paper files and computers to clear out here in London, he could have taken off for Chatham not long after we arrived in London," said Josh.

"We shouldn't have wasted time at that club. We should have been scouting Evonatura from the moment we arrived." I balled my fists and drove them into my thighs, cursing my carelessness.

"Can we finish this conversation later?" Ilya flicked his eyes to the cab driver and gave me a wide-eyed 'shut-up-and-don't-incriminate-us' frown.

The cab pulled over at the train station and my tension melted into relief.

"That'll be ten pounds fifty please, Miss."

Melissa paid as we filed out of the cab. She led us to a ticket window where she again paid our way. She doled out six tickets keeping the seventh. "We need platform eighteen. The next train leaves in ten minutes, so we should keep moving."

"That's great timing." Ilya seemed back to his old self, a small mercy in our mess.

"Yes, we timed our disastrous encounter with our deadly former friends pretty perfectly," said Jonah sarcastically.

"We've been lucky so far, but that won't last." Cole shouldered his way through the crowd. His wide frame easily carved a path for the rest of us.

"I heard Ivan and Tatiana talking about population tests. We should expect a few small incidents before they launch Terra Nova on a widespread scale." Melissa stopped under a sign for Platform 18. "This is our train. Everyone on board."

"Too bad you've never been to Chester," said Ilya as he passed Melissa.

"You should make us a list of places you've been so we know where we can hop to via portal," said Josh.

"Yeah, just think of the travel possibilities!" said Faith.

"Once Terra Nova is neutralized, we'll have to chase down the rest of *The Compendium* projects anyway and who knows where that will take us," I said.

We plodded through the train until we found a pair of empty tables on either side of a less crowded car. Two pairs of facing booths were more than enough seating. We each stuffed our bags into the net-enclosed overhead shelf and wedged into the bench seats.

"I'll help you get around to Compendium sites as much as I can," Melissa said once we'd settled in. "The more that time passes since I left Ivan and Tatiana, the more I realize I'd been working for the devil." Melissa sat down next to Josh, who straightened his posture in response.

The train's electronic bell chimed and we began to move.

Leaning across the table at Melissa and Josh, Cole whispered, "Do you know anything about how contagious Terra Nova is?"

"I saw test results in documents that compared contagion rates for rabbits and rats. All were between five to ten minutes for transmission from a sting-infected host to an animal breathing the same air. They haven't tested extensively on humans yet, at least I don't think they have." Melissa knitted her fingers together resting her hands on the table.

"So it is airborne. We were pretty close to a coyote that contracted and died within minutes of being stung." Cole rubbed the back of his neck as he fixated on a point outside the window.

"If even one of us had become a carrier after that exposure, we would know by now," said Jonah. "But we have to assume that the bee sting is only how they'll introduce the virus to a population. It wouldn't be an effective way to infect masses if that was the only method of contracting and transmitting the virus." He spoke as hushed as the rest of us, but I still skimmed our surroundings to ensure no other passengers were listening.

I locked my arm in Jonah's for comfort as I felt a chill shiver through my body. Across from us, Ilya and Faith were cuddled as well. I felt a moment of longing for the European couples' trip Ilya had promised me.

Envy roiled in my gut for every other blissfully ignorant group of friends backpacking around Europe. I perused the city as the train plowed through it. I pictured streets full of people dying from Terra Nova and I shuddered again.

We had four hours to kill before we would arrive in Chester. I didn't want to spend the whole trip wringing my hands and speculating on just how bloody the end of the world might be. I stood on my toes to reach my backpack on the overhead shelf and fished out my tarot cards.

I propped my elbows on the train table and began to shuffle. I tried to picture what might wait for us in Chester and the face of Ivan's pet snake popped into my mind. Had the snake been named for the town? If so, why? Was the site important?

The train dissolved around me I stood in a glowing golden field outside a small village of cone-shaped thatched huts. It was a peaceful scene, free of the complications of modern urban life. At the center of town was a brick well with metal arms reaching over the opening. At the far end of the settlement stood a small pavilion made with rows of tall white pillars. It suggested a temple of some sort. A woman in a white robe emerged from one of the homes and approached the well. As I watched her walk with a large vase on her head, a flash of red caught the corner of my eye.

A ball of flame rocketed across the field on the other side of the village. It left a trail of smoke that stretched up into the stratosphere. The red ball hit hard and the ground vibrated under my feet. Smoke rose from the patch of wheat around the impact point. A soldier ran past me, past the well, to the crash site.

A rumbling sound came out of the field. An armored thing burst out of the wheat and in one swoop of his metal-plated arm, knocked the soldier to his knees.

The woman dropped her vase. Several villagers ran out of their homes only to stand frozen in shock as the armored person stopped in the middle of their town.

The thing rubbernecked around for a few moments. Its helmet was a smooth metal dome with a dark black slit where the eyes should be. The figure reached to either side of its neck with three-fingered metal hands and released the helmet from the rest of the armor.

The thing lifted its helmet and revealed a reptilian cobra-like head with bright red eyes full of wrath. The cobra man's skin was black with a metallic sheen. Individual scales glittered in the sunlight.

The cobra man bore into me with hateful eyes and made something like a smile with his mouth. He moved one step to his side just as a young boy appeared out of nowhere and plunged a huge sword into the cobra man's chest. The blade that should have impaled the man, or bounced off his armor, somehow crumpled like butter leaving not so much as a scratch on the strange metal. The cobra man knocked the boy aside, sending him flying with one swipe.

The village flickered and jumped forward in time. The huts had all been burned and only their blackened foundations remained. A line of chained people shuffled past me, wearing nothing but loincloths. Each person hung his or her head, struggling to find the energy for another step.

The small temple at the end of the village was gone. In its place, a shining white monument had been erected. The top of the structure was a platform where the cobra man sat on a marble throne, surveying his work. Two hooded figures stood on either side of the cobra king, who still wore his armor on the throne.

I watched the scene spellbound, as one of the purple figures threw back her cloak. A beautiful woman chanted something that sounded like Latin. The cobra king moved to rise, but something held him. He tried to turn, but an unseen force held him rigid.

The woman in purple chanted louder and the cobra man gripped his head with both metal-plated hands. He hissed. She chanted louder still, yelling as she continued.

The cobra king hissed and hissed as the woman in purple pulled a small dagger from her robes. She stepped behind him, reached around his neck, and cut the cobra's throat. Black blood oozed up over his armor and his body lay motionless. Chained villagers looked up and cheered.

I focused on the dead cobra king and willed my viewpoint to the top of his monument. I surged forward and rested above the cobra king's face. Recognition flickered behind my eyes. This was the creature I had seen sitting at Ivan's dining room table back in his cold Victoria condo. Those were the red eyes that haunted me at the Capital City Motel. This was what lived inside Ivan. Somehow. Instinctively I took a step back and the field fell away. I slid through time back onto the train to Chester.

"What did you see?" Jonah stared at me with a furrowed brow.

"Honey, you're shaking." Faith reached out across the table and put her hand on my arm.

I took a deep breath.

"She saw a snake beast," said Ilya, frowning as he harvested the vision from my mind. "Some … thing that crashed to earth and annihilated a village. She saw it come out of a ball of fire and take over and then get killed by some ancient priestess. Holy shit, sis, what the hell?"

"At least someone else can see what I saw," I said to Ilya, calming down. "I think there's more to it. Weeks ago, I dreamed of Ivan and my mother on their honeymoon. They went from Roman ruins to an old church from the Middle Ages. There was a moment where Ivan acted like something possessed him. I think the town I just saw in that vision was the original life of those ruins. I won't know for sure until we get there, Chester could be on top of that ancient village. After we go to Chatham Park, we should find these ruins. That creature got into our father somehow. Maybe we can get it back out again."

"This just took a turn into the Twilight Zone." Cole blew out a long breath.

"And that's saying something for people like us," said Faith.

"Let's worry about Terra Nova. Then we'll think about doing an exorcism on Ivan," said Melissa wearily as she unclipped her hair and rested her head against the back of the booth.

* * *

The British countryside flowed past the train window as I cuddled into Jonah's shoulder. With every stop, passengers came and went. Our group sat under a thick blanket of tension as we wondered how our next – and maybe last – day would end.

A recorded voice announced that our next stop would be Chester. My stomach lurched before the train came to a halt.

"You guys wait at the station while I rent a car. Melissa, if your card is valid, come with me in case they reject mine." Josh watched Melissa expectantly.

We found benches outside the station. I scanned the street in both directions, searching for some sign of the ruins or the church.

"Do you think I have time to look around?" I said to Jonah.

Concern wrinkled his nose. He knew what I wanted to find.

"I think the source of Ivan's madness will be moot if we don't stop this virus from being released."

I paced while gripping my backpack straps firmly.

Josh pulled up alongside the curb in a mint green Volvo van.

"Is this what you call inconspicuous?" Ilya slid the van's side door open.

"We have a seven-seat minimum. It was this or rent two cars. Are you footing the bill?" said Melissa curtly.

"Nobody's sniffin' a gift fish here." Faith used her most appreciative tone.

"Good. Everybody in?" Josh turned around from the driver's seat, observing us with authority as though we were children. "Buckle up, kids."

Josh hit the gas and I lurched forward. "This driving on the wrong side of the road thing is freaking me out."

"Are you sure you want to drive then? I'll give it a try." Cole sounded eager to take the wheel.

"I've driven in the UK. Why don't you let me drive?" Melissa reached towards the wheel.

"No, I'm fine! I can drive the stupid van!" The impatience in Josh's voice made my stomach churn. He drove too fast for someone so unsure.

"If you change your mind, please do so before you crash into a telephone pole," said Melissa crossing her legs and shifting in the seat.

"Just keep the directions coming and I'll be all right." Josh risked a glance at Melissa.

"Look for an exit to the M56. From there, it's a straight shot to Hartford Lane. According to the map, we'll go right past the entrance to the Chatham Park estate." Faith had adopted Nellie's tablet before we left Utah, and the device mercifully still worked in the UK.

More quaint countryside scenery rolled by as we drove. Picturesque hedges and old-world stone walls traded places until we came to a huge grove of trees and a two-story stone arch.

"This must be the place." Josh turned off the lane onto the gravel drive that led to the arch.

A cool breeze drifted through the van as we entered the shade of the trees.

"Aaaaiiie!" Melissa squealed, suddenly flailing for all her worth.

"What? What? Oh shit!" yelled Josh.

I heard a buzzing and I knew what terrified them. Josh hit the brakes and clapped his hands together with a BANG.

"Was it-" I started, but couldn't finish.

"Did you kill it?" said Jonah frantically.

Josh pulled his hands apart. A large dead bee lay crumpled in an oily smear on his palm.

"Burn it." Josh's voice was dark and angry as he glared at the dead insect. We all knew he spoke to Faith and that he could handle the flames.

Faith complied by reaching out her hand. A brief blast was all it took to eradicate the remains.

"Let's end this place." Cole gripped the door until it crunched.

# Chapter 9

J osh pulled into a parking spot at the outer edge of the estate's visitor parking. We were all rattled. I calmed myself knowing we'd found the right place and the Terra Nova ordeal would end soon. Everything else we dealt with after that could be managed without the human race on the line.

"We'll need new disguises." Melissa seemed the most level-headed of us as she carefully re-clipped her hair. "We should be tourists, preferably from a non-English country so we can easily keep to ourselves."

"How about a large Asian family?" said Ilya.

"Bring it!" said Faith.

The telltale feeling of cool wet air filled the van. My friends blurred around me and slowly resolved. Heads of black hair surrounded me. I glimpsed the glass window next to me and saw the reflection of a pretty teenage girl with full lips and a soft white sweater.

Next to me, Jonah's hair remained black, but bone straight

and sculpted with gel. His crisp collared shirt and khaki slacks weren't all that different than something he would normally wear.

Cole, Faith, Ilya, and Josh were all wildly atypical in their preppy outfits and clean-cut hair. Melissa turned around and I saw a lavender outfit exactly like one I'd seen her wear at Innoviro. I began to understand more concretely where Ilya's illusions came from. His mind projected pieces of items and faces he remembered. How intentional those projections were, I'd have to find out over a coffee someday.

"Don't wander off too far and we'll be good for the rest of the day," said Ilya.

"Take a moment and memorize the other faces in this van. If we have to split up and find each other again, you don't want to grab the first dark-haired person you see." Josh seemed far less serious with his new face. Fortunately, Ilya hadn't attempted to change any voices this time.

"I'm sure this goes without saying, but Evonatura's labs will be well hidden. We should be able to gain access from the main manor house and some point out in the adjoining woods. We probably won't find the entrance in the woods, but let's try to find a way into the house's basement level." In her lavender outfit, Melissa regained some of her former snootiness.

Josh examined his face in the rearview mirror. "This is a tourist facility, so off-limits areas will be marked. We can't go by the map on the estate's website because that only showcases the spots they want people to check out. Look for a basement door or stairwell with a rope or sign for private or restricted space."

"Do you still have the tranquilizer guns? It'll be faster than using our abilities to neutralize any security we encounter."

Jonah's eyes, both familiar and strange, connected with mine.

"Our abilities worked just fine back in London." Cole glanced at his sister and massaged his palms, this time with new hands. I wondered briefly if he was jealous that Faith had been the one to kill Adelaide. The thought chilled me. The next adversary who underestimated this man would probably die.

"Shouldn't we assume Casey, Ivan, and Tatiana are on-site, along with all the Evonatura people from London and this facility?" Faith ignited a test flame on her disguised palm. Satisfied, she closed her fist.

"And my sister? Won't Gemma be here too?"

"I'll listen for her. I should hear Casey and Aunt Tat for sure. I won't hear his thoughts, but I'll be able to sense our father." Ilya paused as discomfort distorted his face. Was he connecting the primal snarl he had always sensed from Ivan with the cobra-like monster I'd seen in my visions?

"Melissa and I still have the tranquilizer guns, but we don't know exactly what we'll find. We may have another Soho on our hands if we're confronted. Remember what we're after here. If we see Ivan or Tatiana and there are no witnesses, we should take the opportunity to take them out," said Josh.

"What about innocent people caught in the crossfire?" Jonah's voice got a little louder.

"Anyone involved with Terra Nova is not innocent," said Melissa, calm but firm.

I couldn't help but remember Melissa's role in Terra Nova. Would she seek revenge today?

"We're not getting any younger. Let's do this!" Faith opened the van's door.

The rest of us piled out behind her. As I took stock of our

party, I thought we resembled a small high school class more than a family. Regardless, we would not be what the Innoviro or Evonatura people were hunting.

Faith and Melissa led the way to the small ticket booth on the other side of the arch. Melissa pulled out her wallet again. I considered her reaction if I asked her where the money came from. Had she been that well paid at Innoviro? Or was she able to create a portal into a bank vault and take what she needed, like her surprise black dress in London?

The Chatham Park manor house was a grand Victorian home. Its gray brick and stone pillar exterior implied a library rather than a home, but little touches gave it away. Vases and knicknacks adorned windowsills on the upper level. A restored horse buggy had been posed next to a carriage house.

We crossed the estate lawn via the manicured stone path. The royal vibe from Regent's Park emanated from Chatham too and I half-expected a well-tailored aristocrat to stride past momentarily.

"Good afternoon!" said a short round woman dressed as a Victorian housekeeper. "Have you dears been given your tour yet? We're just startin' another group now. Come on."

The housekeeper tour guide didn't wait for our reply. She seemed not to expect a dialogue. She gestured fervently and we obeyed. Josh frowned at each of us and I knew he meant for us to keep quiet. Since none of us spoke any Asian language we all stayed silent. The housekeeper ushered the rear of the tour group we joined into the house's lobby.

The Chatham Park house was as impressive inside as out. Two staircases curved together connecting two sides of the main lobby to a landing on the upper level.

The main tour guide was a man in a black tuxedo with a

white bowtie and white gloves. His clothing had seen better days, almost a genuine antique as well. "Now, ladies and gents if you'll just follow me, we're on our way through to the main sitting room. We'll go through to the library and dining hall from there."

As our group began to move, I gave Jonah a gaze of approval and I thought to my brother, *This could work in our favor. We get to thoroughly examine everything in the house and we won't be suspected of anything sketchy.*

Ilya rolled his eyes but began to ponder the idea.

The tour guide described the duke and duchess who last lived in the house, their family's heritage, and why the home was eventually donated to a public trust.

It would have been an enjoyable tour if I had been free to lose myself in the drama of old-world aristocracy. The house was beautiful, full of the echoes of fancy people leading privileged lives over a hundred years ago. It looked like a charmed existence that evoked mixed feelings as we moved from room to room.

We shuffled from the sitting room into the library, through to the dining hall, which led to the huge kitchen ringed with bright copper cookware hanging from hooks. We followed our guide up a narrow stairwell to the servant's quarters. We pushed along an upstairs corridor to the family's wing of bedrooms and guest rooms. It was hard to imagine that somewhere in this massive house Ivan and his accomplices were manufacturing the horror of Terra Nova.

Several hallways not taken and doors not labeled caught my eye throughout the tour. Each time I saw a potential door to a stairwell or hall to a secret passage, I shouted mentally at Ilya. It did no good for our route though. Our housekeeper guide remained vigilant in making sure we didn't stray off course.

Back on the lawn in front of the house, the tuxedo guide finally announced the tour's conclusion, and the group dispersed.

"You dears have a lovely time at Chatham Park. Ask at the front gate or find one of the staff if you need anythin' at all," she said a bit too loudly before she bowed and left.

Faith craned her neck around to watch the woman leave. "What was with that bow?"

"Maybe she thinks we're Japanese." Cole shrugged his shoulders.

Melissa smoothed her pencil skirt and adjusted her blazer. "Does it matter?"

"No. That woman has nothing to do with anything. Did we all get a good look at the doors and halls with the potential to connect downstairs?" Josh watched the building as though it could still convey information.

"We should split into three groups. Melissa and Cole, with me on that stone corridor off the kitchen. Irina and Jonah, take that wood door in the-," Josh stopped short as a cry came from the main house behind us.

A shrill shriek followed the cry. The sound was as unnatural in that opulent building as if a lion roared in the middle of an urban mall. Another scream pierced the air and more vocal alarms rang out.

A woman ran out the front door. It was the Mojave coyote in Utah all over again. Her eyes and mouth spewed blood. She clawed at her shirt neck helplessly. The woman vomited. A foamy blend of blood and digested food flowed from her mouth. She heaved again, a gagging cough. Then, she fell to the ground in a lifeless heap.

I stepped closer to her. I stopped as I caught sight of a shiny clump on the woman's back. I barely made out the shape of a large bee before the insect melted into oil and slid off the knit fabric.

More tourists poured out of the manor house in varying stages of extreme illness. Men and women ran in all directions, flailing, vomiting, and shouting. Bees buzzed around them hovering and darting in, received by more shrieks and cries of pain. I felt utter helplessness as the dying crowd panicked around us. Instinctively we formed a circle, backs in, faces out.

"How do we stop it?" Faith yelled over the cries, gurgles, and screams of the victims.

"We can't!" Josh's arms shot out, protecting Melissa on one side and Faith on the other.

"We don't have a cure. We don't even know if there is one," said Jonah.

"Downstairs! They might still be here. We have to catch them!" yelled Josh.

"Irina! Gemma's here. Over there! Follow me," Ilya pointed to a wood shed behind the carriage house.

Josh, Melissa, and the others ran into the manor house after the Innoviro and Evonatura demons responsible for the massacre unfolding in front of us.

I followed my brother to the shed. We reached the door and saw it chained before we could even try the handle.

"She's terrified. They left her here as bait."

"Gemma! It's me! It's Irina! We're here. You're going to be fine," I shouted through the door. To my brother, I added, "Change us back so we don't scare the hell out of her." I felt cool air around me and saw my brother as his normal self.

Out of nowhere Cole elbowed me out of the way and ripped the chain away like ribbon. He yanked the thick wood door off its hinges and swooped into the shed, picking up Gemma effortlessly. Her long straight hair fell behind her like a curtain of wheat. She gaped up at him with a mixture of fear and awe.

"Who are you?" Gemma asked shakily, her face pale.

Cole carried her a few steps onto the lawn and put her down when he realized she was unharmed.

"He's with me. He's a friend from Innoviro," I said.

"I went to Victoria to look for you. Ivan found me and told me everything. He said you got caught up in some kind of cult. He wanted me to help you if we could find you. What's … happening here? Tatiana said that your brother, I mean our brother, would try to brainwash me. They said I'd only be safe here," said Gemma. Her frightened eyes held my gaze until something in her clicked. "You're not in a cult, though, are you?"

"Let's worry about setting the record straight after we bring this place down." I turned to my brother. "Take her to the van. Stay with her." To Cole, I said, "We need to find Faith and get her to torch the basement."

# Chapter 10

The screams ended. Bodies lay on the lobby floor, in an obscene mixture of blood and vomit. I didn't see any bees. I scanned the doorways to my right, left, and straight ahead frantically searching for some sign of my friends. "They must have found the basement."

"We'll try that stone hall off the kitchen." Cole headed quickly but carefully through the bodies and made for a shortcut under the curved stairwells straight to the kitchen. The stone hallway had a steel door at the end. Cole ripped it off like tearing down a curtain.

Dark stairs led down to another steel door. I felt a sense of déjà vu and thought of the Innoviro lab level in Victoria. Only this home had much more history and a darker past than the sewers of BC's capital. This home's lower level had been built by a man participating in an actual cult. I pictured the cobra king again and shuddered. What legacy had that creature left behind? A soul? An essence? Offspring? How had the demon persisted through the millennia? Was that thing somehow, impossibly, inside Ivan?

We reached the second door and Cole popped it open by ripping the doorknob out of the lock assembly. "Nice that this old house doesn't have vault-style deadbolts. Those are messier."

The hall was dark, and an ambulance-style red light flashed above us. I saw figures ahead, past glass-windowed walls. "Josh? Jonah? Faith? Melissa?"

"We're here. We've got her! And that damn snake!" yelled Faith.

Cole and I ran down the hall and my friends' faces came into focus in the dim red light.

We came level with an open doorway and saw Tatiana, frozen in place behind the barrel of Josh's tranquilizer gun. She held a smooth metal canister. She had Chester the snake wrapped around her back, head on one arm, and tail on the other. I saw Josh's real gun poking out of the back of his jeans.

Melissa held her gun relaxed at her hip. Casey lay flat on his back behind Tatiana. Faith and Jonah glared at Tatiana helplessly. Josh stayed cool and motionless as he kept his gun pointed at Tatiana. Cole stood beside me, both of us poised to strike.

"Give us the canister and we'll leave you alive," said Josh.

I knew he was lying, but did Tatiana?

"You think this is the last canister? Kill me or don't. We've already sent Terra Nova to the final launch site. From there, we'll distribute globally. So make your move. Shoot," said Tatiana with a defiant sneer.

"We've gone to a lot of trouble to bring an end to *The Compendium*. Because we know variants can co-exist with humans," said Josh, eyeing Tatiana over the barrel of his gun.

"There isn't a need for what you and Ivan are trying to pull off. It's beyond genocide. It's an extinction the planet won't survive. You haven't thought it through. You can't control the level of geological and biological change you're planning," said Jonah.

"Why not hold off on launching Terra Nova? We can re-evaluate *The Compendium* and work together on creating space for variants," said Melissa. Tatiana glared at her former subordinate.

I knew we were trying to keep Tatiana talking, but I couldn't understand why. I tried to will the canister from her hands telekinetically. It moved, but Tatiana held on tight. I tried again. Her grip was too strong for me.

"We wanted to preserve variant life, where possible. In your case, it seems it is no longer possible." Tatiana glowered at me with malice in her eyes. "Except for Ivan's children. You, we need."

"Where is the final launch site?" Melissa asked impatiently.

"You didn't need our help to find Soho or Chatham Park. Why should I spoon-feed you anything more?" Tatiana spat the word 'spoon' with contempt.

"How many other test sites are there? Where are your secondary introduction points?" Josh impressed me with his calm tone of voice.

I, on the other hand, felt as though my head and heart were about to explode.

"This is getting boring. You have one shot and two targets. I suggest you put me down and play with Chester. Then again, it is a risk. You don't know what either the snake or I am capable of, do you? Or you could let us pass and cut your losses." Tatiana smiled a dark green grin.

"Cut our losses?" screamed Faith.

"You killed every human being on this property. The contagion may still spread after help arrives. You might have introduced the virus already!" I shouted, feeling rage swell inside me.

"You're an evil bitch! You and Ivan and your psychotic Compendium partners all deserve to die!" yelled Faith.

"That's a valid point. If you want to stop the spread of the virus here in England, you should probably have your little friend here burn this estate to the ground," Tatiana spoke directly to me, smirking.

Josh glanced up from his gun for a moment to better assess Tatiana. He made his choice and lifted the tranquilizer back to eye level. Josh fired and a dart hit Chester the snake in his meaty neck. The snake reared and then dropped to the ground.

Tatiana pulled seeds from her pocket and breathed life into a torrent of vines that burst at all of us.

Josh and Melissa were knocked to the ground and covered in a thick blanket of foliage. Tatiana broke into a sprint and tore off down the hall ahead. A wall of wiry branches and thick leaves sprang up and blocked the rest of us from following her.

Cole tore through the vine wall and Faith reached out to shoot a thick stream of fire after Tatiana. It was too late. Her pounding footfalls faded away. Cole ripped the thick vine bonds off of Josh and Melissa.

"We can't let her get away!" said Melissa.

"She's right. We need to contain this site. Faith, if you don't incinerate this place, a medical investigation could launch the plague." Jonah had a firm grip on Faith's arm, giving her a hard do-this-now stare.

"Get everybody out to the van. Or I'm the only one that's going to survive this." Clasping her hands, Faith stretched her arms overhead.

She thrust fire around the lab until a hot orange flame consumed the room. Casey and Chester lay motionless on the ground as their bodies caught fire. A lone canister on the back counter caught fire and exploded hot blue liquid.

The liquid transformed into bees mid-air, catching fire as they flew in a frenzy around the room.

"Go! Now!" she yelled.

"Get upstairs! We'll cut Tatiana off in the woods!" said Josh, already running.

"I'll go for the van." Melissa opened a portal, stepped through, and shut it behind her.

The rest of us raced back up the dark stairwell, through the kitchen, and out the back door into a sculpted garden with a large koi pond and a fountain at the center.

Several men and women had tried to escape, scrambling out of the building into the garden. They lay in macabre positions near the pruned shrubberies and rosebushes. At the end of the yard, a wall of green hedge closed in the back of the property.

Cole reached the hedge first and tore a hole which grew back quickly. Josh joined in and the two started tearing uselessly as the hedge branches clawed into the gaps intertwining again in moments.

Faith caught up with us and I looked back at the house. She had done her job well. She shot fireballs at each of the bodies on the ground.

Jonah beckoned the fountain's water up into the air and doused the ground and the trees around the house. I hoped his experience keeping Faith in check would still serve us on this scale.

"Should I take out the hedge too?" cried Faith over the crackling of the house fire and the surging fountain water.

"We can't risk a forest fire!" shouted Jonah.

"I've almost got it!" shouted Cole as he tore another huge hole in the hedge and ripped into the earth pulling out a handful of roots.

Cole's gap was large enough to run through and I made a break for it. I sensed Jonah and Faith behind me. I turned around to see Cole and Josh bringing up the rear as the hedge grew back behind them.

I caught sight of a path ahead and ran to it. The dirt trail disappeared into the trees in both directions. I saw a flicker of movement on my right and bolted to it.

The earth crunched as my friends hit the path behind me. Our van rumbled behind me, but I ran towards the movement.

Tatiana's green-streaked head bobbed between the trees and dropped out of sight. I ran as hard as I could to the spot where she disappeared.

I reached a mound with wood shutters flat on the ground and I stopped short. There was no lock, but I paused to puzzle over where the tunnel led. I took a deep breath and placed my hand carefully on the seam between the shutters. I pictured Tatiana's face and the woods melted away.

I was in the tunnel with her, my view bouncing behind her as she ran through the dark. I forced my perspective ahead and slid through the black tunnel. A sudden burst of light blinded me and I stood on a lawn behind the ruined brick chapel from my parents' honeymoon. Ivan's face appeared in a space between crumbled walls and disappeared again.

I lifted my hand from the shutter door as the van pulled up behind me. I closed my eyes and showed Ilya what I saw in the tunnel.

"We can beat her to the chapel!" said Ilya.

Cole slid the van's door open. Ilya peeled out. The van rattled through the narrow forest trail until we burst back out onto the country lane. My brother turned the steering wheel so hard that the van flipped up on two wheels. Then, it slammed back onto the road with a bang, racing ahead.

"Where are we going?" Faith gripped her seat as she leaned forward.

Ilya swerved to pass around a car and veered back narrowly missing an oncoming station wagon.

"Are you trying to get us killed?" said Cole.

"Ivan's still in town at that ruined chapel. If we beat Tatiana to the church, we'll catch them both!" I said.

Ilya turned back onto the M56 highway, speeding as he wove through regular traffic.

"We're going to wind up in a police chase at this rate." Josh glowered at Ilya.

"Tatiana has a canister of Terra Nova! And wherever they're going next, they've got more waiting. If we stop them now, the whole Compendium grinds to a halt," said Ilya over his shoulder.

"We don't know that for sure," said Jonah.

"This is our best shot," I said, pleading, hoping Ilya would stay on target and keep blazing into Chester.

"I am so sorry Irina! I had no idea they were cooking up a virus! I thought they were trying to help variants. All those people died so horribly. I could have done something. I don't know what, but something. Tatiana sounded so convincing about helping you – all of you." Gemma's plaintive lament wasn't comforting anyone.

"Kid, save your confession for another day." Faith scowled at Gemma.

"Cut her some slack." Cole slapped Faith's shoulder.

"Stop it, all of you," said Josh as Ilya cranked the wheel hard again.

# Chapter 11

Ilya screeched into the parking lot of the large Gothic church. Hard late afternoon sun glowed on the red brick ruins, exactly as I'd seen them in my vision of my parents' honeymoon.

We poured out of the van when Ilya lurched to a halt.

"Spread out! Look for a shed or shutters or a trap door," I shouted.

"Dad? Dad, are you here?" Ilya ran through the parking lot to the back end of the church. He grabbed my attention; my twin rarely used the word 'Dad' for Ivan.

I raced after him with Jonah a step behind me. I knew Ilya was headed in the right direction.

We rounded the corner and there were the cellar shutters, just like the ones we saw at Chatham Park. They were closed. Ivan and Tatiana were nowhere in sight.

"She couldn't have beaten us here? Where are they?" I cried desperately.

"I can't hear either of them. They're not here," said Ilya,

utterly dejected.

Josh and Cole appeared around the far corner of the church. Faith, Gemma, and Melissa were on their heels.

"Where did they go? Irina? Ilya?" said Josh. His tone accused us of something.

"Maybe Ivan went in and turned Tatiana back? Then they're on their way to Chatham Park," said Cole.

"Or she did beat us here and they took off already. Even if they were on foot, it wouldn't take long to disappear from the street," said Josh.

"Fuck this! Fuck everything to do with this!" screamed Faith.

"Shut up!" I told her. "We don't need this right now."

"We're not at a dead end. We've got a telepath and a psychic here," said Jonah. He took my hand and his calm energy pulled me back from the brink of panic.

"There's nothing more I can do," said Ilya.

"Irina, you can try to see what happened." Jonah's tone soothed me, but I still wanted to punch something.

Instead, I closed my eyes and pictured Ivan's face behind the brick ruins.

A black blink later I was on a train with Tatiana and Ivan. Ivan's complexion had faded to pale ashen gray-pink. He had always been pale, but this was different. Death had kissed him, reducing his strawberry blonde hair to near platinum.

"We can't keep running. The treatment won't work much longer. You're taking higher doses more often. It's time for the transplant." Tatiana fussed over a blanket on his lap.

He rested, eyes closed. "We're not ready. Jinhua must do their part and they haven't even started Phase One."

"Why don't we release Terra Nova now? The test was

successful. Your children will be much easier to catch once they can't hide in human society."

Ivan opened his pale hazel eyes and stared at his sister with bloodshot anger. She met his gaze and broke contact quickly. Ivan resumed his resting position.

"The complexity of *The Compendium* requires the participation of industry and individuals that will be obliterated by Terra Nova. It must be our very last step. My true brothers from my real home cannot thrive here. Variants cannot thrive here. *The Compendium* can only be achieved if we stay on schedule and keep to our plan."

"Shall we move on to ground zero?" said Tatiana.

"Yes. And the more we discuss this, the more ammunition you give my daughter." Ivan turned slightly away from Tatiana to face the window and the countryside.

"We should assume they know everything as it is. Melissa very likely shared *The Compendium* outline with them. They have all the research, execution, and implementation plans we had in Utah."

Ivan turned back to his sister, but instead of meeting her gaze, he found my astral self. His face conveyed rage and for a brief flicker, his pupils flashed the bright red of the cobra king's eyes.

I jumped back and fell hard on my butt with my hand outstretched at the closed cellar shutters. The shaded lawn behind the church was cool under my legs where I landed.

"They're on a train. Ivan is sick, like possibly dying sick. His body is rejecting that thing inside him. I don't know what kicked that off, but he *needs* to change the planet. The thing inside him wants a new host. And it's planning to bring friends from its home, wherever that is," I said, shaking as my brain fought to both understand and expel the images.

"So, what is the status of Terra Nova?" said Jonah, gently but firmly.

"Where do they plan to release it?" Josh stepped forward as though he might throttle the information from my head.

"Ivan said they need to finish other projects before releasing Terra Nova. The timeline is in The Compendium. They're headed to a 'ground zero' location, but I didn't see that part," I said, grinding my fingers into my temples.

"Of course you didn't. That's helpful." Faith's purple dreads splayed in the air as she tossed her head.

"*The Compendium* is too complex to set in motion without human infrastructure. Whatever earthquakes and floods and poisonous shit he's planning to unleash, he needs the unwitting accomplices working with Innoviro and Evonatura and Jinhua."

"We should spend more time with *The Compendium* documents. We were tracking Terra Nova because that was the worst of it, but if they're putting that off, we need to know what comes next." Melissa skimmed the ground around her as though the answers lay there.

"Especially if it's disastrous enough to pave the way for more creatures like the one you've described," said Jonah.

"Where did it come from? This thing that's got Ivan," said Cole.

I replayed the scene in my mind, to share it with Ilya again and refresh my memory.

"A fireball that fell to earth thousands of years ago," said Ilya.

"A meteor then," said Jonah, rubbing his chin.

"I guess so," I said, exhausted.

"Okay, they're on a train. They're not releasing Terra Nova right now. We have some time." Josh scanned the buildings around us, evaluating.

"Where do we go from here?" Melissa looked to Josh for the answer.

"I'm starving. We're going for dinner," said Faith flatly.

"There's a pub across the street." Cole pointed at an awning with faded letters.

"Are you sure that's a pub? Or open for business?" Jonah squinted at the door and a man in a newsboy cap exited.

"It'll do." Cole started towards the pub and the others followed him.

"You guys go ahead. I'll catch up," I said.

Jonah took my hand and smiled. I was glad he wanted to stay. Unless I was lying in bed, I felt safer checking out of reality for the length of a vision with someone around to watch my back.

I walked through the red brick ruins, now totally under the shadow of the office building down the street. I found the altar where I had seen Ivan, my father, place his hand and get possessed by what I could only assume was the essence of a long-dead alien monster.

My hand hovered over the crumbling stone altar for a moment. I hadn't specifically told anyone how Ivan had picked up his inner demon. If I told Jonah now, he wouldn't let me touch it. But, it would spark a vision. It would reveal something awesome, something amazing, wouldn't it?

I stared at the stone. *Who are you? Where did you come from? Why here? Why us?*

I touched the cold limestone slab. Nothing happened. I wanted to cry out like Faith. Instead, I let tears roll freely down my cheeks. My voice shook. "This altar was supposed to have the answers."

"This is where you saw Ivan and your mother?" Jonah asked softly.

"That thing; I don't know how it got into him, but it happened here," I said, fully crying.

"Maybe you should take your hand off that stone now." Jonah's empathetic tone comforted me.

I reluctantly complied. I let him lead me across the street and into the pub. It was mostly empty so we saw our friends right away.

The entire establishment was silent, focused on the television screen behind the bar. The volume had been turned up so we could all hear the newscast.

"BBC correspondent Janine Knight is on location in nearby Shanghai. Janine can you tell us exactly what is happening out on the Taihu Lake right now?" said the anchorman.

The screen was split between the anchor sitting behind his desk and a woman holding a microphone standing in front of a government building.

"Well, Roger, I can tell you that this disaster is very far from being resolved," said Janine hurriedly. "Chinese officials disclosed that a plastic manufacturing facility and a nuclear power plant both suffered small fires earlier this morning, not successfully contained. What makes this disaster so frightening is that two nearby wind farms on the shore of Taihu Lake, one near each fire site, have somehow funneled the toxic fumes and radioactive fallout into an air current broadcasting poison out into the open ocean. If it continues at this rate, evacuation orders will be issued for the entire south coast of Japan. The attempts to evacuate Greater Shanghai have come to a virtual standstill on major highways. Air and sea evacuation efforts are ongoing, but hospitals continue to overflow with people sick and dying faster than authorities can move people out. I am going to have to evacuate after this broadcast." Janine did not attempt to mask the terror on her face.

"That is heartbreaking and terrifying, Janine. Has there been no attempt to shut off the wind turbines of each of the farms directing the deadly fumes?" asked Roger the anchor.

"Officials have been desperately trying to coordinate with a company called Jinhua Energy, a subsidiary of Jinhua Enterprises, but the representatives of the wind farms insist they could not possibly be responsible for the deadly air current. The next step will be for the Chinese government to take military action to shut down the wind farms. It's a devastating step when China has been making so much progress in moving to green energy sources. But, that's all I have time for, Roger. I'm getting the signal that it's time for me to board a helicopter." Janine cast a panicked glance at someone off camera.

"We won't keep you. Thank you for taking the time to share this update, Janine. Have a safe journey," said Roger, who continued his commentary as I turned away.

I leaned on a pub table reaching vaguely in Jonah's direction. My friends stood nearby. They all stared, jaws dropped, at the terrible disaster coverage.

The TV screen displayed a map of the Chinese coast around Shanghai. Red fog represented the patch of earth affected by the poisonous cloud. It fanned out like an inverted comet.

"Did she say Jinhua?" said Melissa.

"Goddamn it!" Faith pounded the table with her fist.

"On the train just now, Ivan said that Jinhua hadn't started Phase One, but he was waiting on it," I said as I sat bolt upright.

"Is *this* Phase One?" Jonah stabbed his hand at the television.

"I sure as hell don't want to see Phase Two!" Cole paced in front of us.

"We can pore over Compendium documents for the next month and still not achieve the big picture already humming with precision in Ivan's mind. If we don't have time, I say we keep going after Ivan and Tatiana. At least we know what we're up against there," said Josh, checking each of us for agreement.

"You're willing to allow mass destruction? Ecological disasters?" Melissa didn't take her eyes off the screen above us.

"I'm saying we cannot stop it. There are seven of us. Maybe, just maybe, we have a chance of killing Ivan and Tatiana." Josh spoke as quietly as he could. We had already drawn the attention of nearby pub patrons.

"I know you still don't want to hear this, but I'm sorry I didn't see through those two before. I'll make up for my mistake. I'll do anything to help." Gemma's voice sounded younger than I remembered. I had to keep reminding myself we had her now.

"Keep your voice down!" hissed Faith.

The bartender lifted his head and evaluated us.

"If we decide to keep chasing Ivan and Tatiana, we need to know where they're going." Josh eyed me impatiently.

"I've already tried. Ivan's getting smarter about keeping things from me."

"That's bullshit. He doesn't have the power to stop you from seeing reality. Remember, you're not listening to people's minds, you're tapping into something bigger than that." Ilya, of all people, knew what Ivan was capable of, but I thought it was wishful thinking that my gift could perfectly fill the gap left by his.

"You just need to focus. If they know where they're going, and they do, you'll find a way to see it." Jonah leaned over, kissed me softly, and pulled back.

A thought occurred to me. I got out of my chair and walked over to Gemma. I hugged her and it felt good. I pushed the images of our parents and our home out of my mind.

I held my sister and closed my eyes. I thought about Ivan and Tatiana on the train. Nothing happened. I pictured the shiny steel canister from the lab under Chatham Park.

A gust knocked the wind out of me and I stood on a brick plaza facing a multi-faceted cylindrical tower topped by a disc. Flags bordered the plaza. Next to the tower, unfamiliar trees surrounded a large metal cone-capped hut. Dark-skinned pedestrians passed back and forth across the plaza. Instinct told me I was somewhere in Africa.

A shiny black plaque caught my eye and I willed myself to it. My viewpoint surged forward and the inscription came into full view.

THIS CONFERENCE CENTER WAS OPENED BY HIS EXCELLENCY

MZEE JOMO KENYATTA CGH MP

FIRST PRESIDENT AND COMMANDER-IN-CHIEF

OF THE ARMED FORCES OF THE REPUBLIC OF KENYA

ON TUESDAY 11TH SEPTEMBER 1973

IN THE TENTH YEAR OF OUR NATIONAL INDEPENDENCE.

Kenya? I assumed the city was Nairobi.

Ivan and Tatiana crossed my path coming from behind me and I refocused on them. Ivan had recovered somewhat from his state on the train.

I hung a pace behind them as they walked. Ivan brushed his shoulders as if something irritated him. Perhaps he'd been improving his ability to sense my mind. They rode an elevator to the twenty-second floor and exited. They arrived at a door marked Kisumu Laboratory Services. Ivan swiped a card through a reader next to the door handle and a red light turned green.

They went into an empty office and turned down a hall. They entered a room with cabinets and containers. I had come to know a specimen library when I saw one. Tatiana extracted a tray of vials from a mini fridge while Ivan rolled up his sleeve

Tatiana wasted no time in injecting a full vial into Ivan. He unrolled his shirt sleeve and buttoned the cuff before unlocking a cabinet above them.

Dozens of mirror-finish steel canisters glinted in the fluorescent light. They were exact copies of what I'd seen Tatiana remove from the basement of Chatham Park.

Ivan lovingly ran his finger across the canisters with satisfaction beyond confirming the unchanged inventory. He caressed them. The vision ended when he locked the cabinet door.

# Chapter 12

"They're going to Kenya." I released my sister from our embrace and stepped back.

I scanned the pub and breathed a sigh of relief. The bartender busily polished the bar while the two pairs of aged patrons played an electronic lottery game.

"They're going where?" said Ilya.

I closed my eyes and recalled the images for my brother's benefit. The faceted tower, the metal hut, the trees, the plaque.

"She's not kidding. They're going somewhere called the Kenyatta International Conference Center."

"And they've got a huge supply of Terra Nova stashed there," I said quietly.

"How are we going to get to Kenya?" Cole crossed his arms accentuating their size.

In unison, we all turned our heads to Melissa.

"I've never been to Kenya. I've never been to Africa period." Melissa's furrowed brow and sorrowful eyes filled my heart with pity. It wasn't her fault we had a long road ahead.

"Does anyone have a valid passport with them?" Jonah plunged his hand into his black hair.

"We're not going to Kenya, are we?" said Gemma excitedly.

Faith regarded Gemma with an angry frown. Gemma stared down at the table.

"The Evonatura office will likely have a collection of stolen or fake passports in their safe. Innoviro did," said Melissa.

"Shit, are you serious?" Cole frowned with disbelief.

"Why should anything surprise us now?" Jonah dropped into a rickety pub chair.

"But stuff like that would have been lost in the fire. Or seized by the police," I said quietly, leaning into our group.

"Not necessarily. If Claude used anything like the fireproof wall safe that Ivan did, it could have survived the fire and remained hidden." Melissa fished her lip balm out of her purse and reapplied it nervously.

"We never did see how bad the damage was." Cole took a seat with Jonah at the table.

"How will Ivan travel to Kenya?" Jonah asked Melissa.

"He'll probably fly, as direct a route as he can, as soon as possible. I think he'll stay within the law if he can, albeit with an unlimited budget," said Mellisa.

Josh nodded in agreement.

"He's like, crazy sick now, right? Will that change anything?" said Faith hopefully.

"He was better when I saw him in Kenya," I answered. "Tatiana's injecting him with something that keeps his illness in check."

"If he did it for me, of course, he'd do it for himself," said Jonah.

"Maybe that's what he wants with us. He needs to study us

or harvest something to cure himself." Ilya rubbed his eyes and my heart broke for him. Ivan was my father too, but I'd never known him. Ilya had been peeling back layers of the man who raised him, finding more and more rot.

I remembered the word 'transplant' and my core grew cold as I realized who the intended new host was.

"I can't tell what's wrong with him," I said. "From what I saw, it's bad. Being invaded or possessed or whatever happened, can't be good for a person. When I said that thing inside him wanted a new host, it was because Tatiana said that it was time for a transplant." I looked at Ilya to make sure I didn't have to say it out loud. My brother nodded and looked down at the table.

"Back to these passports. Can you create effective illusions from the photos? Can you turn us into whoever we need to be?" Josh said to Ilya.

"It'll be good enough for a customs officer. I'm more concerned about how many passports are there. If I created an illusory passport, it wouldn't stand up to an airport security scan. Passports have digital crap in them nowadays. I can't fake that. However many passports we can get, that's how many go to Kenya."

"We should get back to London before we worry about how many go and who." Jonah's blue eyes lit up with a flicker of anticipation.

"Yeah, there's no point in arguing until we know what's in that safe," said Faith.

"That's one leg of the trip I can shorten," said Melissa. "I think I can open a portal discretely enough in the ruins across the street. Especially at night."

"What about the van?" Ilya looked at Josh, handing the keys

back.

"We'll take it back. If they're closed, I'll leave it in the rental parking lot," said Josh.

"Your rental, your call." Cole's muscles flexed involuntarily as he shifted his stance. I caught Gemma staring at him and I almost laughed.

Melissa went to the bar and paid for our beers. Josh retrieved our van from its parking spot and took Melissa with him to the rental office. The rest of us went back to the church ruins to wait.

"So is this your boyfriend?" Gemma offered her hand to Jonah. He shook it with a polite smile.

"I wish I could say I'd heard so much about you, but my sister hasn't exactly kept in touch," said Gemma.

"You had your memory wiped! How could I just call you up?" I said indignantly while trying to keep my voice down. The streets of Chester looked empty, but I couldn't be sure.

"Well, I didn't know I'd lost my memory. I didn't even know I was a healer, but if you'd taken a moment to reach out, maybe I would have gotten my memory back sooner." Gemma's familiar sing-song tone of reproach went directly under my skin.

"How could I possibly have known you were a variant, let alone capable of self-healing your amnesia? As far as I knew, my variation came from my father – and we don't have the same one. Remember?" I struggled with the frustration erupting in my belly.

"Oh, your variations *did* come from him, but he also gave Mom some kind of 'booster' to make you guys more powerful. Didn't you know that? How is it that *I* know that and you don't?" Gemma snarked at me, oblivious to the stares of my friends.

"Should we maybe have just left you in that shed? Would you be happier back with Ivan?" I said through a hard glare.

A second later it clicked that Gemma said 'variations' in the plural. She was up-to-date. That meant Ivan and Tatiana were too.

"It does make sense. If your mother didn't have a natural genetic variation, and Ivan introduced a gene-altering agent during her pregnancy, it could have remained in her system and affected subsequent children," said Jonah.

"I'm glad we got that figured out." I glared at him and he closed his mouth.

"Ivan said you had two variations. I wonder if I can do more than healing. Is there a test you guys can do?" Gemma looked from Jonah to Cole and Ilya. All of whom looked bewildered by her.

"Let's worry about that sometime down the road." Jonah put his arm around my shoulder. I felt him trying to calm me.

Melissa and Josh popped out of the air mere feet away. A few minutes later, we were stepping out of another portal back in London.

# Chapter 13

We emerged from Melissa's portal in an alley down the street from Evonatura's office. I could smell the charred wreckage on the summer breeze. The foul odor was stronger than the scents of the alley.

"Give me a second." Ilya listened to something in the distance. "Nah, there's nobody in their building."

"Gemma, you stay here. Jonah, guard her," I said flatly.

"I don't need a babysitter. I'm only sixteen months younger than you. And Ilya." Gemma's mouth formed the petulant pout she always used to get her way.

"You're still a kid, barely eighteen," I said.

"I'm old enough." Gemma eyed Cole again and that time, he noticed. "If you're so worried about me, leave the strong guy here," said Gemma, gesturing at Cole.

Cole opened his mouth to answer, but I raised my hand. "We need him to bust open the safe if we find one. Jonah is plenty strong enough to take on anyone who comes near you." I smiled at him, confident in his recovery. Jonah grinned back at me.

"I'll stay too," said Ilya.

Cole considered Gemma sympathetically, but I shoved him forward.

Melissa gave the street a quick scan and opened a portal. I followed Cole, Josh, and Faith. We came out inside the Evonatura sitting room. In the dark, I couldn't properly see how badly the fire had damaged the structure. But the smells of charcoal and melted plastic were strong.

"Start checking picture frames. And look for locked cabinet drawers or doors," said Melissa, peeking behind an abstract splash of color.

I left the sitting room paintings to the taller guys. I wanted to seize my chance to see what was down the hall of offices on the other side of Evonatura's lunchroom.

The hallway smelled far less pungent than the rest of the office space. I took a deep breath as I walked.

Three doors were ajar and I peered into the first office, an administrator's room. A plain wood desk with a hutch took up the corner. A single guest chair sat on the other side. There were no pictures on the wall or personal effects on the table.

I moved on to the next office. It was almost the same as the first. The hutch rested flat along the wall, not backed into a corner. There were two guest chairs.

The last office was Claude's. A window displayed a court-yard hidden from the street. His chair was a tall leather corporate throne, padded for comfort. He did not have a hutch, but a long glass-on-wood executive desk with a simple blotter at the center.

Two pictures hung on Claude's wall, a panorama of London and a painted portrait of Claude in a suit, sitting in an armchair, hands clasped in a gesture of satisfied achievement. The painting was just the sort of thing a self-involved CEO would commission. I lifted it off the wall and punched through the stiff canvas. I dropped it when my eyes registered a wall safe where the portrait had been.

"Cole, get in here!" I called.

Heavy footsteps plodded down the hall.

"You found it?" Cole gave a rare smile of delight.

I pointed at the metal door with a numbered knob.

"Awesome." Cole shoved his fingers between the drywall and the edges of the safe. He pulled the huge heavy metal box out of the wall with a loud scrape.

He placed the container on the carpeted floor, door side up, and punched the front of the safe. The blow allowed Cole to peel off the damaged door like a sticker from a page. He upended and shook the safe like a kid with a box of crackers. "Let's see what Evonatura thinks is worth hiding."

The others came into the office. Cole picked up the safe contents and spread them across Claude's desk.

Several wads of currency rolled away and onto the ground. British Pounds. American Dollars. The largest roll was Euros. I hastily gathered up the money and stuffed it into my backpack.

"Now someone other than me can pick up the tab," said Melissa, hand on her hip.

Josh sifted through the papers and envelopes on the desk. "We've got passports!"

"How many? From where?" Faith closed the distance to the desk.

"Hang on, let me gather them." Josh brushed a few envelopes to the ground and cast more papers aside. "Two American, two Canadian, four British, one German, and I think three Russian. We've got more than what we need, so we should study them and match them up as closely as we can. It's not just for photos; if we're getting on a plane or a boat or anywhere they check passports, we'll need to talk about where we were last, when, and why."

Cole picked up an American passport and opened it. Faith picked up a Canadian passport and started flipping through it. Josh set the Russian passports aside and flipped through the rest one by one.

"Denmark, April eighth, O-two. Back to Britain, April fourteenth. Korea, September twenty-second, O-seven. Back again on that one. The most recent stamp is for Athens, Greece on March tenth of this year. No stamp back in though."

Josh threw them down on the table and kicked the leg.

"What's the problem? We've got passports," I said.

"According to the stamps, these passports never left Greece back in March," said Cole.

"So how the hell are they here now?" said Faith.

Josh swept his hand above the scattered booklets. "It doesn't matter! We can't use them in London!"

"I can get us to the Greek island of Santorini." Melissa picked up a passport and turned it over in her hand. "I went on vacation there with my parents as a child. It was a long time ago, but I can get us there."

"I could kiss you!" blurted Josh.

"Buy me dinner first," said Melissa with a wry smile.

"Grab the passports and let's go," said Cole.

Gemma was as excited to go to Greece as she had been for Kenya. I admitted to myself that, circumstances aside, it was amazing to travel like this. If only we could go sightseeing. I felt stress and fatigue setting in as we huddled in a muggy London alley.

"So what's our game plan once we arrive in Crete?" Faith asked Melissa. Faith adjusted her eyebrow ring as she thought, to Melissa's disgust.

"We need a place to stay. Time difference aside, we'll drop dead from exhaustion if we don't sleep," I said.

"I'll put us on a hillside just outside a town called Fira. I don't remember the streets well enough to know where the alleys, corners, parks, or other hidden spots will be. And it's been about twenty years, so a lot could have changed."

"What if the hillside is a suburb now?" Jonah took a drink from his water bottle.

"I'll test it. I haven't walked into a wall yet. Let's hope this isn't my first time," Melissa opened a new portal and eyed it for a beat before plunging an arm in. "So far, so good." She stepped through and we waited. An excruciating long minute passed. And Melissa finally reappeared. "We're good to go."

Her swirling silver oval hovered in the air, imitating liquid metal as we watched. Melissa walked back through. The rest of my friends followed through the silver pool. I lingered. I wanted one more vision to show me we were on the right path. I hesitated, thinking I should be able to see past Ivan's arrival in Nairobi. If I concentrated hard enough, would I see the outcome of *The Compendium*? I saw nothing but black behind my eyelids, so I stepped through the portal.

A torrent of dust and sand engulfed me. Coarse brown curtains filled the air. I tried to open my eyes. The sand burned my skin and choked me. I walked forward. My foot hit something hard, knocking me off balance. My backpack lurched against my shoulders. I hit the ground, face-first.

# Chapter 14

The sandstorm beat my body. I choked. I curled my arms around my head, shielding my face. I cupped my hands around my mouth, desperate to breathe.

A large hand grabbed my bicep and yanked me to my feet. Jonah opened his jacket, enveloped me, and put his lips to my ear. "Something went wrong."

"You think?" I shouted back.

"We have to find Melissa to get out of here. Cole has your sister. Ilya and Faith are here too, but we haven't found Melissa or Josh," Jonah bellowed against the wind.

He lifted his jacket enough for me to see Cole with his arms wrapped around Gemma. Ilya had his shirt over his nose. Faith had pulled her dreadlocks around her face like a veil.

"We should find shelter and wait out the storm," Jonah yelled to the group.

"Bad plan," Cole yelled back. "The storm could last for hours. Melissa and Josh could be anywhere, moving away from us."

"Can't you hear them?" I yelled at Ilya.

He shook his head and yelled back at me. "No better than you can 'see' them!"

"Try again! Concentrate!" Faith shouted at Ilya.

"Wait, I have an idea," I blurted.

I closed my eyes to focus and burrowed into Jonah's jacket to escape the storm. I pictured the sand stopping mid-air and dropping to the ground, dust and all. I pictured us inside a bubble of calm air like a glass dome around us in the swirling mass of loose dirt. The crackling chaos around us went silent.

"Irina!" yelled Ilya, way too loudly.

"Nicely done!" said Faith at regular volume.

I pulled away from Jonah's jacket and I saw the reality of what my telekinetic ability had produced.

There was no glass dome. Not all the sand had been pushed away. It was like being inside a beige snow globe. Granules of dirt and dust floated as though moving inside a liquid.

The sandstorm carried on in the distance. Invisible walls around and above us kept the wind and debris from entering our space. Faith shook copious amounts of sand from her hair and the rest of us brushed grainy dust off our faces.

"There they are!" said Cole. He released an arm from around Gemma to wave, beckoning them into our fragile shelter.

As they moved closer to us, I saw Josh towing Melissa by her hand. He broke through into the bubble and took a desperate gasp of air. He pulled in Melissa. She gulped and fell to the ground coughing.

"Where the shit are we?" Faith shouted at Melissa.

"I don't know. I think ... I must have been thinking about the Syrian sandstorms I read about in Compendium files." Melissa coughed a few more times.

"You brought us to a fucking sandstorm?" yelled Ilya.

"We would have been better off swimming to Greece!" shouted Cole.

"I'm sorry! It was an accident. My memories of Santorini are faint at best so I must have slipped off course. I'll try again."

"Damn right, you're gonna try again!" Faith continued knocking dust and dirt out of individual dreads.

"Would you mind testing it first before the rest of us go through?" said Jonah.

"Of course, she's going to fucking test it!" said Faith.

"It's not her fault. We're lucky we have her with us. You know anyone else who can open a portal between two points in space?" I yelled at Faith.

Faith glared at me and resumed shaking sand out of her dreadlocks.

"Melissa, I don't want to make this worse, but I'm not sure how long my little miracle bubble here will last."

"I'm ready. Just give me one more moment." Melissa dusted herself off and rubbed sweaty dirt off her face. She closed her eyes and took a deep breath, coughed, and recovered. She breathed in and out and in and out. Then she swooped her arm slowly and carefully through the air until her liquid silver oval came back to life. She plunged through the uncertain gateway.

We waited nervously for a moment. No one spoke. Suddenly Melissa came back through the portal smiling. "Come on guys, it's a sunny day on Santorini."

She stepped into her oval and I followed first, hoping my confidence would inspire the others. Jonah kept hold of my hand and slipped through behind me.

The bright sun blinded me for a moment. As my eyes

adjusted, a cliff-top plateau of dry grass unfolded around me. Melissa had chosen her spot well. We were isolated from the town which clung to a cliff far away. Beaches below were full of sunbathers too distant to notice the flicker of Melissa's portal.

Josh brushed dirt from his vest and pants. "We should find some water and clean up first. If we head into town looking like we just escaped a sandstorm, we'll attract attention."

"I've got this." Jonah walked to the edge of the cliff. As though he pulled a rope up from a climb, he guided seawater up a channel on the side of the cliff facing away from the tourist hub. He pulled and pulled until a pool of murky seawater swirled beside us in mid-air.

"That's the best I can do on an arid Mediterranean island." Jonah shook off his dirty jacket and plunged his arms into the floating basin-less bath. He splashed his face. The water pleased him and he immersed himself leaving only his calves and feet bare.

Faith plunged in and I gingerly touched the edge of the pool. The water smelled of salt and seaweed, but it was warm. I splashed my face a bit and retreated since Jonah's jacket had kept the worst of the storm off me.

Once everyone had their fill of wetting and washing, Jonah eased the water to the ground. Water flooded our feet and then gushed back down off the edge of the cliff.

"Everybody ready to explore Greece? Meet some locals?" said Ilya.

"We'll find more tourists than locals around here," said Melissa.

"Just walk." Faith frowned as she untangled a long strip of seaweed wrapped around one of her thick locks.

The Mediterranean sun dried us quickly as we walked along a dirt path to the cluster of whitewashed cube and dome homes at the edge of town.

Our group didn't appear as though we'd just come from a sandstorm, but we weren't tidy. I wanted to stop and buy clothes. I wanted a shower and a bed.

More than that, I was starving. "We should grab some food before we find this ferry. I'm assuming most people on this island will speak English?"

"Yeah, that's a safe bet. We should buy some souvenirs too. If we start spending money quickly, no one will care that we look like vagrants," said Josh.

"I've still got those rolls of Euros and American dollars," I said.

"Then, lunch is on you," said Faith.

The town rose in front of us as we crested the last hill. Roasting meat and drum beats greeted us. I was so happy I nearly cried. I held it in and tied my hair back into a ponytail.

We passed several bright white homes on the outskirts before the buildings connected and stone stairs descended into the commercial area.

A cobblestone street wound past a resort that emanated a vibe far too posh for the likes of us. Bright blue and yellow paint on window frames and doors shone in the strong sun overhead. Hanging baskets of bright flowers outside high-end boutiques betrayed the ancient age of the island.

We pushed on to where the white paint had faded to dingy ivory and sun-bleached baby blue peeled off the shutters. A general store had fruit in carts outside and enough young sweaty tourists milled about that we weren't quite so odd.

I angled through a group of Spanish-speaking girls around

my age and I started filling a wire basket with food. A box of crackers, a loaf of bread, a bottle of water, some cheese, a jar of olives. I picked up a canvas tote bag, paid for the lot, and stuffed it all into the bag which hung nicely from my shoulder. My friends continued milling around outside, except for Josh who talked with the Spanish girls. I admired his seemingly flawless Spanish while Melissa watched suspiciously.

Jonah stopped a lady pushing a souvlaki cart and bought a dozen skewers of meat. Out of the corner of my eye, I saw Ilya's head perk up before he ran off into a crowd.

We found an unoccupied brick ledge and sat down to eat our meat. I passed around chunks of the loaf of bread I'd bought. Faith bought six bottles of beer from a nearby pub and handed them down the line.

I pulled my phone from my bag and checked for a signal. The top left corner simply said Vodafone where it had been Rogers before. Josh saw me and frowned.

"We should pull our sim cards from our phones, in case Ivan is tracking one or more of us. I should have had us do this in London, but I got distracted," said Josh.

Each of us obeyed promptly.

"One of us should get a burner as soon as possible," said Cole.

"Lets hope the airport sells phones," said Jonah.

"Where did Ilya take off to?" I asked Faith.

"We should find that ferry." Josh took a large bite of his skewer and ate hungrily.

"He thought he heard a variant," said Faith calmly.

"What?" Cole frowned as he chugged on his bottle of beer.

"And he just took off hunting her?" I said.

"Him, I think. Ilya said he'd be right back." Faith's face

conveyed contentment as she chewed on her bread and cheese.

"Jerk," I said into my skewer of chicken. The meat and beer and bread tasted so good I couldn't stay angry.

We finished our food while the street bustled around us. Finally, Ilya appeared in the crowd with a small olive-skinned man in tow. The man seemed much older than us, although he was several inches shorter than Ilya.

"Hey, guys, this is Giorgio," said Ilya.

"And this is happening, why?" Josh warily eyed Giorgio.

"Don't be rude. I'm Melissa." She stood up and extended her hand. "That ill-tempered man is Josh. These are our friends, Faith, Cole, Jonah, Irina, and Gemma."

"Nice meeting of you," said Giorgio in a thick Greek accent.

"It's nice to meet you too, but we're not staying long on Santorini." Jonah pushed back his wet hair from his face. I noticed his blue eyes matched the ocean water.

"Can you point us in the direction of the ferry to Crete, preferably Heraklion, specifically," said Josh.

"I take you on my boat." Giorgio nodded with an air of finality.

"Uh, I'm sorry, but we don't know you well enough to hop on your boat. I don't know what Ilya told you, but we're in a hurry. And we've got a very important job to do." Cole tipped his bottle and finished the last of his beer.

"Yes, is important to stop Evonatura from causing many more problems." The features on his face were stone-serious.

"Giorgio knows what's going on," said Ilya.

"All the same, we're happy to take the ferry," I said cautiously. Hairs on the back of my neck prickled. *This is way too easy*, I thought to my brother.

"Ferry goes only in morning now. Only one ferry business

left from better days. Costs too much for many trips. You want to go fast, you come now with me," said Giorgio.

"He's telling the truth. He's a pyrokinetic. That's how I heard him. He was keeping his temper in check to stop from burning down his ex-wife's shop. Not unlike someone else I know." Ilya playfully lifted one of Faith's purple locks. She sneered at him.

"You're serious, aren't you?" I said directly to my brother.

"His boat is the only way off the island until tomorrow and that certainly puts a new spin on things," Ilya said.

"Don't you think it's a bit convenient that this guy happens to cross our path?" Cole pointed at Giorgio with contempt.

"How do we know he's not working for Evonatura? Or God knows who else at this point?" I had a bad feeling and I needed Ilya to share it.

"I think he seems like a nice guy." Gemma sipped from her bottle. She looked from me to Cole and back again.

I wondered if she could still count on one hand the number of beers she'd ever had. "Nobody's trusting your judgment for the next decade, not after where we found you," I told my sister. I reached out my hand to Giorgio. "Let me see what I can see."

Giorgio sized me up and then took my hand. Santorini melted into a sunny hilltop vineyard. I saw Giorgio talking with a man in a suit. I recognized Claude Mueller from his portrait in Evonatura's London office.

Giorgio wore overalls and a dirty brown T-shirt. He cleaned his hands with a cloth as he spoke. "Replacing grapes with new plants will kill business."

"You will be very well compensated for participating in our work. Whatever you earn at your winery will be doubled by me. I will pay you in cash. Declare only what you want to the Italian government," said Mueller.

"And what you want me to grow?" Giorgio looked at Mueller with distrust.

"That's on a need-to-know basis. Until you're part of our project, you don't need to know. Keep in mind, doing business with Evonatura comes with the added security our staff can offer. On the other hand, not doing business with us is risky. What if someone down in Messina learned about you and your wife? This is not a part of the world that embraces oddities, particularly of the non-human variety. What if a local found you out? They might decide you're a demon and that your wife is a witch. Wouldn't that be sad? Frightened and superstitious people are dangerous." Mueller's cold expression promised to deliver on his hypothetical nightmare.

"You don't make threats to me. Fine, I grow your crops for one year. Then you leave again. Is that deal good enough for you?" Giorgio glared at Mueller.

"We need five years. Minimum. We'll pull our plants when we're ready. You'll allow us to convert your winery to laboratory space as well." Mueller looked pleased with himself.

"My wife is going to be angry. The winery is in her family for many generations." Giorgio's glower softened as he accepted the deal.

"Help her understand this is how she can keep it for many more," said Mueller. "If she doesn't go along with what we want, she won't have a vineyard for long."

I released Giorgio's hand and returned to Santorini. "Yeah, he's not onboard with Evonatura," I said to the group. To Giorgio, I added, "I'm sorry they destroyed your wife's vineyard. I don't know how you ended up here in Greece, but that was unfair."

"Many years ago now. She is not my wife anymore. Forget my past. Now, we go to Crete."

I picked up my backpack and nodded. "Lead the way."

# Chapter 15

Giorgio's boat was a small fishing trawler that could barely transport nine people, including its captain. By the time everyone was onboard, there was standing room only. I no longer cared for comfort, though. The anxiety eating away at my insides made rest impossible.

I consoled myself with the thought that we were at least moving forward. My unease persisted, but Jonah's arms helped. I buried my face in his chest and curled up on his lap. With so few seats, it was a childish indulgence I didn't have to excuse.

Giorgio steered us out of the harbor and into the open ocean of the Mediterranean Sea. The water was a soft warm blue, bluer than Jonah's eyes. He looked more alive than I had ever seen him. He basked in his element out on the sea. Only his pale skin which refused to tan gave away that he didn't belong in the Mediterranean.

The afternoon sun-ripened to a golden hue as it descended. Our journey went quickly. Less than two hours later, Giorgio docked at a marina outside Heraklion exactly as we'd asked. The day unfolded so neatly that I felt like we were finally on the right path.

"I take you to airport too. Pickpockets are bad in this city. You get lost, maybe you get into trouble," said Giorgio.

We pushed through the bustling marina to the swarming main waterfront road where Giorgio instantly hailed a minivan taxi. Fortune stayed on our side. If Santorini and Crete had not been busy tourist destinations, we might have remained stranded even after fighting our way out of a Syrian sandstorm.

"Do you know how often flights leave for Cairo? Or anywhere in Eastern Africa will do as long as it's not too far from Nairobi," I asked Giorgio as I followed him into the minivan.

"Airport here is like ferries. Nothing goes as often now with money troubles. Tourists still come but it is not enough," said Giorgio.

"We need to get to Nairobi as quickly as possible." The urgency in Jonah's voice wasn't lost on Giorgio.

"What about a private charter? There must be services that fly on demand if the price is right." Melissa sounded desperate too.

"Throwing money at the problem might not be the right answer. We can't keep a low profile if we're tossing cash here and there. People remember you that way." Josh nodded at the taxi driver.

Melissa rolled her eyes.

Cole laced his fingers together and cracked his knuckles. "I'm starting to care less and less about our profile."

"Yeah, I'm ready to burn them all on sight. I don't care if

we're in the middle of an international plaza." Faith snapped a flame to life and blew it out instantly.

"Okay, save it for later," said Ilya.

I heard a twinge of hurt in his voice and I remembered that not so long ago Ilya held out hope of turning Ivan back from his psychotic plan to annihilate most of the planet.

The taxi-van pulled up at the N. Kazantzakis Heraklion Airport. The signage was in two languages, English and Greek. The Greek letters enchanted me, ΚΡΑΤΙΚΟΣ ΑΕΡΟΛΙΜΕΝΑΣ ΗΡΑΚΛΕΙΟΥ Ν.ΚΑΖΑΝΤΖΑΚΗΣ. My heart ached for everything I'd passed by too quickly since we spilled out into that smelly London alley.

"I come with you. I will talk for you if is needed." Giorgio rattled something quickly in Greek at the cab driver and slipped him some Euros.

"You don't have to do this, but thank you," I said.

Giorgio remained in the cab exchanging more words with the driver. Their discussion heated up, so we exited quickly.

As soon as we piled out of the cab we noticed the lack of activity at what should have been a hopping airport. The sliding glass doors should have been opening and closing to people coming in and out. But they weren't.

"Something's wrong," said Jonah.

I evaluated the main entrance. Someone had taped two large hand-written signs to the inside of the glass.

The English version read: *Heraklion Airport is closed for business until further notice. Operations will resume under new management as soon as possible. Please contact your air carrier provider for refunds and rescheduling. We apologize for any inconvenience.*

"The airport is closed," I called back to the group.

Giorgio and the cab driver were now yelling at each other.

"What do you mean it's closed?" said Ilya.

"It sounds like they went bankrupt. Or something."

"Perfect!" yelled Faith.

Giorgio got out of the minivan and the driver tore off down the road.

"I take it he knew the airport was closed before he brought us out here," said Josh.

"Man is greedy jerk. He knew. He brought us and says he does what we tell him. Nobody ask him if airport is open or shut."

"Great. We're stuck," said Cole.

Melissa and Gemma sat down on the curb. Jonah and I did the same. Exhausted, defeat weighed me down more than the Mediterranean heat.

"Giorgio, I hate to ask, but are you able to take us on to Cairo from here. Or maybe over to Turkey where we can get a flight to Cairo?" said Jonah.

"This shit is taking too long!" blurted Faith.

"It's not like we have any choice!" Ilya shouted at her.

"How long will it take us to get to Cairo by boat?" Josh asked Giorgio.

"My friends, we cannot go by boat. Not by my boat. I am a fishing boat. Very small. Not enough fuel to cross the sea. I cannot go to Africa," said Giorgio.

"Damn it!" yelled Cole.

"Is too bad. If you can get to Egypt, you can meet my friends in Cairo. Many variants live there, even some from America. Some worked for Evonatura for years. They know how bad the company was. Caused problems for many people, especially in Europe and the Middle East. They would help you if you can get to them. I take you to Athens. Airport there will be open of course," said Giorgio.

"Wait, have you been to Cairo?" I asked.

"Yes. I go many times after Evonatura kick me and my wife off our land," said Giorgio.

"Ilya, can you take images from one person's head and put them into another?" I said.

"Not exactly. But I think I could create an illusion from someone else's memories. Not perfectly, but believably."

"Could you search Giorgio's mind and build us an illusion of Cairo? From there, Melissa might create a working portal."

"No, it's too dangerous. I almost got us killed the last time I tried a destination I didn't know very well. And I had actually *been* to Santorini."

"You have to try, Melissa. We can't afford more delays. Who knows how long it will take us to get up to Athens and then get on a plane to Nairobi?"

"I can't generate the portal if I don't have a clear picture in my mind. It won't even form."

"Can't you try one more time?" said Cole.

"We'll need a guinea pig. Someone to go through and test it, like we did for our second attempt at Santorini," said Jonah.

"I'll do it," said Josh.

"What about our passports? Don't we still need stamps departing Greece?" I said.

"Aren't you people listening to me?" Melissa blurted. "It doesn't matter either way. No matter how hard I tried, we simply couldn't trust the portal."

Ilya ignored Melissa's protests and walked to Giorgio. With a curious expression, Giorgio took Ilya's hand.

"Think of Cairo. What is your best memory? Is it a hotel

room? A restaurant? A street? When you think of Cairo, what part of the city pops most quickly to your mind?"

Giorgio stood in dumbfounded thought.

"Excellent. That should do nicely," said Ilya.

My brother assessed the airport parking lot. The few people walking around the property were not interested in us. Ilya closed his eyes.

It was almost like one of my visions. The airport and the landscape around us grew fuzzy and dark. I blinked and blinked until I stood in a tall corridor of clay and brick.

A horn honked in the distance although we stood in a pedestrian corridor. Laundry hung between windows over our heads. Sun bleached dust floated in the few shafts of light that cut through the buildings into the canyon ahead.

Men and women in ivory and beige robes moved around others in linen shirts and crisp slacks. All the hair I could see was black. People moved briskly, but not harried, knowing their destinations without the whip of time constraint behind them. The sheer volume of people prohibited real haste. I examined each of my friends. All of us except Ilya were bewildered at suddenly standing in Cairo.

"Giorgio, can you take us somewhere secluded?" said Ilya.

Giorgio was struck dumb for a moment, but then he spoke. "Um … uh … follow me."

We wove through the human traffic and a pang of panic hit me. Were we actually walking through the Heraklion parking lot, possibly wandering into the peril of real auto traffic back on Crete?

"No, calm down. We're not moving that far," Ilya called back to me from the front of the pack.

"This is good spot. It is my friend's home," said Giorgio as we reached a gap in the tainted whitewashed facades.

We turned down an even narrower corridor. Only one person could walk at a time so we fell into single file.

"This is his door. His name is Tarak," said Giorgio.

"Should we try to go in?" said Cole.

"Popping out in someone's kitchen or living room is too risky. Better to stick to a quiet alley like this," said Josh.

"This alley is a narrow window for me to hit. I usually choose open spaces. If I can manage a portal, it could lead right into one of these walls. It'll probably kill whoever goes through." Melissa pushed the heels of her hands into her eyes. She took a ragged breath, visibly distressed.

"Take a long hard look. I trust you," Josh said to Melissa.

"Let's give her some space."

Melissa observed up and around and down. She touched the wall. She knelt down and brushed the hard-packed bare earth. She crouched down. She closed her eyes and smelled the air. She tilted her head, listening to the world around her. "Ilya, you can shut it off now. I've got as much a feel for the place as I'm going to get."

A moment passed and the feeling of cool wet air washed over me again until we were all back in the parking lot of the Heraklion Airport.

I whipped my head around evaluating what onlookers, if any, were witnessing. We merely seemed to be a stunned group of weary travelers, perhaps in shock that we would not be getting on a plane. A scenario that was essentially true, excepting our collective fake trip to another city.

Melissa closed her eyes and stood still for a long moment. Eyes still shut, she swooped her arm around and nothing happened. She drew in a long deep breath and made the shape of an oval in the air again. The second time her gift worked and the now familiar silver window hung in the air at the center of our circle.

# Chapter 16

"Giorgio, is there any chance you can get your friend on the phone and ask him if there's a floating liquid mirror outside his front door." Josh eyed the portal. He'd keep his promise to test it, of that I was sure, but he was too smart not to try an alternative.

"I do not keep a phone. Too much money for me. I catch fish, I sell fish at the docks. No phone," said Giorgio.

"Awesome. Buddy's probably got his head out the window checking a weird thing in the air, just getting ready to call the cops," said Faith.

"Well, it's now or never." Josh put his hand into the portal, waved it around and withdrew it. "No wall so far. Here goes."

We took a collective gulp of air as Josh fully entered the portal. Melissa concentrated on keeping it open. No one said a word as we waited.

Minutes passed. I paced around in uneven circles. Faith busied herself lighting weeds on fire. Jonah extinguished each fire as quickly as Faith started it. Cole slowly kicked apart a parking barrier.

"It's been too long!" I snapped.

"Should someone go in after him?" asked Jonah.

"If one of us was in danger, the person I'd send in would have been Josh," said Ilya.

"This was a moronic plan," said Faith angrily.

"He could have gotten tied up if he bumped into someone coming out of the portal. Our best option is for me to keep it open as long as possible." Melissa strained to concentrate.

I opened my mouth to protest and closed it again. Action was needed more than words. I approached the portal, ready to plunge through, and collided with Josh as he came back out.

"Just about to lose patience?" said Josh.

"Where the hell were you?"

"Exactly where I was supposed to be, in Tarak's house," said Josh.

"You were supposed to go through, and if it was safe, come right back and tell the rest of us. Go and come back, that was the deal!" I yelled, stabbing my hand back and forth.

"I knew it was going to be safe." Josh winked at Melissa and smiled.

"You're braver than the rest of us." Melissa relaxed a little knowing her portal was stable.

"Let's get this show on the road. Giorgio, are you coming?" said Jonah.

"You might get stuck in Cairo for awhile," said Cole.

"I'll make sure he gets home before the end of the day," said Melissa confidently.

"What does Tarak say?" Giorgio asked Josh.

"He would like to have us all over for tea. He says there are quite a few variants who would probably like to meet us, but they're more likely to trust us if Giorgio comes."

"Will they help us?" I asked Giorgio.

"I cannot speak for others, but some friends like Tarak will want to do right thing." Giorgio's eyebrows lifted high with optimism.

"We need a plan to get to Nairobi as soon as possible. Then we'll have tea," said Jonah.

"Follow me." Josh walked back through the floating mirror.

One by one we popped through the portal and crowded into the alley in front of Tarak's door where Josh already knocked.  Ilya had been right.  His recreation of Giorgio's memory wasn't perfect. The street was louder with chattering voices and vehicle traffic nearby.  The air was full of spice, sweat, and dirt. The sun was fainter under a mildly overcast sky.

I made a note to myself not to try a stunt like that with Melissa's portal skills ever again. There were plenty of places other than brick walls and sandstorms where popping into existence could kill us.

Melissa emerged and closed her portal in a smooth movement before she collapsed. Josh dropped to the ground to help her.

"Come in, please. You are all welcome." An older man with a neat goatee and a beige tunic opened the door. Giorgio took his hand and the two pulled into a friendly embrace before making way for the rest of us.

"If we travel by portal again, keep in mind those doors take a toll when they're open for too long," Melissa said wearily.

Josh helped Melissa to an armchair in Tarak's living room. "I wasn't thinking. I'm so sorry."

A sudden tenderness in his voice caught me off guard. I could tell he meant it. Melissa wasn't in the mood to smile, but she nodded in recognition.

Gemma tugged my arm. "I'm not very good at it yet, but I could try to heal her."

"That would be lovely. Anything you could do would help." Melissa reclined in the armchair and closed her eyes.

"Okay, um, hold still," said Gemma.

My sister moved her hands along Melissa's body, starting with her feet and ankles, up her calves and thighs, over her abdomen and down her arms. None of the golden energy given off by Camille's healing came out of Gemma's hands.

*All variations are different*, I thought. *Cut her some slack.*

Gemma reached Melissa's head and it happened. Shimmering pulses shot from my sister's palms into her patient's temples. Melissa remained motionless for a moment and then opened her eyes with a deep breath.

"Ahhhh, that feels so much better. You really are a little miracle worker," said Melissa with a bright smile.

"Aw, thanks. I'm still learning." Gemma flipped her wheat hair, acting much younger than her eighteen years. I swelled with pride anyway.

"Sorry, is this Egypt-Air? Yes, I'd like to book eight seats on your next flight from Cairo to Nairobi." Cole held a cordless phone to his ear, walking to the hallway door. "I'd like to pay in cash if possible. Will you hold the seats with my credit card, but allow us to pay cash at the desk? ... Euros."

"I'm sure we'd have a lot of fun meeting the North African variant community, but I agree with Cole. We've got to keep pushing to Nairobi," I said to Jonah.

"The next flight with open seats might not be until tomorrow." Ilya took a step to join us.

"What if we can't go for days? Maybe we should meet these local variants and do the destination-memory-transfer-thing again." Faith shoved her hands in her pockets.

"It's an option, but there's still a chance one of us could wind up at the bottom of the ocean or stuck on glacier. If she's off by just a little, there's always the brick wall problem," Jonah said.

"I think I've had my quota of blind leaps of faith for the day." Josh took a chair and let tension melt out of his body.

"If you stay the night in Cairo and meet variants here, you can share the load of what you do," said Giorgio.

"I agree with Giorgio when it comes to Evonatura. From what little Josh communicated to me, it sounds like *The Compendium* is a complex endeavor, equally complicated to undo." Tarak stroked his goatee as he appraised us.

"At this point, our first priority is stopping them from releasing the Terra Nova virus," I said.

"Share your Compendium data with me and my friends and you'll have more arms tying up more loose ends." Tarak gently brushed creases from his tunic.

"We just met you. How do we know you don't work for Ivan or Claude?" said Faith.

"Not to disrespect you in your own home, but it's a good point. Will you let me listen?" Ilya tapped the side of his head and extended his other arm to Tarak.

Obviously offended and a little angry, Tarak glowered at Ilya.

"You have time to take tea and enjoy my friend's hospitality. Meet more friends." Giorgio shifted, glancing at each of us. "You trust Giorgio, now you trust others here."

"Ilya, poke into his head anyway," said Faith, whispering, but still audible to everyone.

Tarak's expression softened and he took my brother's hand.

Ilya regarded Tarak with unwavering eye contact as he pulled stories and images from our host's head. "He knows people from Innoviro. Before my time. The first ones to leave the sewer. And he knows other Evonatura refugees. A man that got fired for asking questions at a lab in Madrid."

"So we call friends, yes?" said Giorgio.

"Please do," said Ilya.

"Okay, we're booked on a midnight flight that has a layover in Addis Ababa," said Cole, returning from the other room to join us.

Tarak nodded and took his phone back from Cole.

"We still need to deal with the passport problem. Are we just going to fudge the fact that we have arrival stamps across the board for Greece with no departure stamps?" I said.

"In this part of the world, many travelers come and go through ports with very low-tech customs officials. Many entry and exit points do not stamp. You should be fine," said Tarak.

I wanted to clarify that we had the added liability of using fake or possibly stolen passports, but I thought better of it. And then I remembered Melissa had never been to Africa at all. If we hadn't detoured through Greece, we would never have met Giorgio and might not have found our way to a friendly home in Cairo. Was life funny like that or was I experiencing fate? I shook my head at the prospect of contemplating something so unknowable.

Tarak dialed a number and started speaking rapidly in something I thought was either Arabic or Farsi. Tarak paced through his back rooms as he spoke. He made another call in French and finally a call in English. I heard the words, "variant warriors" and "bring a hard drive" before Tarak returned to us.

"I have invited all the variants I know in the city. They will come quickly. They know your situation and that you are leaving in the middle of the night," said Tarak.

"I'm starving. Have you got any dates? I always hear about Egyptian dates." Faith clasped her hands eagerly and Ilya rolled his eyes.

Tarak laughed. "We will have a full dinner soon, my friends."

# Chapter 17

Tarak began dumping ingredients into pots and saucepans, pulling loaves of bread and bags from his pantry. He filled plates with crackers, fruit, and cured meat. We relayed platter after platter to the dining room table.

I quickly understood that Tarak had invited us for 'Tea' in the British sense. He meant for us to eat dinner with him. A knock at the door interrupted the soothing simmer of a spiced lentil dish on a hot plate.

Tarak escorted an extremely tall man to his living room sofa. The man had to lean slightly while standing inside the room.

"My friends, I would like you to meet my neighbor, Monsieur Bonne Nuit," said Tarak.

"I suppose we needn't ask what his variation is then," said Jonah as he rose and extended his arm to shake the man's hand. Jonah's six-foot two-inch stature was utterly dwarfed by Monsieur Bonne Nuit. Even Josh at six-foot-five looked up to the man.

"Regrettably, we cannot shake hands, sir," said Monsieur Bonne Nuit with a subtle French accent.

"Yes, my friend delivers melatonin through contact with his skin. He will put you to sleep if he touches you," said Tarak.

"Worse things could happen." Cole yawned, stretching his thick arms above his head.

"I can prepare some crackers for you to take on your flight, to ensure you are refreshed when you arrive in Nairobi," said Monsieur Bonne Nuit.

"Sweet! Between that and the awesome dinner goin' on here, this stop has been a total score." Faith grinned and popped a date in her mouth.

"Monsieur Bonne Nuit is a fugitive from Evonatura. Like Giorgio, Claude Mueller was very keen to take something from him. Only in my tall friend's case, obtaining his value would have required extensive testing and therefore long term incarceration," said Tarak.

"Tarak has graciously hosted me on a number of occasions when we detected Mueller's men in the city," said Monsieur Bonne Nuit.

"No offense, but what makes this house so safe?" said Josh.

"We can indulge in a little demonstration," said Tarak and a thin smile stretched above his beard.

He picked up an empty glass beer bottle from the back of his kitchen counter. He rinsed a metal sauce pan that had been emptied of its sautéed vegetables and placed the glass in the middle.

Tarak fixated on the bottle. His brown eyes began to shine with a red-orange ember-hot hue until two laser-like beams shot out into the glass, melting it on contact.

"This is a small scale demonstration. It took me many years

of being trained and tested to hone my skill to this degree. I hid in countries all over the Middle East, piggybacking on the horrors of war to test my craft. Evonatura will not dare come to my home," said Tarak.

I saw regret in his eyes and heard shame in his voice.

Another knock at the door drew our attention.

"Mr. and Mrs. Monroe, how good of you to come," said Tarak.

A woman in a leopard print niqab entered followed by a plain man in his forties. The woman took a seat in the last unoccupied chair in Tarak's living room while Mr. Monroe and Giorgio exchanged a hug.

I tried not to stare, but something was off about Mrs. Monroe. It looked like another layer of cloth hung over what little of her skin showed around her eyes.

"Remember my love, we're among friends here. You can remove your cover," said Mr. Monroe.

"At this point, we've really seen it all." I tried to sound reassuring and accepting.

Mrs. Monroe unpinned something under the fold that hung beside her left cheek. She peeled back the fabric and revealed the chestnut-brown face of a feline human hybrid.

"Amazing!" said Faith.

I hoped her hearty enthusiasm was well received.

"Agreed," said Cole. He and his sister both gawked at Mrs. Monroe with ardent fascination. Jonah smiled as well and extended his hand.

"I hope *you're* able to shake hands," he said.

Mrs. Monroe accepted and took Jonah's hand gently. "Thank you. It's always a pleasure to remove my veil in mixed company." Her silky voice suited her golden-orange eyes.

"We chose this part of the world so that my wife can cover up in public without drawing negative attention," said Mr. Monroe.

"What's your variation, if you don't mind sharing?" Ilya asked Mr. Monroe.

"I can make metal. Iron is usually easiest, but it depends on what I'm working with," said Mr. Monroe.

"How about this?" Faith passed a plump date to Mr. Monroe.

He turned it over in his hand. In a flash he held a small oval chunk of bright copper.

"Impressive!" said Jonah.

"Wow, what does it take to make gold? Or silver?" said Faith.

"You must be pretty flush for cash," said Ilya, arching his eyebrows with a knowing nod.

Mr. Monroe gave the copper date to Faith who examined it with wonder. "I'll admit it does come in handy," he added.

"We work primarily to further the interests of variants, as opposed to achieving financial gain," said Mrs. Monroe.

"You're the couple that used to work with my father at Innoviro," said Ilya.

"You must be Ivan's son," said Mr. Monroe.

"We're both Ivan's children," I said.

"And you're at odds with him now?" said Mrs. Monroe.

Another knock at the door startled most of the room.

"Shira! Thank you for coming, my dear," said Tarak.

Shira exuded elegance with full flowing black hair and a simple white linen T-shirt dress. She allowed Tarak to kiss her hand. And then she disappeared in a blur. Shira reappeared a moment later with a bottle of wine in her hands.

"Sorry, Tarak. In my haste, I forgot the wine." She smiled a flash of bright white teeth against red lips.

"Where did you come from?" said Faith.

"My home is in Heliopolis, just outside Cairo. Not so far really," said Shira, smiling bashfully again.

"You just crossed the city and back?" said Ilya with marked incredulity.

"No, my dear, I went to a nearby bazaar." Shira turned to Tarak, handing him her bottle as though they shared something meaningful.

"I think this is everyone who will join us tonight," said Tarak.

"My friends, there are more variants in Cairo for sure, but we must see who we can before we put you on your plane," said Giorgio.

"I understand there is something big happening between Innoviro and Evonatura," said Mr. Monroe.

"Big is the understatement of the year. This is the single most dangerous plot the world has ever known," I said.

"Dial it back a bit, sis." Ilya nodded at Gemma who had shockingly remained silent.

"She's not exactly exaggerating," said Cole.

"It's called *The Compendium*. There is another corporation in China involved, Jinhua. That disaster going on in Shanghai right now? It's Compendium-related. The earthquake that ruined San Francisco? One of Innoviro's Compendium projects," I said.

"Don't forget the sandstorms in Syria," said Melissa.

"How could we?" said Cole, lifting the bottom of his dirt stained shirt as evidence.

"The worst is yet to come and that's why we're headed to Nairobi," said Josh.

Giorgio, Tarak, the Monroes, Shira, and Monsieur Bonne Nuit all listened without a motion or a sound.

"A virus called Terra Nova will be released soon, possibly any day now. Once Ivan is satisfied that enough catastrophic terra-forming damage and environmental ruin has been instigated, he's going to let loose a pathogen that will wipe out every non-variant on the planet," said Jonah.

"He says he's trying to create a world where variants will thrive and dominate. He's selling it as some kind of utopia for people who'd have an easier time of it if judgmental humans weren't here." Cole gave Mrs. Monroe a knowing glance. Her furry face did not conceal her embarrassment.

"She's already rejected him. She's on the right side." Ilya frowned at Cole.

"We're not talking about expanding our group traveling to Nairobi, are we?," asked Melissa.

"We want you should share your data. There are many things to stop, yes? You give us leads. We will work together," said Giorgio.

"Have we got anything to lose?" I eyed my brother. He shook his head.

"Then it's decided. You will leave us a copy of your Compendium files. And now, we eat!" said Tarak, clapping his hands merrily.

Faith barreled towards the dining table with abandon. I was so hungry that I was hot on her heels. I'd been snacking on meat and cheese and bread, but the chance for fresh, hot homemade food was becoming a rarity for us.

Tarak opened Shira's wine and passed around bottles of beer with a pyramid on the label. I took a glass of the red wine expecting sharp tartness. Its sweet, light, fruity flavor made it go down too easily. I soon felt light-headed and joined in on the laughter as we ate our fill.

"Little Miss Irina," said Giorgio as he put his hand on my shoulder. "I hear you have a talent for telling futures that come true."

My cheeks already felt warm from the wine, but I could still sense the extra flush. "Yes, I'm able to see things from a person's past or future. It's one of the reasons Ivan turned my life inside out."

Giorgio nodded. "Like my wife's ability to grow things. This is what Evonatura really wanted from us. They steal our land, yes, but they do many, many tests on my wife. She leave me because I could not make it stop, not the tests or the theft of our land."

Tatiana's fake 'green thumb' variation invaded my mind. "It wasn't your fault. I'm sure she's just hurt. Give it time."

"This is what I am asking. Can you tell me what will happen, in time?" Giorgio's eyes pleaded his case more effectively than his stilted albeit sincere words.

"Are you sure you want to know? Sometimes hope is better than certain knowledge. And I still don't know that the future I see is written in stone. Just because I see something doesn't mean it will come true no matter what."

Giorgio blinked at me with an inebriated smirk. He rolled his eyes and held out his hand. I took it. Perhaps if I saw his wife with another man, or a new woman in his own life, Giorgio could move forward.

I saw Giorgio and his wife back in their vineyard. They were grooming and pruning vines on a sunny day, smiling at each other under wide-brimmed straw hats. I'd gone in the wrong direction. I released Giorgio's hand and came back to

Tarak's dining room.

I shook my shoulders and arms out to refresh my tense muscles. I pictured Giorgio's wife alone and took his hand again. I stood with her behind a cash register in a trinket shop, I assumed back on Santorini. Her worried brow and the increasing volume of alarmed voices outside the shop told me I wasn't about to witness her reunion with Giorgio.

A teenage girl in a sundress burst into the shop and slammed the door behind her. She whirled around to peek through the blinds back out into the street. Blood weighed down her hair with debris tangling her bone straight locks.

The girl began to dry heave as she turned to face Giorgio's wife and me. Suddenly the girl's stomach contents came up and poured out onto the floor. Blood leaked from her eyes and nose as she pulled herself along the bookshelf that lined the wall between the door and the cash register.

Giorgio's wife looked past me to the end of the counter, her only escape from this girl. Instead of making a break for it, she reached under the counter and pulled out a gun. She shot the girl point blank in the chest. The girl choked on her own blood as she collapsed to the ground.

The shattering of glass shocked me as a barstool came flying through the picture window of the shop. Two very sick men crawled in through the broken glass and ambled angrily in our direction. Giorgio's wife fired and missed. I let go of Giorgio's hand.

"What you see? What is she doing? There is another man now, yes?" said Giorgio. I knew my face had a horrified gape.

"No, Giorgio, I didn't see another man. I saw that we need to go to Nairobi now. Your wife is in danger. You must go to her right away. She needs you."

# Chapter 18

I told Jonah and Josh that I had a vision of Terra Nova loose on Santorini in what seemed like the near future. Josh called a taxi service and booked us a van to come as soon as possible.

"Okay folks, we need to get going so we don't miss our plane." Josh handed me my backpack and reached for Faith's bag next.

"Thank you, Giorgio and Tarak for all your help and hospitality," said Jonah.

Gemma eagerly nodded her agreement from behind him.

We took turns shaking hands with our new allies, passing over Monsieur Bonne Nuit each time who bowed gracefully instead. Faith and Melissa instructed Mr. Monroe on how to navigate files from *The Compendium* which they'd copied to his sleek cutting- edge tablet.

Tarak gave my sister a small satchel he said was full of food. Monsieur Bonne Nuit presented me with a small plastic bag containing the melatonin-infused crackers he'd promised us.

Our van honked in the street outside and we scooped up our belongings. The driver seemed a little confused that we had not one suitcase among so many passengers, but he got over it quickly.

Tarak said something hurriedly in his native tongue and slapped the top of the van.

Most travelers leaving a major urban destination have their first sampling of local traffic after arrival. Most travelers don't arrive by interspatial portal. Gemma and I squeaked and squawked little sounds of alarm as our driver aggressively wove through Cairo's post rush-hour traffic.

The sun set while our driver stopped, started, and shouted out his window at the drivers around him. For the half hour we were in the taxi-van, I had something other than Terra Nova to fear.

We arrived at the Cairo International Airport and came to an abrupt stop in front of a rounded ribbed metal roof with Arabic and English characters.

"Your friend pay. All you go now, thank you," said the taxi driver through a very thick accent.

"Thank you sir," said Cole, pleasantly surprised.

We piled out of the van and regrouped on the curb. Our taxi-van lurched forward without a backward glance from its driver.

The Cairo International Airport was a bustling travel hub that evening. People swarmed throughout the halls. We pushed our way through the crowd. I was grateful not to be hauling a suitcase.

"Okay, we need the Egypt-Air check-in desk." Cole inspected the facility, craning his neck up to read the signage that stretched along the wall just under the ceiling.

No sooner had the words left his lips than I sensed danger. I whipped my head around, back and forth, scanning the crowd.

"It's Rose and Sage!" Ilya blurted at me over Gemma's head.

"Maybe they've changed their minds and they're going to help us talk Ivan out of his plan." Hopeful desperation filled Gemma's voice.

"There is literally zero chance of that," I told her impatiently.

"Where did you see them?" Jonah scanned the sea of heads with me.

"I dare those bitches to come near us!" A flash of rage filled Faith's eyes. "I'll teach them to mess with us."

"Not in the bloody airport!" said Ilya, rounding on his powerful girlfriend.

A security officer in a blue police-like uniform frowned at us from the doorway of a canteen nearby. He put a radio to his mouth and his lips moved.

"I think we might be drawing some unwanted attention," I said as anxiety rose in my throat.

"The twins aren't going to make a move in the middle of the Cairo airport." Josh's dismissive tone failed to sate me.

"Then why are they here?" Cole scanned the crowd with the rest of us.

"There's only one Irina. Ivan can't magically know where we are or what we're doing. They're probably just supposed to verify that we're on our way to Nairobi," said Melissa.

"Then let's not be seen," said Jonah.

"We need to transform into our passport others before we check in," said Ilya.

Two Panama hats over smooth platinum heads popped out of the sea of veils, caps, turbans, and bare black heads ahead.

"Guys, we're running out of time. I can see the twins up

ahead." Frantic adrenaline charged through me as the hats got closer.

I glimpsed the security guard standing against the wall nearby. He hadn't taken his eyes off of us.

"I see him too," Ilya said to me. "Everyone, bathroom now!"

Ilya led the way to a tiled joint entryway to a pair of men's and women's bathrooms. As soon as we broke line of sight with the guard, Ilya immediately shrouded us. The transformation felt like a slow motion shower.

The guard rounded the corner and came face to face with a completely different set of faces. He blinked and gave his head a shake, then pushed past into the men's side.

"I saw the Egypt-Air logo farther down the terminal, past where the twins were." Jonah's voice came from the face of a man I'd seen inside one of the British passports. We'd planned to use the English-speaking passports first to make questioning easier. Luck had matched four women and four men with the photographs in the passports.

"The faster we check in, the faster we're out of their reach." Josh peered around the corner to watch the guard continue down the hall.

Jonah led us back through the crowd to the Egypt-Air counter. We passed by the twins in the sea of people. Their bluish white faces were stern, studying the crowd with obvious intensity.

Cole moved ahead and presented our passports along with the sheet of paper with our booking confirmation and flight details.

My stomach knotted tighter and tighter as we waited. My lungs clamped nearly shut as I fought hard to pull air in and push it back out.

We had our tickets and retreated back into the crowd. The twins' hats were coming back towards us. Could they possibly have some way of detecting us inside our illusions?

The security screening line was long and we had no choice but to stand and wait. None of us dared to speak as Rose and Sage closed in on us.

People shuffled forward drearily. The twin Panama hats edged closer. I glanced back at the sliding glass doors at the far end of the terminal where we'd entered.

Incredibly, I saw a copy of my brother waving both hands in the air, trying to get the attention of the guard whose interest we piqued.

Ilya replicated himself perfectly and the illusion worked. The guard blew a whistle and shouted something in Arabic. He started to run, yelling something into his radio.

Rose and Sage caught sight of the scene and pushed their way through the crowd until they were running hot on the guard's heels.

The fake Ilya slipped behind a luggage cart and disappeared. The guard skidded to a halt and heaved his way around the luggage cart, much to the surprise of the young family surrounding the pile of baggage.

Rose and Sage stopped short, just in time for another security guard to appear out of the crowd and grab them by their arms. I contemplated the possibility their wings would come out in public today. The first guard joined the man holding Rose and Sage. The four marched down a security corridor and out of sight.

Our line inched forward again and again until we were finally ushered through the baggage x-ray and metal detector.

***

A tense few hours consisted of our motley crew of fake travelers alternately sitting and pacing around the Cairo airport's Gate 53 for our red-eye flight to Nairobi.

A question burned in my mind. How had Rose and Sage known we were at the airport? How they had traveled to Cairo was no mystery. They had built-in transportation. But how did they know where to find us? The puzzle only had one solution.

There seemed no alternative but someone at Tarak's house had betrayed us. I searched my mind for any potential liability in having shared Compendium files. If they were working with Innoviro or Evonatura, it probably wouldn't be new information anyway.

After mere glances at our passports, we boarded our 737 air bus and took up a row and a half. I stuffed my bag into the overhead bin. I stretched in an attempt to soothe the sore muscles of my back and legs. My dry eyes burned, aching to close. I curled up in my seat and shut out the world.

I woke to Jonah's magnetically warm hand gently squeezing my shoulder. I'd slept through the layover in Addis Ababa and it was time to get off the plane.

I blinked awake and saw the faces of strangers around me. It took a moment for me to remember that Ilya had disguised us to match our passports.

Then a strange new sensation churned in my gut. I did not feel good. At all. I felt odd, nauseated. A wave of sickness hit hard and I grabbed the paper bag tucked in the seat pocket in front of me. I emptied the contents of my stomach into the bag and took a breath. Another wave came and I opened the bag again.

My friends stared at me, along with our flight attendant. The plane had emptied and they were waiting on me to get moving.

"Sorry. It must have been something I ate." I managed a weak smile.

"Let's get some fresh food into you then." Jonah's furrowed brow and outstretched arm motivated me to move.

We stood in another security line, this time to be admitted to Kenya. Our passports passed muster again and we were all stamped quickly. Josh paid our entry fees with the last of our American cash.

Melissa made arrangements for an airporter to take us to Tarak's friend's hotel. I kept quiet about my suspicions regarding our allies in Cairo. We had few choices left. I took the remainder of my assorted cash to a kiosk and exchanged everything for Kenyan shillings while Cole herded everyone back together.

My stomach churned relentlessly as we all piled into the van. I began to worry as I buried my envelope of shillings at the bottom of my backpack. Was I seriously ill? Had I become a carrier for Terra Nova? If so, how long until I started to make people sick?

"If you were a carrier, all hell would have broken loose already," said Ilya from the back seat of the airporter van.

"Irina, you couldn't possibly be. You were right the first time, you've got some kind of bug." Jonah laced his fingers into mine, transferring energy. The sensation felt right.

"I'll heal you when we get to the hotel." Gemma's doe-eyed sincerity broke down the last of my resolve, despite the fact that she spoke from behind another girl's eyes.

"Let's hope that's all it is." I looked up at the van's rearview mirror. The driver watched me with concern. I rooted in my bag and then distributed shilling notes to each of my friends.

I leaned against the window next to me. I watched the buzzing hazy city of Nairobi rushing to meet us alongside the highway. A bubble of nausea rose up through my belly and I sucked in air to shove it back down. Before anything else, I need to get to that hotel and the toilet in my room.

# Chapter 19

The Nairobi hotel owned by Tarak's friend was an oasis in our dismal journey. Free from the motion of the airporter, my equilibrium returned. The little voice that kept promising me Compendium-free travel experiences told me to enjoy the bright East African décor.

Open French doors on either side of the lobby allowed an equator-warmed breeze to sail lazily through the space. A giant slow-moving ceiling fan helped circulate the air giving the whole building a fresh atmosphere. We waited at the front desk while padded linen armchairs beckoned our weary bodies. Palms rustled in the wind on the patio outside a wall of windows.

Melissa and Josh claimed our six rooms with our passport and disguise combinations still intact. We agreed to drop our bags and meet in the hotel bar at the far end of the building.

"Are you feeling any better?" said Jonah as soon as we entered our room.

I paused to review the now familiar sandy-haired man who

stood in my boyfriend's place. The only signs of concern I read were arched bushy eyebrows. "I'm fine. Now that we're here, I'll be okay. I'm more concerned with how we track down Ivan and Tatiana. I've been thinking about it, and I'd like to start by finding the plaza from my vision. We can ask for it by name, so we should get in a cab and start there," I said.

I started towards our door and Jonah followed me. I paused again and took in my reflection in the body-length mirror. I had long wavy red hair, gray yoga pants, and a tan scoop-neck T-shirt. I had to admit it wasn't a terrible ensemble.

Jonah put his hands on my shoulders and made eye contact with my reflection. "We should all go together. We can't be sure how much backup Ivan has here in Nairobi. If he's got a lab with a stash of Terra Nova and whatever gene therapy supplies he's using on himself, there could be a large variant presence here."

"You think it's another Evonatura or Innoviro office?" I asked wearily.

"Could be. Or it could be nothing more than a couple of fridges and cupboards. What else can you tell me about what they were doing there?" said Jonah.

"All I saw was Ivan getting an injection and checking on a shelf full of steel canisters. There were no other staff and not much there, not that I saw anyway." I sat on the crisply made bed and rubbed my temples.

"I'd love to pinpoint how your brain accesses information remotely. Why do you see some events and not others? When your brain goes hunting for a piece of information, it usually makes a connection. Sometimes that connection is a better answer, sometimes it's not so telling. If we understand why, we could improve your results." Jonah rested against the room's desk and crossed his arms, looking at me with scientific curiosity.

"Now you sound like Ivan." I pulled my wallet out of my bag and slipped back into my shoes.

"Don't think of it that way. Ivan gained so many variant followers because he could make a logical argument for advancing variant science. And in terms of artificially generated variations, who wouldn't want to be stronger, and more adaptable to a post-climate change world? Accelerating climate change is unacceptable, but there are some nuggets of value in Ivan's work," said Jonah.

"We'll have to agree to disagree on that." I rolled my eyes and left the room. Jonah hastily caught up with me, locking our door behind us. I scanned the balcony walkway connecting our room to the stairwell back to the lobby. We were alone as far as I could see, but I felt uneasy.

"All I'm saying is that we should hang on to any research and development these corporations concocted. That way it wasn't all for nothing. And maybe we can fulfill the promise they never intended to, Irina." Jonah sounded sincere and I was increasingly irritated all the same.

"I'd like some wine. And you're buying," I said firmly.

We walked into the bar and I glanced around for our friends.

"Jambo! Karibu! Good Afternoon." The bartender wiped the bar with a cloth.

"Two glasses of house red. The gentleman will pay," I said to the bartender without looking at Jonah.

"Yes, Madame." The bartender nodded as he poured our wine. "You are looking for friends?"

"We are. Have they come and gone already?" Jonah placed

a few Kenyan Shilling notes on the counter.

"There is a group on the patio now, sir. I believe they're part of the group you came in with," said the bartender.

It struck me that the hotel probably saw frequent groups of safari-goers and student travelers. If my friends on the patio hadn't concocted a cover story already, I knew what we'd say.

Jonah smiled at the bartender and took our drinks. He followed me through the patio doors. Light rain pattered on the tarp overhead making the foliage surrounding the patio even more tropical.

Josh, Melissa, Cole, and Gemma sat around a wicker and glass bistro table with their own glasses of wine.

"One of these days, we're going to have to take a trip that isn't about saving the world," said Jonah.

"Speaking of our trip, I thought we could say we're here to go on safari. If anyone asks," I said.

"Sure, sure, sounds good." Josh waved off my topic of conversation.

"Now that we're here, where to?" Cole eyed me squarely.

"I've thought of that. We should start at the Kenyatta International Convention Centre. I'm sure all the cab drivers know where it is," I said.

"And if we find the supply of Terra Nova? What then?" said Melissa.

Faith and Ilya joined us, both disheveled.

"I'll burn it to ash, that's what." Faith decisively placed her glass on the table.

"Can we be sure the canisters here are the total of Ivan's supply?" said Cole. He did not share Josh's relaxed attitude.

"I'll use one of the canisters to jog a vision. I'm getting better at pinpointing the information I need when I launch a vision."

I shot Jonah a wide-eyed stare meant to silence him.

"I've noticed you're getting better too," said Josh.

"What are we waiting for?" Melissa plunked a shilling coin on the table and rose to leave.

Jonah and I quickly finished our wine. The warm rush and my gurgling stomach gave me a moment of pause. I steadied myself and followed at the back of our pack.

"We can't all fit." Josh stood alongside a taxi sedan, the only one in the hotel's parking lot.

"Who can stay behind?" said Cole.

"You don't need me," said Melissa.

"What if we need a quick exit? You could land us on the road outside this hotel in seconds," I said.

"I'll stay," said Gemma.

"Me too. I'll make sure she stays safe." Jonah ignored Gemma's offended huff and put a reassuring hand on my shoulder.

"Josh, we need your know-how. Cole, your strength, Ilya, your ears, Faith, your fire. We'll have to squish and hope the driver doesn't care." I ushered everyone in and got in the front seat. Only I had seen the tower and could describe it if we got lost.

"The Kenyatta International Convention Centre please," I said to our driver. He regarded me with a glass-eyed inquiry.

"It's here in the city. Big plaza. Tall tower." I pointed down for here, made a circle with my hand for the plaza, and signed my best approximation of a long cylinder.

"Sawa sawa. Okay." Our driver put the car into gear, shot out of the driveway, and zipped down the road.

The golden afternoon sun made Nairobi's brick and plaster buildings warm and inviting. The barbed wire and razor wire topping every other fenced home suggested an alternate reality. Was it all necessary? Were criminals and militants around every corner? If they only knew the real danger lurking in this metropolis if we failed.

A few twists and turns through the hotel district produced the plaza from my vision. We paid our driver and thanked him.

"He's close," said Ilya shakily.

"Remember, that thing you hear is not our father," I said firmly.

"I never really knew him, did I?"

I couldn't think of an answer for my twin brother. We stood on the edge of the plaza looking around helplessly.

"So where is he? I mean, where is *it*?" said Josh.

"It's coming from the tower. They must be there now." Ilya observed the building with apprehension.

"Any chance they'll recognize these faces? We don't know where or how Evonatura got these passports," said Cole.

"There's no way to find out now." Melissa glanced behind her uncertainly.

"Hang on! Nobody move!" I grabbed Josh's sleeve as I saw the figures of Ivan and Tatiana exit the conference tower ahead.

Ivan carried a large black duffle bag. He and Tatiana cast furtive glances around before slipping into a silver sedan that had been waiting for them at the curb.

"Shit! That was it! They've got it!" said Cole.

"We need to follow them!" Melissa took a helpless step to the car.

"And do what? Attack in broad daylight? We'll spook them and they'll release the virus." Josh grabbed Melissa and pulled her back.

"Concentrate, Irina. Where are they going?" Ilya's panicked voice set me on edge.

I glanced around at my friends' earnest expressions on strangers' faces. I closed my eyes and willed my viewpoint to follow the silver sedan.

The black behind my eyes melted away and I saw Ivan and Tatiana parking on the edge of a giant low-income community. A patchwork of rusty tin and sun-bleached fiberglass rooftops stretched to the horizon.

They walked into a shack set apart from the rest. Ivan turned back and looked directly at me with red eyes full of malice. I felt a blast of wind push me backward. I refused to let go, concentrating on seeing what Ivan and Tatiana were trying desperately to hide.

The scene switched back on again but jumped into the future. Somewhere on the outskirts of the tin-roofed community, Tatiana walked along a ditch broadcasting seeds. Ivan followed behind pouring oil from a canister onto the seeds. He acted different somehow. I willed myself to get closer. It wasn't Ivan helping Tatiana, it was Ilya! How could this be possible? The vision had to be wrong!

I watched as my aunt and brother finished their seeding. Tatiana plunged her hands into the dirt and a stream of plants sprouted up in the ditch. She moved her hands in the earth and the plants grew. Ilya grinned alongside her while he evaluated the blossoming ground. Tatiana retracted her hands and Ilya patted her on the shoulder as they walked away.

I watched as Tatiana's sprouts shot up into shrubs. The sky flickered as the midday sun rapidly shifted to a deep blue sky, then inky black. Twilight broke and a long thick hedge stood where the ditch had been.

Tiny buds throughout the wall of green suddenly bloomed into pearl flowers in unison, each releasing a single oil-slick rainbow bee. The bees flew up and over the hedge, down into the quilt of shacks.

My vision jumped to a man being stung and swatting away the bee. He didn't get sick instantly the way I'd seen at Chatham Park. Time lurched forward again and the sting victim was visibly ill, but no longer in the shack town, instead, walking through a Nairobi street. He wretched on the ground and a passerby stopped to help him.

# Chapter 20

"I know how they're going to release the virus! They're in a low-income area somewhere outside the city. Tatiana will grow a giant hedge, pre-loaded with Terra Nova oil. Once the hedge is fully grown, those little pearl flowers will bloom, and when they open, infected bees will swarm the community." I took a deep breath. "And you're going to help them, Ilya."

"What!" he blurted.

"I saw it. Read my mind and see for yourself." I stood nose to nose with my brother, doing my best to offer up my brain.

Ilya studied me, searching behind my eyes. "It'll never happen. I'd never do it!"

"The future isn't written in stone, right?" Faith slid her hand into Ilya's and clamped it tightly.

"Something happens between the time Ivan and Tatiana enter that community and when Ilya helps launch the virus. Ivan pushed me out somehow. When I reconnected it was suddenly Tatiana and Ilya instead. In my vision, Ilya had a variation like Ivan's. He shot energy from his hands," I said hurriedly.

"I can't do that! It's not possible!" said Ilya.

"Not yet." Josh eyed us warily.

My memory retrieved the conversation between Tatiana and Ivan about the latter needing a transplant of some kind. A black hole formed in my gut and I tried to push the images inside before Ilya could sense them.

"There's no way to know how much time passed between when Ivan pushed my mind away and when Ilya joined their side," I said. "We may have some time to figure this out."

"Stop saying that! I'd never join them!" Ilya's tone was full of shame and anger.

"Whatever happens to Ilya hasn't happened yet. So we guard him. Between all of us, we can make sure he's not on his own, not until we've got every last canister from Ivan." Cole pointed to the ground as though our future remained in our hands.

"Melissa and I should find this neighborhood. It'll be hard to miss. It's a huge patchwork of tin and fiberglass shacks." Nausea swirled inside me again and I swallowed.

"The rest of us will be a human shell around Ilya. I won't leave his side. Our combined abilities will rain hell on anyone who comes near him." Faith's ferocity matched her brother's.

"We should focus on getting Terra Nova away from them. If we break an earlier link in the chain, Irina's vision will be moot," said Ilya. He put his arm around Faith's shoulder reassuring her as best he could.

"Once Irina and I find this place, I can bring everyone out through a portal. We'll have our full fighting strength quickly." Melissa sounded confident and I believed her.

"I'll grab us a cab." I ran to the edge of the plaza where a sky blue car with an unlit "Hire" light on top.

"Sir, hello, are you available," I rapped on the window.

The driver rolled down the window. "Jambo! Where would you like to go?"

"This is going to sound strange. I'm not a tourist. I'm here with a non-profit. I need to get out to that huge low-income community outside the city."

The driver's smile evaporated. He frowned at me. "You mean Kibera. It is not a place to visit."

"Yes, I understand that. As I said, I'm not a tourist. I know it's not safe. I'm not sight-seeing."

"I will not take you to Kibera. I will not be responsible for you if you go." The driver rolled up his window and drove away.

I cast a quick glance back at my friends who had anxious expressions on their passport faces. I crossed the street to a white taxi which also waited for a fare. I made the same request and got a less courteous decline. In my peripheral vision, I saw Ilya approach.

"This is bullshit. We're going to rent a car instead." Ilya beckoned me back with a brisk wave.

Cole had already ducked into a strip mall on the other side of the plaza. Ilya and I returned to the group, but Cole was already on his way back. The stranger's face he wore exuded rage.

"They won't rent the car to me. I've got a passport that doesn't match my driver's license and credit card," said Cole.

"I'll try another cab," I said.

"We could be at this all day. Let's ask at the hotel." Melissa ducked behind a large orchid-covered shrubbery, opened a portal, and disappeared.

I followed her. "So what exactly can we say to the manager, that'll convince him to get us a ride to Kibera? That's what the skittish driver said the patchwork community is called."

Cole and Faith popped out of the portal behind me. Her arched eyebrows framed fretful eyes.

"We'll try your aid worker story again," said Melissa.

"What if he doesn't believe us?" said Cole.

"So we convince him we need to borrow his car." Josh rubbed his cheek thoughtfully.

"And what reason would that be?" Ilya glared impatiently.

"I hate to say this, but maybe we need to steal a car," I said.

"How do you suggest we quickly and quietly steal a car in the middle of Nairobi?" Cole's tone bordered on sarcasm and I suppressed a snarky quip as a new idea hit me.

I ran out of Melissa's door and whipped my head around to get my bearings. She was on the third floor. I ran to the stairwell, bounded down one floor, and sped to mine and Jonah's door.

My boyfriend and my sister were sitting out on the balcony playing cards. They looked at me with curious expressions.

I plunged my hand into my backpack and felt for the plastic bag Monsieur Bonne Nuit had given us. I flipped it out. Success! We had a handful of turbo melatonin-spiked Egyptian crackers ready and waiting to help us scoop a car.

I ran back to Melissa's room with Jonah and Gemma on my heels. I burst through Melissa's door and flung my hand out gripping the plastic baggie.

"We've got the sleep crackers!" I exclaimed.

"Fat lot of good that'll do. It takes too long for those to kick in," said Faith.

"We'll hire a tour van and say we want to go to the Rift

Valley. I've seen a few posters for that in the lobby." I gestured our route through the air, digging deep for convincing enthusiasm.

Faith picked up her tablet and started tapping away.

"This is a bad plan. In a stolen vehicle we could end up arrested," said Jonah.

"It's not likely. Nairobi's crime rate combined with the resources of their urban police force make it unlikely they would find us quickly, if at all," said Josh.

"I found it!" said Faith. "Kibera is on the way to the Rift Valley. We could get a tour guide. Anybody with a van can take us out there. We'll go to a lookout or a roadside stop, get him to eat the crackers, and stall until he falls asleep. We'll choose a food stand or a trinket trap so the guy's not stranded. Then we'll double back to Kibera. From there Ilya can listen for Tatiana and Ivan." Faith's features finally relaxed with the start of a solution in sight.

"What if he doesn't want to eat the crackers?" said Ilya.

"Then we're screwed." Faith rolled her eyes with a toss of her dreadlocks.

I pulled my backpack back on and marched out the door. I hopped down the stairwell and bounded into the lobby, nervous and afraid. I hoped the combination would come across as excitement in the eyes of the people at the front desk.

"Jambo!" said a young male clerk behind the counter.

"Can you recommend a tour operator to take my friends and me to the Rift Valley? We need someone to take us to a viewpoint," I said.

"Ah, yes, Rift Valley is very nice for pictures," said the clerk.

"Yes, we'd love to take some pictures," I gushed with enthusiasm.

"You take Karibu Kab Tours?" said the clerk, pointing at a poster.

"That would be perfect. Can I borrow your phone? Or can you call them for us?" I said.

"You sign up here. He takes groups of eight to ten. If you are not enough people in your group, you wait until more sign up," said the clerk.

"I have eight people ready to go now. When will he let us know?" I tried not to sound panicked.

"I call right now," he said.

"Okay, that's perfect." I was humming with nervous energy as I paced around the lobby. After a fifteen-minute eternity, a jolly man with a wide straw hat came in expectantly.

"Good afternoon, miss! You go to Rift Valley?" said the man, beaming warmly.

"Are you our driver?" I said optimistically. I sized him up in more detail. He was tallish and strong, but not so giant that we couldn't affect his body chemistry. He wore a linen shirt and crisp khaki shorts. I prayed he wasn't so nicely dressed as to attract thieves or worse once we left him alone by the road.

"I have Karibu Kab Tours. You have a group to go for a drive?" said the driver happily.

"You bet! I have eight people. When can we leave?" I said.

"You pay by credit card before we go?" The driver tilted his head hopefully.

"I can give you cash."

The driver's face brightened and he grinned again. "In that case, we go now if you like."

I rounded everyone up and got us back down in the lobby in less than ten minutes. I wasn't taking any chances on the Karibu Kab driver changing his mind.

He waited for us outside the lobby in a small white passenger van. I counted out twenty-five thousand Kenyan Shillings while my friends climbed in. I didn't have the heart to tell them we were almost at the end of our financial resources. We had bigger problems on our hands anyway. I took the front passenger seat next to our driver.

Once he re-counted his fee, we were off and bouncing through Nairobi traffic. We sped through old European cars, glossy Asian cars, and strange vehicles I had never seen before. The towers of Nairobi were unmistakably urban and yet nothing like the Canadian cities I knew. We rounded a corner and a sea of aluminum and fiberglass squares stretched unevenly into the horizon. I let out an involuntary gasp.

"This is Kibera," said the driver, displeased at the sight.

"How many people live here?" I asked.

"Some say as many as a million. At least hundreds of thousands. It is a very bad place," the driver regarded Kibera with contempt that startled me.

We left the community behind and Nairobi's urban density faded. We passed single and double-story strip malls made of dusty buildings with old paint. Hand-painted signs in English and Swahili over stained cement storefronts were paired with fragile straw-capped wood huts. Traffic thinned out and many people were on foot, carrying plastic bags or baskets.

The road relaxed into golden rolling hills. Outside the city, dry grass and shrubbery stretched around us. Small trails headed off into the wild here and there. And then a huge gulf of green yawned in front of us. Fluffy white clouds cast shadows over the lush grassy plain, a patchwork of farms and tiny buildings.

"Welcome, my friends, to Kenya's Rift Valley. You take many

pictures. I will take you to buy souvenirs and food and art. You will have much fun." Our driver knew how to maximize the profit from his tour drives in the area.

I smiled at the change of pace he would soon experience with his current passengers. Worry quickened my pulse. I smiled uncomfortably.

"Are you feeling well, my friend?" The man's features remained concerned as he returned his attention to the road.

"I'm well. Enough."

"Good, good. This will be your favorite part of your trip. Relax. You are safe here."

# Chapter 21

We pulled over at the Samburu Curio Shop, a pair of bright red wood buildings with vibrant yellow trim. The colorful structures overflowed with wares. Striped and patterned fabric hung in layers from racks. Drums, plates, and bowls were mounted on the wall above the large open doors. Inside sculptures and carvings covered every inch of the first two tables I saw. Batik squares of canvas covered the wall behind it.

"You look, you buy," said an older woman who approached me out of nowhere. She held a painted wood lion and thrust it at me. I took it from her, caught off guard.

I took in my friends one by one. Each of us had a salesperson chattering away about buying, buying, buying.

"Handmade. Good deal," said another lady, older than mine, tugging on Jonah's arm.

"Gifts. Treasures. Take many," said a little boy, no older than twelve who held up two shell necklaces, one in each hand in front of Gemma. She took a necklace and smiled.

"We don't have much money. We can't stay long." Cole frowned at the man showing him a painted soapstone keepsake box.

Melissa browsed inside, miraculously unattended and Faith had slipped away to the bathroom shed. I handed back my lion and excused myself to the van.

I pulled our melatonin crackers from my backpack and said the only thing I could think to say to our driver. "Sir, can I offer you a snack? I packed these crackers for myself, but the sun hit me funny. I'm still not feeling well."

I held out the plastic baggie casually, pleading with the universe, willing him to take the bag while trying to come off as nonchalant as possible.

"Thank you, miss. You sit. You feel better, you shop again." The driver set the crackers down on the dashboard of the van and said something in Swahili to my saleswoman who rapped on his window.

I imagined she complained because I hadn't bought her lion. Maybe, one of the others had told her I had all the money, which in terms of cash shillings was mostly true.

A handful of excruciating minutes passed and then our driver did the unlikely. He absent-mindedly reached into the bag of crackers and pulled one out. He ate carefully. Then he picked up the whole bag and ate the rest. Ten crackers laced with concentrated melatonin.

Another tour bus pulled in and two dozen American schoolchildren stomped out squealing. The salespeople rushed to greet the eager children.

I tiptoed back to the front of the van. Our driver slept deeply. I inspected the parking lot. Josh and Cole were on their way to the van. The rest of my friends followed.

"Is he asleep?" Josh poked his head in the door.

"Don't you think he'd speak up if he wasn't?" I answered.

"We'd better hide him quickly. These people are obviously his friends." Cole opened the driver's side door and slipped his arms under the driver's legs and behind his back.

The rest of my friends got into the van quickly. I stole a glance at the curio shop. The kids and their chaperones were the perfect fit for the aggressive salespeople piling trinkets and keepsakes into wicker baskets for anyone who would hold them.

I watched Cole carry the driver to a nearby tree, out of sight from the storefront. He laid the man in a seated position back against the trunk. It looked like an afternoon nap. It was perfect.

"Time to go." Josh slid into the driver's seat. He started the van and Cole hopped into the front passenger seat. Josh pulled out onto the road and we sped back to the city.

"Ilya, can you please get rid of these passport personas?" I needed to be myself again.

"Wait, take the next dirt road. We need practice." Jonah pointed to a path. Josh peered ahead and shook his head dismissively.

"We can't waste time working out," I said.

"We've still got Ilya, right? So nothing's gonna happen until they get their hands on him," said Faith.

I paused to consider her logic and it did make sense.

"It's a fair assumption." Melissa sounded impressed.

"I hate not knowing. If I don't know what's coming, how can I stop it?" Ilya's concern moved me.

"This one! There's a stream!" exclaimed Jonah as we passed a sign for a recreation area.

Josh hit the brakes and turned hard. Inertia shoved me against my seatbelt. We bumped our way up the hill and crossed the stream. The road curved around a bend to a plateau on top and we found a pond surrounded by rushes and several baboons bathing in the pool. I froze in my seat as Josh parked.

One of the baboons ambled over to our van and Cole stepped out. The baboon eyed him up for a moment, assessing every square inch of Cole. Then the animal let out a primal scream of rage that rattled me to my core.

"Bring it!" said Cole in a deep angry tone.

Sensing the challenge, the baboon rushed Cole. But Cole was faster. The baboon leaped into the air, springing from its powerful hind legs. Cole snatched it and tossed it down the hillside behind us.

Josh hopped out of the van in time for another baboon to pounce on him. The baboon swiped. Instead of rending flesh, a sickly scrape was followed by a whimper as Josh's fist connected with the baboon's face and sent him flying. The remaining two baboons ran off down the hill after the animal Cole had thrown.

"Come on out. It's safe now," called out Cole.

"Are you sure this is a good place to practice?" My glance darted around the space, waiting for something to materialize behind a tree.

"Could you see this pond from the road?" said Josh.

"What if someone comes up here sightseeing?" said Melissa. "Or a local?"

Ilya stared back the way we'd come. "Then they'll find the illusion I just threw up of a barricade with biohazard symbols," he said.

Faith shot a thick stream of fire into the ground. She pressed energy from her hand into the earth until only a molten crater remained. The edges cooled, shiny and dark while the rest of the giant fresh glass bowl stayed red hot. She lifted her arms to the sky triumphantly. "That felt awesome!"

"You're getting better." Ilya leaned in over her handiwork.

"How about aim?" I levitated a fist-sized rock in the air above Faith's head. She shot a thin stream of fire at the rock, knocking it into the distance.

Jonah sent a column of water after it quenching the rock with a hiss before it hit the ground.

"It's a good thing you two usually go hand in hand," said Josh.

I frowned. I saw his point, but I wanted to change the fact that my boyfriend and his ex were a better fighting team than he and I would ever become.

"That may be the case, but he'd no more go back to her than she'd go back to him. I wouldn't stay with Faith if I didn't know she was into me a hundred percent." Ilya stood next to me watching the show.

"I need practice too," said Gemma indignantly.

"You want one of us to intentionally get hurt?" said Melissa.

"If you want me to get better at healing different things quickly, then, yes," said Gemma. There was that pout.

"Can you heal regular humans?" The carnage at Chatham Park popped into my mind. The lobby, the front yard, the back lawn. So many bloody bodies.

"I think that's outside her control." Ilya frowned at me fiercely.

"It is for now. I've grown, maybe she can too," I said.

"Let's hope it doesn't come to that," said Ilya.

Cole stretched his bare arm at his sister. "I'll go first."

"Are you sure?" she asked.

"Better take your shot now." Cole gave Gemma a gaze of approval and she blushed.

"This is going to hurt." A smirk of satisfaction and a frown of deep thought wrestled on Faith's face as she contemplated how best to burn her brother. She shot a thin stream of fire barely the width of one of her fingers straight into the fleshy muscle of Cole's forearm.

Cole grunted as he bore the burn.

"That's enough!" Gemma ran to Cole.

A patch of Cole's arm was a ruin of bloody red flesh and bubbling black blisters. He dropped to his knees and braced his wounded left arm by squeezing the bicep above with his right hand.

Gemma's hands shook as she hovered over Cole. She panted with panic until she took a deep breath. She focused, staring hard at Cole's arm. Golden light shot out of her hands and onto his burn.

Relief washed over Cole's face. The burn diminished. Red faded to pink and back into the hardy beige of his regular skin.

Gemma released the energy and stepped backward, grinning at her handiwork. She rubbed her hands together waiting for Cole's response.

"How do you feel?" Jonah's eyebrows arched as he assessed Cole.

"Good. Better. The pain is gone." Cole made a fist and flexed his arm.

I had a new idea and picked up a small rock, stepping away from the group. I levitated the rock, this time picturing the stone being crushed inward, crumbling into dust under the weight of nothing. It turned over and over in the air. And then it began to crack. One crack turned into a handful of fractures. Suddenly the rock exploded sending fragments everywhere.

"What the hell was that?" yelled Faith.

"Nicely done!" Jonah walked over and patted my back.

"I hope Ivan and Tatiana don't know just how much you're capable of," said Josh.

I looked down at my hands, my tiny unremarkable small hands. I took a deep breath and tried not to solve the mystery of understanding exactly where my powers came from or how they worked. That knowledge wasn't what I needed for the fight ahead.

# Chapter 22

I sat on the dry, packed earth as I watched Jonah perfect his pressurized water jet attack. Fluffy clouds drifted across a bright blue sky, and I was almost relaxed when I heard a low growl. It had a chilling familiarity, a sound I never thought I'd hear again.

"Look out!" shouted Melissa.

The growls turned into aggressive snarls as two scorpion dogs crested the hill. Cole tackled one and Josh pounced on the other. I turned away in time to hear a squeal and the crack of a breaking neck. Then a sickening crunch as the second creature was crushed.

"That wasn't a fluke encounter. He must know where we are," said Jonah.

"I'm sure he has more of them," I said, forcing myself to ignore the dead animals.

Cole and Josh dug quickly with their bare hands and buried the horrible bodies.

"How long should we wait?" Faith glanced around, her feet

planted in a wide stance.

"It's already here," said Ilya, listening to the hillside.

A wave of chills shot up my back at the sound of a fleshy thumping overhead. A grotesque black stain in the sky had the wings of a huge bat and the head of a cobra, eerily similar to the alien demon from my vision. Its thick abdomen was much like a snake, but it had two clawed feet separating body from tail. The creature was larger than any eagle I'd seen in Northern BC.

The giant snake-bat hissed and a long blue tongue darted out to taste the air as another creature flew in behind it. And another and another until four demons circled our group.

Faith shot a stream of fire into their midst sending them scattering with a chorus of hissing.

Melissa raised her arms to open a portal in front of one. The creature dodged it artfully and fixed its gaze on Cole. The thing flexed its mid-section and sent a wave of spiked darts at Cole's head. Cole dodged, enraging the animal. The giant snake-bat broke into a dive and swooped at Cole, mouth gaping, fangs dripping with neon yellow liquid.

"Don't let it bite you!" I tried to focus on the creature long enough to hold it still. The thing fought hard and I felt agonizing pressure inside my head.

Cole whipped a rock at the bat's head and it made contact with a loud crack. The blow sent the creature into a downward tailspin.

Another creature dove at Cole, but a molten stream of Faith's fire knocked it off its trajectory and engulfed it. Flames spread from the body into the fleshy wings like liquid death. The bat hissed, curled into a ball, and fell. The other two bats broke away and flew southwest, back to Kibera and Nairobi.

"Fuck them! Fuck you, Ivan!" Faith yelled up at the sky.

"Back to the van. Now!" shouted Josh.

Jonah took me by the arm and I let him. We ran back to the van. Josh had us rumbling along the highway in minutes.

I rummaged in my bag, suddenly needing to take inventory of my possessions. Did I have my toothbrush? Extra socks and underwear? Lip balm? Tylenol? Tears welled in my eyes at the ridiculousness of my stress. I knew supplies wouldn't matter if Ivan's mutated abominations kept getting worse.

Josh turned hard on each corner on the highway back to Nairobi. My pulse raced and I panted as I leaned forward into the van's speed. The faster we got to Kibera, the closer we were to the end. I almost wanted the end more than the outcome. A small part of me thought that when I saw Ivan, I would just walk out to him and surrender, letting him crush my throat with his telekinetic power. I visualized it for a moment.

"Don't you dare!" Ilya rounded on me from the row of seats in front of me.

"Aren't you tired? Aren't you afraid?" I said.

Jonah put his arm around me. "We're all afraid. But we're strong."

"Stronger than Ivan," Cole told me. "We'll beat him, Irina."

"Speak for yourself." Gemma sat on my other side, gazing out the window, more afraid than anyone in the van. The roof tapestry of Kibera emerged on the horizon.

Josh pulled over in a field full of trash on the outskirts of the area. He fished under the seat and retrieved a steering wheel club. He fitted the security device into the steering wheel, locked it, and removed the key.

"Take everything with you. Stuff your pockets. We need to

prepare for this van to be gone when we get back," said Josh. "I don't know how long it will last here."

"I can get us to the hotel with a portal," said Melissa.

"We might not want to go back to the hotel either. Once that driver gets back into the city, the hotel where he met us is the first place he'll check," said Jonah.

Outside the van, Josh took stock of all of us, appraising our condition more than making inventory.

"Can you pick Ivan or Tatiana out of the crowd? How close do you have to be?" I asked Ilya.

My brother grimaced as he listened to the sea of minds in Kibera. His face contorted. I wondered what he heard, but I tried to keep my mind as quiet as possible. Not speaking was a given, but it was hard to not think either.

"There are too many people. So many are sick already from malnutrition. So much misery." Ilya lifted his hand and pointed. "Over there, a woman is desperately worried about her baby. She's sick and she isn't making enough milk. The baby is sleeping too much. She thinks it might die."

Ilya shifted his gaze and closed his eyes. "There's a man nearby who's planning to kill his brother over a girl. He's very drunk. He's drinking something called Changaa. A little boy is crying. His brother just hit him, hard, for eating the last of their bread. Their father died and now the big brother is in charge while their mom is at work. It was for him to say when they ate and they were supposed to share. They're both young. The little one just turned ten. The older one is thirteen."

Ilya did something I'd never seen him do. He began to cry, quietly and softly.

"Okay, there's too much going on here for Ilya to pick out a single mind in the mess," said Jonah.

"Yeah, this is lame. We should move on foot until we find something." Faith studied Ilya with uncharacteristic sympathy and it made my heart ache too. He wiped his face, blinked rapidly, and steadied himself.

"Should we go in 'bare' or should we try a new look?" Cole watched Ilya who wiped tears off his face.

"I'm more worried about being stopped by the residents than being seen by Ivan," I said.

"Good point. Our passport alter-egos will stand out as much as we would," said Josh.

"I'll turn us into the staff from the Samburu Curio Shop," said Ilya.

"Perfect!" said Faith.

Ilya's wet foggy air engulfed us and when my reflection sharpened in the van's passenger window, I saw the older lady who had tried so hard to sell me a wood lion. It was possibly the strangest disguise Ilya had given me yet. Just when I thought I had been someone else for the last time. "Should we stay together or split up?"

"We will cover more ground if we go in pairs," said Cole.

"If we split up, we may never find each other again," said Josh.

"If Ilya can't single anything out and we can't split up, how the hell will we find anything in here?" Her new persona conveyed as much fury as Faith herself.

"Anybody pick up any Swahili?" said Jonah through yet another strange face.

"Are you serious?" said Ilya.

"We should start by doing a circuit of the perimeter," said Melissa.

"Good idea. Let's start by rooting out an entrance to

something underground. Ivan won't keep animals like those scorpion-dogs or snake-bats in some pen above ground," said Josh.

"I think I'll recognize the ditch where they're growing that hedge and releasing the infected bees," I said.

"Once we find ground zero, we can stake it out and wait," said Melissa.

"I might be able to hear my father or aunt if we're close enough to them," said Ilya.

"What's the plan if we come across them?" I said.

"We don't know if they'll have backup, or in what form." Josh rubbed his new chin deep in thought. "This stage is extremely important to them. They'll have security measures to ensure their plan happens on schedule. And then there's Ilya's conversion. Everyone, keep a close eye on him. And if any of us sees Ivan or Tatiana, take them out."

"Are you suggesting we disregard civilians?" said Melissa.

"I'm not willing to throw innocent people under the proverbial bus," said Jonah.

"Nobody wants that," said Faith flatly.

"But remember, if you've got a civilian between you and one of the Krylovs, it's the rest of humanity at stake," I said.

"Today could be the day this finally ends," Ilya breathed deeply, re-centering his mind. Faith hugged him.

"We've talked this through again and again. If you don't think you can make a kill when the time comes, get back in that van right now and stay out of the way," said Josh.

We followed him away from our stolen vehicle to the border of Kibera, possibly the place where we would all die.

# Chapter 23

We evaluated each other, taking in our mutual anxiety written on a fresh wave of strangers' faces. I pushed through the group, walking parallel to the outer edge of the sea of shacks. Gravel crunched behind me and I knew my friends followed.

Kibera was my first in-person experience of extreme poverty. In my childhood, I'd encountered people living on the street at home in industrial Prince George and later in Euro-inspired Victoria. Apart from the variants living in Victoria's seaside urban sewer, when I had seen people sleeping on sidewalks, cold and hungry, I thought that was the bleakest way to live.

Vancouver's East Side educated me during our initial search for *The Compendium*. I saw people in the throes of violent addictions and suffering from diseases of the mind.

Nairobi's roughest urban terrain represented something else entirely. Kibera was not a part of town where homeless people dotted an otherwise structurally normal area. As we walked around the outer border, the makeshift buildings slowly drove a crack into my soul.

We passed a small shack made of wavy fiberglass, stained by the sun, and another made of plywood with a rusted metal roof. Some buildings had the stability of brick and mud mortar walls. Decaying mounds of discarded clothing, plastic bags, bottles, cans, cardboard, and layers of rotting muck fringed the exterior of these homes.

Two children walked past holding hands. Little boys in shorts and nothing else, barefoot and bone-skinny, probably not unlike the pair Ilya had heard arguing about bread. They glanced at us briefly and turned down a path bordered by more trash piles.

I wondered why they didn't ask us for help or money. It took me a moment to realize that my friends and I were still concealed as the salespeople from the Samburu Curio Shop. I blinked out of my haze of disbelief and looked around at my friends.

I had lost track of who was who and I could only pick Jonah out of our group. I decided not to worry about putting faces to names for the moment. I had to focus, like Ilya, on somehow groping my way to where Ivan and Tatiana hid in this crazy maze.

The sun's heat warped the air over the cracked clay ground. I examined my dark feet in worn-out leather sandals. It was surreal, not just to be outside a massive stretch of impoverished housing, but to literally walk in someone else's shoes. I felt a stern resolve to go on, to find Ivan and defeat him so that I could evolve into someone capable of healing more of the world around me.

We walked and walked until we reached the end of the dry

field we had parked in and came up against a huge cement barrier. The wall ahead had to be over ten feet high, and like the pit I'd seen in my vision, it was topped with razor wire. Something in the coiled wire sparkled in the sun. We got closer and I saw a fringe of broken glass embedded in mortar. The residents of this other Nairobi neighborhood wanted very much to keep Kibera on its side of the fence.

Our path was forced inward and I led the way. We turned down a trash-lined alley that cut into the heart of the community. People sat on the bare ground and in lawn chairs. They milled about surrounding oil drums over which some were roasting meat on sticks.

I saw an empty bottle of carbonated water – the exact same brand Ivan had requested so many times back in Victoria. Was it even available for sale in Kenya? And who in the middle of Kibera would bother to waste precious shillings on it?

I bent down and picked up the bottle. Kibera went pitch black around me. I opened my eyes in a pit surrounded by muddy brick walls topped by coiled razor wire around the edges. Two worn wood doors were the only way in or out. Skimming the fiberglass rooftops around me, I was still in Kibera. I heard Ivan's voice muffled by a wall.

The doors burst open. Rose and Sage shoved a thoroughly beaten Ilya out ahead of them, nudging him forward until he collapsed at the center of the pit. Ivan shuffled behind, his face a sweaty white death mask, utterly drained of vitality.

Ivan dropped to his knees across from Ilya. It took all Ivan's energy to face his son. Ilya struggled against an unseen force. Despite his exhaustion, Ivan seemed to hold Ilya in place telekinetically. Ivan grabbed his belly as though he was about to heave his stomach contents out onto the ground between them. Suddenly a red bolt of flesh launched from the back of Ivan's throat, grabbing Ilya by the neck.

The red tendril wrapped around my brother's throat again and again. It slipped up Ilya's neck and into his mouth, forcing its way down into his abdomen.

Ivan's body collapsed as a tail of red wiggled free and snapped against Ilya's chest. My father lay in a lifeless heap while my brother struggled uselessly against the parasite that slithered into him.

Terror and disgust held me frozen in place. Every fiber of my body was paralyzed as I watched Ilya flinch and twitch through the last of the transition. His eyes flashed red and my brother was gone. The cobra demon had him. It stood up, squared its shoulders, stretched, and grinned.

The creature reveled in the youthful strength of Ilya's body disregarding whatever injuries my brother had sustained in captivity. It flexed Ilya's arms and spun on the spot. It walked over to Ivan's corpse and kicked it hard in the gut.

I finally forced my hand open and dropped the green glass bottle that connected me to the worst vision I had ever seen. Back on the outskirts of Kibera, I regained my bearings. I studied my friends' unfamiliar faces, trying to reconnect with who was who. Even with a stranger's features, I saw the fear in my brother's eyes as he flipped through the images in my mind.

"Well, now we know why it's me helping to release the killer bees." Ilya's grave manner set Faith back on edge.

"You can't seriously think we'll allow that thing to take you?" I gave my brother a reassuring stare.

Ilya slipped into a narrow alley and I followed with the others right behind me. I felt a rush of moisture in the air and we were all ourselves again.

"There's not much point in hiding anymore," said Ilya.

It was refreshing to see the faces of my friends again, but I felt nervous about being exposed.

"What thing?" Jonah frowned at my brother, before turning to me and asking, "What's going to take him?"

"The demon. The alien. The whatever-the-hell creature living inside Ivan. He's sick because his body is dying. That creature controlling him wants *my* body now." Ilya stared at the ground to avoid eye contact with Faith.

"Never gonna happen!" Faith crossed her arms angrily.

"When we find Ivan and Tatiana, I'll go with them. I'll remind them that I can heal. I can help Ivan so he doesn't have to hurt Ilya," said Gemma.

"No, we finally have a real bargaining chip with Ivan and Tatiana." Ilya took a deep breath and lowered his voice. "We can trade my body. We'll find Ivan and you can use me to get their entire supply of Terra Nova. Even if we assume they've already got seeds laced with the oil and ready to go, it'll be a one-shot deal for them if we destroy the rest of their Terra Nova. Once that creature's got a hold of me, I can fight it. Ivan isn't telepathic – I am. I have a weapon he didn't."

"Don't you fucking try it!" Faith glared at Ilya with rage in her eyes.

"No! No, no, no! You don't know all the abilities and powers our father has. And you don't know which come from our father and which are from that … THING!" I shouted.

"It's going to happen. I'm going to be possessed. You wouldn't have seen it repeatedly if we could avoid that path. We should roll with it and make it work to our advantage." Ilya glanced between me and Faith.

"Horseshit! You're not rolling with anything! Over my dead body!" Faith's voice got louder, but nobody tried to shush her. I lifted my hand, wanting to calm her. I withdrew and turned back to Ilya.

"What I saw in my vision before was you helping Tatiana release the virus. Even if you can fight the creature off eventually, the damage will be done by then. What's the point in fending off that demon if Terra Nova is already loose?"

"We can't be certain this single release point is enough to spread Terra Nova worldwide. I don't think it could be. They have to move on from here." Ilya's amber eyes brimmed with a blind optimism I couldn't fathom.

"Hang on. A pandemic *can* have a single point of origin. And something this virulent is hard to predict. If they've adjusted the incubation period properly, combined with the likelihood of infecting nearly a million people within a day … I don't want to err on the side of wishful thinking," said Jonah.

Ilya rooted around under his shirt. He produced the silver medal Faith had given me to hold back in Victoria. He held it out to me. "Wear this and you'll keep a strong psychic and telepathic link with me."

"It's not enough." I took the chain from his hand and Faith shot daggers at both of us.

"I have never successfully prevented a vision from coming to pass. If we go with your plan, we need to contain the release of those bees. We need to be there with you and Tatiana when the hedge is grown. And I didn't see that in my vision. I would have seen it. I'm sure I would have seen it!" I pleaded with my brother knowing it was futile.

"You just said it yourself. You can't prevent your visions. You can't stop the creature from taking me. And we need to deal with containing another outbreak." Ilya struggled to remain calm, but the slight shake in his voice betrayed him.

"Let's back up a bit to the location you saw," said Josh. Faith shot her hands in the air and stormed off at the mere hint of entertaining Ilya's plan.

"This incident you just saw with Ilya – was it near here?" said Cole.

"I think so." I took long deep breaths trying to reject the image of Ilya's possession and see the setting around him.

"Describe it to us. Those of us who can't see inside your head," said Jonah.

"We're looking for a ring of razor wire around a deep pit made of brick. Like a fighting arena. There's something underground connecting to that pit. From the street, all we'll see is the wire. It's surrounded by fiberglass rooftops."

"This whole place is made of fucking fiberglass!" Faith marched back into our midst.

"But the razor wire is only on that wall back there," said Cole.

"That we've seen so far," Josh said cautiously.

"This place is huge. We've gotta narrow that down somehow," said Cole.

"Can't you listen for Ivan's mind? That demon thing I mean?" Gemma asked Ilya.

"Wait, I saw it in my vision of Tatiana growing the hedge too. Their base won't be far from their ground zero. Wherever that pit is, it's near the outer edge of Kibera."

"But that heinous wall of razors and glass cut us off from making a circuit of the area," said Faith, bringing her temper back to normal with visible effort.

"It did to the north. If we retrace our steps back out and

past the van, we can follow around the border of Kibera in the other direction," said Josh.

"Backtracking isn't the stupidest idea we've ever had," I said.

"Let's get on with it then." Ilya marched back out of the alley and the full force of the mid-day Nairobi sun hit his head. He flinched, fished some money out of his pocket, and gave it to a woman sitting at a folding plastic table selling hats. She smiled and started offering him one grubby used hat after another.

Ilya started passing hats around to each of us. I assessed the residents' faces. It had not gone unnoticed that a group of white twenty-somethings had just walked out of an alley where a pack of locals had entered minutes earlier.

Several men were glaring at Ilya. Josh and Cole surveyed the scene. Before I could stop him, Cole picked up a piece of old rebar off the ground. He bent it into a knot as effortlessly as a child playing with a drinking straw.

More people stopped what they were doing or stood in their tracks to watch us.

A barefoot little girl in a stained sundress walked up to Gemma and gave her a small hand-carved cross. "Christian?"

Gemma smiled at her.

"Good idea. We're missionaries," I whispered into Gemma's ear.

Gemma took the cross and turned it over in her hand. "Yes, we are, bless you, darling. You keep this." She put the cross back in the little girl's hand and folded her fingers around it.

Cole led the way back down the trash-lined street and past the glass and razor fence.

I heard a flutter and whipped my head up, looking for a bat creature. A seagull caw-cawed and sailed away.

A sudden rustle and a low growl in a pile of trash sent my heartbeat into overdrive. A mangy tail emerged and then a tattered brown mutt backed out of the bags.

"It's almost over," said Jonah, sensing my panic as he walked beside me.

"It has to be. I can't take much more of this," I said as I laced my fingers into his hand which dwarfed mine.

# Chapter 24

We found our van exactly where we left it. I thought the police would have gotten to it or our Karibu Kab driver would be on the scene. But no, our stolen vehicle remained ours if we wanted it.

"We should keep the van. We can't rely on portals to get us everywhere we need to go," said Jonah.

"And it's nice to have shelter. We're vulnerable in this heat," I said.

"Hey, speak for yourself," said Jonah.

A cloud formed over my head and began to rain on me. It felt nice in the midday sun.

"Neat trick!" Josh reached out to touch the droplets.

"Buddy, I didn't know you could do that." Cole patted Jonah on the back.

"Hmmmm." I side-stepped the personal shower and wiped my face and hair.

Jonah smiled and drew the moisture back into his hands. "Sorry, I've been waiting for a chance to do that."

"If we can't laugh before the end of the world, then we're screwed right?" Faith's tone gave away her nervous energy.

"Irina, do you have any other landmarks we can go on? If you can see anything on the horizon, we should leave this van where it is." Gemma's eyes flashed confidently as she adjusted her ponytail.

"The kid's not wrong," said Josh.

"Are we more conspicuous in a stolen vehicle or as a bunch of lost tourists?" Cole examined his reflection in the van window and rubbed off some sweaty dirt.

"At this point, I'd rather draw Ivan out. Let him see us," said Ilya.

"You're in a rush to get possessed by an alien parasite?" I snapped.

"We know that if I get taken, events are finally set in motion." Ilya sounded surprisingly level-headed.

"I'm not sold on her visions being written in stone!" Faith shoved a finger in my direction.

"Hey, I've been praying to be wrong at some point," I said. "I've also seen Terra Nova ravaging Santorini. Meaning Terra Nova reaches Greece! We flat out CANNOT let that happen."

"So when we find Ivan, what do we do?" Cole squeezed his knuckles back and forth, demonstrating his intent.

"If Ilya feels he can fight this creature, we could go with his plan to trade his body for their entire supply of Terra Nova. It's a big gamble though. If he can't fight the thing in time and they retain any amount of Terra Nova, we'll need a way to subdue a contagion we already know flashes out of control in minutes," said Jonah as he swept his palm through the air.

"We'll make the exchange and rely on Irina's connection to Ilya to keep us close by. Ilya will guarantee they've given us everything by reading their minds. Faith will torch whatever they give us." Josh shielded his eyes from the sun.

"Screw that. I'll torch them all on the spot before they touch him!" Faith rammed her hands into her hips

Josh flicked his gaze over to Faith, and then up to the sky. Exhaustion took him for a beat, but he bounced back. "If we're on hand when that hedge is grown, that's our chance to destroy it. Once they've released those bees, Faith and Jonah will rain hell on everything in that hedge that moves. Irina, you can use your telekinetic ability to help contain it." Josh accepted a bottle of water from Jonah.

"You and I can run interference if Rose or Sage or anyone else tries to stop them," Cole said to Josh.

"As far as plans go, that's going to have to do," said Jonah.

"No, you forgot something pretty important!" I said. I nodded at Ilya.

"We're not leaving Ilya imprisoned in his own damn body!" Faith planted her feet in the stance I recognized as her battle mode.

"It might end that way. If you've got to take me out, do it," said Ilya quietly.

"Shut up! You're my brother. I'm not leaving you to a demon."

"I swear I will burn this whole city to the ground before I let you die!" shouted Faith.

"If it's my life, or the spread of Terra Nova and the death of almost everyone else on the planet, what the hell am I supposed to do?" said Ilya.

"What if she's right and Terra Nova spreads anyway and you die FOR NOTHING!" screamed Faith.

"We've got a plan. It stands a solid chance of working.

And after every infected plant and bee is dead, we'll turn our attention to restoring Ilya," said Josh.

"Between Josh and me, we'll hold Ilya, no matter how strong he gets," said Cole.

"Let's go before I change my mind." Ilya departed along the Kibera border and everyone else followed.

I hung back for a moment. Jonah stayed with me. His sympathetic expression misinterpreted a need for comfort. I held up my hand to keep him at bay.

I closed my eyes and held Ilya's pendant in my hand. My mind flashed back to that pit where Ilya had just been taken by the alien demon. I pulled back and focused on Ilya, walking ahead of me.

*Ilya, I know you can hear* me, *but I need to know if* I *can hear you. I'm not putting one foot in front of the other until I know I can trust this connection. If it doesn't work now, how will it work once you're trapped, taken over by that thing?*

I waited for a long moment. I opened my eyes. Jonah stared at me. Our friends were getting farther away along the border of Kibera.

*Test. Test. You didn't think I was going to punk out on you, did ya?* My brother's voice echoed in my ears.

*So you knew this would work. Did you do this with Faith before? Why didn't you say something earlier?* I thought hard at my brother.

*Faith is already mad that I gave you the medal. Didn't you see that glare she gave you when I handed it over? If I told everyone we did this all the time, she'd be hella pissed. She's just crazy like that.*

Ilya's voice ended and I steadied myself. The process of hearing someone inside your mind was disorienting. It was a wonder he didn't lose his balance regularly.

*This telepathy thing is freaking me out. But we'll do one last check when we find Ivan, okay?*

*You got it, sis. Just don't lose my medallion. I had to carry that thing for years to get this to work.*

I rubbed my temples and sighed at Jonah. He reached out to support my shoulder. "This thing works after all. We just have to hope it'll still work once that demon jumps from Ivan to Ilya."

We walked and walked as the sun crept towards the horizon. The intensity of the heat did not relent. We darted in and out of pockets where rooftops and the sun's angle created respites of shade. I didn't have the distant view of Kibera's ceiling that would allow me to see the ring of razor wire that marked the end of our road.

The telltale subdermal heat of sunburned flesh radiated from my back and shoulders even in the shade. My burn kept me from braving the sun for a better glimpse at the top of the structures next to us.

Out of nowhere, Ilya's hand shot out in a halt gesture and we froze. Each of us stayed silent. I begged Fate to show Ilya some sign of where our next footsteps should take us. My brother beckoned us forward. "We'll turn in at the next opening. I can hear him, it, the creature. It's not far now," he whispered.

We turned in where Ilya pointed and followed his lead. He took us around the corner onto the first inner street we found.

Two tall, toned men stood guarding a metal gate that led to a corridor. The end of the corridor was the crown of razor wire surrounded by fiberglass rooftops exactly as I'd seen in my vision. My heart leapt up and I gasped. Ilya wasted no time in approaching.

"Hi there! How are ya? We're here to see my father, Ivan. Aunt Tat's in there too. Can you go get them? We'll wait." Ilya's calm assurance impressed me.

My heart pounded in my chest. I watched the man closest to us slowly reach for the latch on the gate, not breaking eye contact with Ilya until the last moment. He said nothing as he turned and went into the compound. Faith vibrated with anger and anxiety, turning my skin to gooseflesh as the other guardsman bore into her with his eyes.

"Come. Just Ilya and Irina," said a familiar female voice.

I peered past Gemma's shoulder down the gated corridor. Rose and Sage stood in the doorway ahead.

"I've got a bad feeling about this. It's all way too casual," I said.

"Cole is coming with us. Irina needs protection," Ilya called through the gate. I knew Ilya meant for Cole and me to leave without him. Panic surged in my gut.

Rose whispered in Sage's ear. Sage whispered back.

"Okay, Ilya, Irina and Cole. No one else," said Rose.

I followed Ilya through the gate and Cole was on my heels. I had to trust that my friends were safe out on the street. I proceeded into a far more dangerous place than run-of-the-mill Kibera.

Rose and Sage led us down a narrow hallway open to the sky at the top, which led to a landscaped courtyard. Ivan and Tatiana sprawled on reclined patio chairs under a blue fabric sunshade suspended about ten feet above them. A table of fruit, bread, and cheese with pitchers of orange and pink juices stretched along the far wall. Only the razor-lined roof on the other side of the courtyard reminded us all where we were. Rose and Sage walked over to the snack table and helped themselves each to a plate of food. They stretched out their wings and sat cross-legged on the ground to eat. Ilya ignored them and approached Ivan.

"So, cards on the table, Dad. Well, not Dad, I mean, who or whatever the hell you are, we know everything now," said Ilya. Cole and I stood behind him speechless.

"Is that so?" Ivan sat up to participate in the conversation. His eyes flashed red and I felt a wave of nausea pass through me.

"We know you're not strong enough to help Aunt Tat launch Terra Nova. We know you need my body."

"And what do you want in exchange for your cooperation?" said Ivan.

"We've come to exchange me for your entire supply of Terra Nova oil. Including the seeds that Aunt Tat has already laced with the virus. We want every drop of what you've got here, with your assurance that there is no more Terra Nova anywhere on Earth."

Ivan and Tatiana both contemplated Ilya with intensity. They eyed each other.

Tatiana cocked her head and then sat up to consider each of us. "What prompted your change of heart?"

"Don't you understand that we have to try? Can't you at least empathize, for a moment, with the rest of humanity?" I said, pleading with my most earnest tone.

"We're not human." Ivan's sly expression suggested he knew more than we did. "You're not going to stop us. It's far too late for that now. Why not embrace the new world?"

"You're right. You're not human. You never were." I said to Ivan and pointed at Tatiana. "But she was."

"My father is in there somewhere. I want to talk to him too. That's part of the deal," said Ilya.

Ivan eyed Ilya carefully. "We can arrange a meeting, of sorts. It'll have to do."

"I want to say hello and goodbye to my father," said Ilya.

"You will," said Ivan.

"Then I'm ready," said Ilya.

I rubbed my face with my hands. This was the wrong time for my brother to finally meet our father, even if this was his last chance.

"For what it's worth, I get why you want to reboot this planet," Cole said to Ivan, before turning to Rose and Sage. "And you two, I get it for you guys too, but it doesn't take much soul-searching to realize that you're not more important than everyone else. Most people – most human people – are good and they don't deserve to die. Those good people would accept and incorporate variants. I know it."

"I don't care what they would accept or incorporate," said Ivan. "Those people would not survive the world we need for ourselves. Removing them now is a mercy. Witnessing the chaos of their slow and painful deaths in new ecosystems would be more unpalatable, I assure you."

"Then don't change the planet!" I blurted. "We can all live here as is. Just let it be."

Ivan opened his mouth to speak but paused and read Tatiana's deep frown. She shook her head and Ivan closed his mouth.

"Okay, we're at a standstill. We don't see eye to eye. Now are you going to make this exchange or not?" said Ilya.

"We'll make the exchange," said Ivan.

Tatiana shook her head and lay back down.

"Rose, Sage, would you please collect our precious Terra Nova canisters and hand them over to Cole?" said Ivan.

"And we'll know if you short us! Don't forget the seeds!" I called out.

The harpy twins set their plates down carefully and flew up and over the razor wire. They dove down into the pit.

Scratching and clanging were soon followed by the twins' landing in front of Cole with two sealed plastic bins. He moved to lift the lid of the top bin.

"It's all there. Ask your mind reader. Every drop of oil we have, plus seeds," said Rose.

Ilya observed the sisters from head to toe and nodded to Cole. I realized it was time for Cole and me to leave. I threw a panicked gawk at Ilya.

*I've changed my mind. I can't just leave you here!*

Ilya frowned at me. *Get out. You agreed. I'll be fine.*

"Come on Irina, it's time to go." Cole touched my arm gently. I shrugged him off angrily. He picked up the stacked bins and waited for me.

I reviewed Ilya one last time and turned back down the hall. Tears flowed. I wiped them off my cheeks, furious. *Stay in touch. If I can't hear you, I'll... Just don't lose touch!*

*I won't. I promise.* Ilya smiled at me and turned to face Ivan.

# Chapter 25

"That sucked." I pushed past my friends on the other side of Ivan's metal gate. Cole followed me closely.

"Is that it? Did you get it all?" said Jonah, craning his neck to see the bins in Cole's arms.

"Even the seeds Tatiana laced with oil. Ilya made them promise this was everything, but I don't think we can be sure." I marched angrily through the street.

"We should set up camp somewhere nearby. I saw a cluster of trees before we came in. It's like a no-man's-land between the apartment towers in the city and Kibera's border." Josh's spiky hair fell limp with sweat and his exhaustion returned with a vengeance.

"I can go back to the Mojave for your camping gear." Melissa emitted fatigue, more dirty, beaten, and ragged than I'd ever seen her.

"Are we going to get hassled by police? Or residents? I'm sure there's a reason nobody else is camping in a patch of urban Nairobi woodland," I said.

"We'll have to take our chances. We are not leaving Ilya here. I'm not. None of you are either." Faith's voice had gone cold. Visibly sticky and uncomfortable, her face dripped with sweat. She stretched her tank top down for relief inadvertently accentuating her mix of muscles and curves. She massaged her face, stopping to rub her eyes, and wiping them with her fingertips. Faith relied on her armor of stoicism, so I knew better than to comfort her.

We left the trash-lined street behind and were back outside Kibera. Jonah and I led the way to the patch of forest Josh had suggested. As we closed the distance, I saw it was nowhere near as dense as I'd hoped. Trash covered the ground where underbrush would normally grow. It was a far cry from the urban woodlands I'd been used to in Canada.

I dropped my backpack and sat down on an old wood box. "Who says nobody's camping here? These woods might get much more interesting at night. If Ilya was here, he'd throw up an illusion and keep us covered perfectly."

"We can manage without him for a few nights. We'll get him back soon. And anybody who bothers us is going to quickly become sorry they did, day or night." Cole set the two bins of canisters down on the ground.

"We can't start a war with Kibera. You can bet there is a system of power and politics in this place. We just don't know what the system includes. Ivan won't share his secrets. We're better off to make friends than enemies." Josh removed his hiking boots and socks to wiggle his toes in the fresh air.

"I'm sure that takes money, which we no longer have." Faith drew a water bottle from her bag as she sat down on the ground. She drank and then splashed her face.

"I'll bring back some tradable valuables and more water

when I grab the camping gear," said Melissa.

My eyebrows lifted as I considered her proposition.

"Hey, don't ask and I won't tell," said Melissa, hands raised defensively.

"In the meantime, I'm going to try to have a vision about this place. I want to see if we've changed the growth of that hedge abomination. Maybe there's a variant nearby. Once we know where things stand now, we'll be in better shape to fight Ivan and get Ilya back." I found my tarot cards in my backpack.

"Be careful. Finding a variant doesn't mean we've got a potential ally. If we connect with anyone already working with or for Ivan, making friends could backfire," said Josh.

"I agree. It's more likely that a nearby variant is working *for* The Compendium, not against it," said Melissa.

"You're the only one who knows anything about Evonatura. And this Jinhua business is a gaping black hole in our knowledge of personnel. We need to spend some time going over anything you can remember about Ivan's counterparts," Jonah said to Melissa. She gave a deep sigh as her shoulders dropped. It was too much for now.

"We will. But I should get on with my trip to the Mojave." Melissa swept her arm and opened a portal. She stepped inside without a word and closed it again after herself.

"Well, I think it's time for a bonfire! How about you guys?" Faith eyed the shining canisters of Terra Nova.

"Wait until we've got the camp arranged. If the canister you burned back in Chester was any indication, these things won't go quietly. If bees are going to fly out, burning and frantic, we should do them one at a time, at night," I said.

I noticed a man walking out of Kibera, headed in our

direction. He had a head of tight black curls with a speckling of gray. He wore a weathered striped collared shirt and simple slacks. A single large tooth dangled from a leather cord around his neck.

"Uh, how can we help you sir?" said Cole.

Jonah stepped between me and the man.

"You are not missionaries. Polle, polle. I am come to help you." His Swahili accent was strong.

"Thank you, but we have things under control here. We know it's not a safe part of town," said Cole. He took a step to our visitor to make his point.

Faith and Josh continued scavenging the area for more wood boxes to serve as seats. Gemma's brow furrowed with a hint of unease on her face.

"I am Mr. Mbele. I am here for Irina."

"What's that?" Cole took a step to the man. Jonah joined him.

Mr. Mbele peered around Jonah and Cole and extended his hand to me as though he expected me to recognize him. Josh and Faith stopped rummaging and fell in beside Cole and Jonah. They formed a human wall between me and Mr. Mbele.

"I am not here to hurt. She will see if she has not seen already."

His soft-sounding voice put me at ease. He was not a large man. Even though my brother wasn't there to verify our visitor's truthfulness, I felt compelled to trust him.

"Stay here," I said quietly to Gemma. I walked around my tall boyfriend and his highly protective friend.

"Guys, it's okay." I made eye contact with Mr. Mbele.

"You should be aware that we're very capable of defending

ourselves," said Cole.

"I know, strong man," said Mr. Mbele. Cole's eyes widened.

"I think you have me at a disadvantage," I said.

In response, Mr. Mbele shook his hand at me, reiterating his offer for me to take it. I hesitated for a moment. I examined the aged, dry hand reaching out to me. I looked at my friends. Nobody knew what to do.

I took the man's hand and the trash-strewn woods disappeared. I was in a dusty village of mud houses with thatched roofs.

A group of three women in bright multicolored robes walked past me and filed into a hut with smoke wafting out a hole in the roof. I crept in behind them. The dark interior was tiny and I felt a wave of claustrophobia.

My eyes took a moment to adjust. They sat along the wall patiently waiting for a man drawing in the dirt on the floor. A few moments later I could see that the man drawing was Mr. Mbele.

He gazed up at me and made eye contact. People rarely looked directly at me in a vision. It unnerved me every time, though it was usually a brief coincidence.

"Irina, I show you this time in my village. These women have come to find out what the gods will make in their lives. The gods show me many things. The gods show me you. They show me I am to help you," said Mr. Mbele.

I stood in shock for a moment. I had never spoken to anyone in any of my visions. I took for granted that I was an invisible invader in scenes from the past and future.

"Can you hear me?" I said. "Can you see me?"

"Yes. I hear and see you. Now, we go to Kibera." Mr. Mbele threw his drawing stick to the ground and took my astral arm.

We flashed back to Kibera and the monstrous hedge from my vision.

Tatiana had nearly finished growing it. Ilya raised his hands and shot pulses of energy into the hedge's roots. The bees were released from the flowers and I looked away. I didn't want to watch it again. Anger flickered inside me knowing we had been betrayed. I knew we couldn't trust them!

"I see these plants grow from those people many times. It brings sickness to everyone here. It is always the same when I see this vision," said Mr. Mbele.

The bees started hitting targets on the other side of the hedge. Cries of pain and alarm rang out.

"If you've seen this, have you seen how to stop it? What are we supposed to do? That's my brother over there and he's possessed? How do we stop this and get him back?"

No sooner than I spoke, the vision-version of Faith stepped forward and torched the hedge. Cole picked up Tatiana by her ankles and thrashed her back and forth on the ground until her bloody body was limp. Josh restrained Ilya and Faith kept burning, but the cries evolved to screaming.

I watched our plan fail in front of my eyes. Ilya gripped Josh and the demon's power engulfed them both in a giant flare of blinding red light. Josh fell to the ground. Ilya rounded on Melissa and shot her with the same energy pulse. She fell instantly. He shot Faith next.

"That boy and the woman must die before this time. If they grow these plants, all is lost."

"There has to be another way," I said desperately.

"You are the only other seer I ever meet. If we do not see another way, there is not one," said Mr. Mbele.

"When does this happen? How long do we have?" I felt

helpless. I was asking how long my brother had left.

"Sun has barely risen. It is morning. Could be tomorrow morning. Could be day after that. We have a person watch this spot." Mr. Mbele pointed at the hedge in our shared vision. "When green woman and red-eyed boy come, we kill them. Your soldier friend and strong man can do it. Fire girl too."

I stood speechless. We needed a new plan, something pre-emptive, but killing Ilya wasn't an option. I pulled my arm away and released the hand I still held in the real world. In a blink I returned to the trashy woods. I glared at Mr. Mbele. I had mixed feelings about trusting his vision.

Why hadn't I seen that far in the future myself? Why had he seen me, but I hadn't seen him? Jonah's words puzzling over why I saw what I saw when I saw it came back to me. I made a fist. If only I had more lavender liquid or some other way to boost my abilities.

"He's telling the truth. He's another psychic," I said while Mr. Mbele watched quizzically.

"We must kill the green woman and the red-eyed demon boy. There is no other way," said Mr. Mbele.

"What? Back that bus up. Hell, no, we are NOT killing Ilya!" Faith hopped to her feet.

"They held back some seeds. I don't know how they fooled Ilya, but they did. They can still grow that hedge. I saw it again, with more aftermath." We were interrupted by Melissa's liquid silver oval portal right next to me. A nylon tent bag came through and I had to jump out of the way. Another tent bag and another and another came through, followed by a large black duffle bag that clinked when it hit the ground. Melissa stepped through the portal and closed it behind her.

"That's everything we left in the Mojave, plus some goodies from a pawn shop in St. George," said Melissa.

Melissa opened one of the tent bags and pulled out its contents as she noticed Mr. Mbele.

"Have we taken on an extra camper?" she said warily.

"I am here to help kill the green woman," said Mr. Mbele.

"Tatiana?  Good, we need all the help we can get," said Melissa.

Josh and Cole joined Melissa in pulling open tent bags.

"Mr. Mbele is a psychic, like Irina," said Gemma, clearly impressed.

Melissa stared at her with a confused brow.

"Don't forget the part where he thinks we've got to kill Ilya." Faith glared at the ring of rocks she was building for our fire pit. "Do I need to say I'm not happy about that?"

"We're going to find a way around that, don't worry," I said.

"If we can't save him, he *did* leave knowing exactly what he was doing," said Jonah as he helped Cole spread open a tent.

"I'm not going to entertain a notion of killing my brother. What I *am* going to do is work on having a vision about that alien demon inside him. It's got to have a weakness," I said, willing optimism into my heart.

"Why don't you check on Ilya?" said Faith.

"Good idea. I'll feel better knowing that he's still himself, for now," I said.

"We must find growth site and have someone start the watch. I will know the place when I see it," said Mr. Mbele.

"Maybe we should make a move to get Ilya out of there now. I knew this was a stupid plan!" Faith scowled at me and turned away quickly.

"I'll try to connect to Ilya and see what our best chance to break him out could be," I said.

"In the meantime, we need to destroy the canisters we already have," said Jonah. He regarded Faith with a mix of urgency and empathy.

"I'll go with Mr. Mbele to find the hedge site. Once we know exactly where it is, we'll take shifts watching it in pairs," said Cole.

"We go now then." Mr. Mbele departed.

Cole frowned and followed him.

Faith dumped a handful of loose twigs into her new fire pit. She shot a small fireball into the wood and the fire sprang to life. "Once the sun is fully set, I'll start burning these canisters."

Jonah and Josh fed assembled poles into collapsed tents. Gemma took a seat in front of the fire. She started unpacking a cooler pulling out bags of flatbread and cans of food.

"When our tent's done, I'll need some time alone," I said to Jonah. To everyone, I announced, "Once I reconnect to Ilya, it's going to be hard to conceal that we want to break him out. He'll fight me if he's still ready to let the proverbial bus flatten him."

"Then it's just too damn bad that we love him enough to fight for him," said Faith. I could tell she meant 'I' love him but was too proud to single herself out.

"Here you go." Jonah unzipped the door to our tent.

I kissed him on the cheek, picked up my sleeping bag, and crawled into the tent. I unrolled the bag and unzipped the entire thing. I laid it out like a large blanket covering the base of the tent.

I looked back through the open tent door to see Faith toss the first canister on the fire. The metal cylinder blackened for a moment and then Faith shot a bolt at it. The canister exploded in flame and a handful of bees rushed out into the night on fire. My entire body tensed and in a heartbeat the bees shriveled and fell back down, hitting the dirt as flaming blobs.

I zipped the tent door closed so I could concentrate. I positioned myself cross-legged in the center of the tent. I took a firm hold of the medal around my neck, rubbing the small coin between my thumb and forefinger. I took a deep breath and closed my eyes.

I sat cross-legged in the dark tent, trying to picture my brother's face so I could reconnect. I prayed that his mind remained his own, able to talk to me.

*Are you there? Are you still yourself?*

Silence answered.

# Chapter 26

The blackness behind my eyes slowly brightened to reveal Ilya handcuffed to a cot in an otherwise empty room. The space was a bare drywall cube with a cement floor. A single bare light bulb hung from a cord above him.

*Are you there? Ilya?*

*Chill, Irina. I can hear you.*

*What happened? Why are you locked up?*

*They're not taking any chances. That demon isn't ready to change bodies yet. It drained both of them when I got to meet the real Ivan.*

*What's he like? Our real father? Can you show me?*

*He's a good man. I wish you'd been with us. I think I can show you.* Ilya closed his eyes and lay back on the cot.

Ilya's room disappeared and I sat in a small one-room log cabin with Ilya and a shaggy old man. Ivan's face was covered in deep lines. Gray and white streaked his ginger hair and overgrown beard.

My brother and father sat at a picnic table covered in books, papers, used plates, stacked cups, and an overflowing ashtray.

Ivan lit a cigarette and took a long breath. He exhaled a cloud of white smoke, which Ilya waved away.

"I wish to be meeting you when you were born, the way a man should meet his son. I have had to settle for glimpses this thing has given me of you over the years," said the real Ivan. His accent was just as I remembered from my vision of him in Chester.

"Where is this place? Where are we?" said Ilya.

"This is my cabin outside McBride. Is in British Columbia, south of where your mother moved for your sister," said Ivan.

"We're in BC? How did that happen?" said Ilya.

"You of all people should know we are not really in BC. You are in my mind. This place is my memory of my cabin. Is where I am trapped for two decades now. Demon cannot get rid of me completely, although many times he tries," said Ivan.

The window outside was full of fresh green trees, just as it would have been in rural BC. A flash of black and red filled the window and a single red eye stopped moving behind the glass. The eye blinked and I knew who it was. It peered into me and its pupil widened. Pure malevolence flowed out of the ruby-red iris.

Fear swept through me and I let go of Ilya's medallion. Back in my dark tent, I heard Gemma's voice asking Faith about roller derby. I heard Jonah and Josh talking too, but I couldn't make out their words.

I closed my eyes and picked up the medallion again. *Sorry, sorry, are you still there?*

*Where else would I be? Why did you bail?* Ilya answered, irritated.

*I got scared and I had to take a break.* I said defensively.

*You can't get scared, Irina. Suck it up. You need to stare this thing down!*

*Okay, but in the meantime, we need to find a way to get you out. I've met another psychic. He had a vision of you and Tatiana at the hedge. Our plan isn't going to work. We have to abort. If that thing takes you, the hedge will come to life.* I showed Ilya a flash of my updated vision.

*Abort? Now?* Ilya's incredulous tone was full of anger.

*We'll get you out somehow. Tell me about your room. Tell me everything you saw in that building after Cole and I left. Better yet, show me.* I tried to sound convincing.

*Maybe I should go through with this possession. Ivan deserves to get his body back. I could try to negotiate with the creature, see if he'll let Ivan live.* Ilya put his head in his bound hands.

*I saw that thing leave Ivan for dead. I saw the creature kicking his corpse once he was in your body. It's a tragedy, but the real Ivan can't be saved.* I summoned all my empathy and tried to send it to Ilya.

*It's so easy for you to let him go. You didn't grow up with him. Or who you thought was him. I've been combing my memory, trying to think if I ever saw the real Ivan. It seems like that never happened, not until earlier today. That's not enough time. That creature owes all of us a lifetime as a family.* Sorrow filled Ilya as he sent me more images of Ivan.

*It's not easy for me! But we can't think of Ivan and Tatiana as family. We need to get you out now. The hedge grows early in the morning. Maybe tomorrow!* I tried to think louder, willing my brother to see the situation my way.

*The creature wants to rest before making the transfer. At least that's what it said to me before I was allowed to see Dad. I don't think he'll do it until tomorrow night.* Ilya sounded certain.

*So are you going to help us rescue you?* I challenged him.

*Not right now. Not yet.*

*Fine. We're coming anyway.*

I dropped the medallion a second time and unzipped the tent door. My friends huddled around the fire. Faith demonstrated a roller derby stance for Gemma.

I sat next to Jonah on an overturned potato crate and slipped my arm around his. I rested my head on his shoulder. "Ilya got to meet our father, the real Ivan. He showed me."

"What was he like?" said Jonah.

"Russian. A bit of a curmudgeon, but he seemed like a nice guy. You can't get to know someone in one sitting though. Ilya's pretty messed up about it. He's not going to help us break him out. He won't try to escape. He's convinced himself that he can save Ivan, or at least get to know him better before the change. I don't trust the creature. Ilya is underestimating it, I know he is." I stared into the flames of our fire.

"Ivan's weak, we know that. Did you see much security inside that compound?" said Josh. Under the cover of night, Josh removed both of his guns from his vest. He began cleaning his handgun with a rag.

"Now that we know our plan won't work, it does seem better to prevent the creature from changing hosts," said Jonah.

"Maybe we can't prevent anything anyway," I said.

"Don't get all lost and despondent like that. It doesn't suit you," said Melissa.

"Can you open a portal inside the compound?" Josh asked Melissa.

"I think so," she answered.

"Ilya's pretty sure the change won't happen until tomorrow

night. The creature told him he needed to rest before the transfer. In my vision, the possession happened under bright sunlight. It could be tomorrow during the day. Or the next day," I said, looking from the fire to each of my friends.

"So when should we go?" said Jonah.

"It's best done at night, but I'd like to have a better idea of what's inside that compound before we go in," said Josh.

"When this Mbele guy gets back, why don't you two put your heads together and try to see exactly where they're keeping Ilya," said Melissa.

Faith and Gemma sat down with us.

"If we're busting Ilya out, I'm going with you," said Faith.

"No chance," said Josh flatly. "I know that's hard to hear, but I should do this on my own. I'm trained, you're not. I'll act calm, you won't." He stared Faith down, waiting for the explosion. She grimaced but stayed silent.

"I want to help too," said Gemma.

"You can help by staying here and being safe so we've still got a healer after it's over," I said.

Cole's figure caught my eye through the trees. His muscular frame was unmistakable, even when barely lit by urban ambient light and our fire. Mr. Mbele walked next to him.

"We found the site. He's sure." Cole pointed his thumb back at Mr. Mbele.

"No one comes for hours, but it is the right place," said Mr. Mbele.

"Then what are you doing back here?" said Josh.

"We were starting to fall asleep. We found an abandoned couch to sit on that's got a perfect view of the ditch," said Cole.

"Okay, I'll take the next shift. Tell me where it is." Josh reached into our cooler and cracked an energy drink.

I suppressed my disgust and tried to replace it with gratitude.

"It's just around the corner. Make your way to where this little forest ends. You'll see a long trench in the ground. It stands out 'cause it's the only patch in the ground not filled with trash. It's freshly dug. You can't miss it," said Cole.

"Strong man is right. The ground is ready. Seeds may not be there yet, but they prepare the earth," said Mr. Mbele.

"I'll go with you, Josh. We'll return faster with a portal if we suddenly need backup," said Melissa.

"Thanks." Josh smiled at Melissa. It was refreshing to see a smile on Josh's face. Our meandering quest had been taking its toll on his demeanor, as it had done for all of us. The two of them walked off into the night.

Cole sat on Jonah's other side, but Mr. Mbele stood firm and stared into our fire, mirroring my focus. An idea broke my concentration.

"Mr. Mbele, I want you to help me remotely explore Ivan and Tatiana's compound. We have to rescue my brother Ilya before that creature inside my father has a chance to move over to its new body." The more I thought about Ilya, the more I realized what a stupid move it had been to let him exchange himself for Terra Nova.

"Okay. We look in the morning. Now is time for sleep." Mr. Mbele took off his backpack and produced a bedroll. He found a bare patch of earth and promptly laid down with his back to us.

Cole flexed his hand and his face filled with a grimace of pain. He opened his palm and revealed a long bloody gash.

"How did you do that?" said Jonah.

"Man that's nasty," said Faith.

"I found a broken bottle inside that abandoned couch. I've been trying to keep my fist closed.  Probably got infected already," said Cole, as embarrassed as he was frustrated.

Gemma sprang to Cole's side. "Give me your hand."  She extended her hand, palm up, with a stern stare demanding compliance.

"It's not all that bad," Cole said sheepishly.

"I'll be the judge of that."  Gemma leaned over and took Cole's thick meaty hand with both of hers. She drew his palm up to her face. She cradled Cole's hand with her left and with her right, she hovered gently above until a golden light shot from her hand into the wound. The gash slowly closed and Gemma released his hand. He made a thick fist and smiled.

"If you guys have this under control, I'm going to bed.  I doubt I'll sleep tonight, but I have to try." Faith slipped into her tent.

"We should all get some sleep. Gemma, you should bunk with Faith. Don't worry, she won't bite your head off." Cole unzipped the door on the largest tent he shared with Josh.

I wondered where Melissa would sleep when she got back. We had two extra bodies that hadn't been with us when we outfitted ourselves for camping back in Oregon.

"We've still got our tent." Jonah leered at me suggestively with the electric eyes that always made my heart flutter.

Every time Jonah and I had a chance to be alone, I wondered if it would be our last. The closer we got to the fight of our lives, the more I had to resist imagining my life without Jonah. Or his life without me. If I started experiencing the tragedy prematurely, I knew I'd fall to pieces.

Not all of us would survive this final confrontation with Ivan and Tatiana. Ever since our plan shifted from thwarting them to ending their lives, I spent a lot of time measuring our powers against theirs. Even in his weakened state, Ivan still terrified me.

"Yeah, I could use a little distraction tonight." I gave him a coy smile.

Jonah pulled moisture from the air and rained it down on the fire while I crawled back into our tent. I arranged our pillows and brushed out the blanket. I wanted the space to look nice. We deserved better. We deserved something comfortable if not plush and romantic. This dusty little tent would have to do.

Jonah crept into the tent and grabbed my waist. I tensed at first. The day's traumas had me on edge. His lips touched my neck and tension melted out of my body. Desire took over as Jonah's hands slid under my top. The sensation of his fingers on my bare skin sent heat into my core.

I turned to meet his eyes. A lock of black hair fell onto his forehead, wild and sexy as hell. He tore off his shirt and I traced the lines of his pecs and his abs.

He kissed me softly and then again passionately. All my worries, stress, pain, aches, and nausea dissolved inside me one by one as Jonah's overwhelming body moved over top of me.

As Jonah's kisses moved down my chest onto my stomach, I celebrated the fact that he couldn't hear my thoughts. That little voice returned, telling me this might be my last night with him. It might be my last night alive. I shoved the voice out of my head and let his lips carry me off into oblivion.

# Chapter 27

The next morning I woke to the crackling sound of the campfire. Jonah slept soundly, so I dressed carefully. The cool morning air made me glad I'd kept my hoodie. I quietly unzipped our tent door.

Mr. Mbele and Faith were the only two around the fire.

"No sign of Josh and Melissa?" I said.

"Not yet." Faith glared at the fire.

I felt a sinking stab of guilt at sharing a night of passion with Jonah while my brother sat captive and his girlfriend worried for his safety. "Why don't you come with us this morning? You'll be the first to know what's happening."

"Of course, I'm coming with you!"

"Fire girl, you must be careful. You are hazard here. Kibera burn very easy," said Mr. Mbele.

"Don't worry about me. I can keep it in my pants." Faith pulled her fabric band from her pocket and tied back her dreadlocks.

"Let's go now. I've got a bad feeling Josh and Melissa fell

asleep at the proverbial wheel."

Mr. Mbele needed no further prompting. He rolled up his bedroll, stuffed it back in his bag, and headed out of the trees to the hedge site.

"Hey, wait for us." Faith jogged after him. I ran to close the distance as well.

The early morning sky brightened. The first few rays of hard sun spilled onto the ground ahead. The shadows of Kibera's rooftops were still long on our side of the community, but I could see the couch Cole had mentioned and the freshly dug trench in the ground.

There was no sign of Josh and Melissa until we got close enough to the couch to see two people slouched asleep. I walked around to face them. Josh had his arm around Melissa whose face was buried in his shoulder.

"Good morning!" I couldn't begrudge them either comfort or rest, not when I had indulged myself the previous night. But I couldn't help being irritated that they'd let down their guard.

"What?" Melissa lurched backward.

"Huh? Shit! Sorry!" Josh leaped up off the couch, blushing deeply.

Faith and I scanned the scene for any trace of Ivan, Tatiana, Rose, or Sage. Only a few early morning trash scavengers were digging. I heard the tink-clink of glass on glass as one woman pulled two bottles from a mound of debris.

"So do we know if there are seeds under that soil?" I asked, nodding at the trench.

"It's unattended. Let's go check." Faith closed the distance between us and the tilled ditch, but she didn't make it close enough to check the ground. She collapsed a few meters from the ditch. She vomited the contents of her stomach in a couple of quick heaves.

"Come back. Just back away!" I shouted.

Faith crawled back until the sickness relented. She sat with her head on her knees. I knew what had grabbed her. Ivan's 'curse' on my old apartment building and the Mojave testing grounds had been implemented here. No wonder it was unguarded.

"Bring me your necklace!" Faith shouted back.

Fortunately, I still had my protective rune pendant around my neck. I'd been wearing it for luck on and off - now every day after the Mojave. I gave a startled laugh as I lifted it off and passed it to Faith. She put it around her neck and charged back to the ditch.

Faith crossed an unseen threshold and dropped to the ground again, clutching her stomach. She wretched and writhed in the dirt. I ran to her and pulled her back by her armpits. I felt a wave of nausea and let go of Faith as I threw up violently.

Both of us crawled backward until the crushing urge to get sick faded away.

"It didn't work," said Faith between gasps.

"Uh huh. I guess Ivan's got more than one kind of curse up his sleeve," I said.

"I'm going to kill Ivan myself." Faith wiped her mouth and brushed sick off her shirt.

"Are we close enough for you to still torch the thing?" I said.

"I think so. But if she hasn't planted those seeds yet, what's the point? Scorched earth? She'll just pick a new site. Can't we stick to the plan where we get Ilya out asap?" Faith steadied herself with slow breathing. I followed her lead as we stood recovering from the powerful urge to vomit.

"You want to find the red-eyed man and the green woman. We do it now," said Mr. Mbele, standing over Faith and me.

I stood up and dusted my pants. Faith did the same.

"How do you usually trigger your visions? I seem to need an item or a person, although sometimes I can manage with concentration alone," I asked Mr. Mbele.

"You need practice then. I will guide us."

Mr. Mbele took my one hand and brushed my eyes closed with his other. He started to hum. The sound was distracting. I couldn't picture Ilya or Ivan.

Darkness flicked away and Mr. Mbele and I were back in Ilya's cell. Ilya slept fitfully. Mr. Mbele walked through the room's only door and I followed. It had never occurred to me to pass through a door or wall in a vision. He was right. I needed practice.

"Your soldier friend may get in here, but something is wrong. I can't see your brother's future once his eyes are red. That demon blocks me," said Mr. Mbele.

I followed as he walked down the hall towards the sound of voices. "I have trouble seeing around that alien monster thing too. But clearly, my abilities are lacking compared to yours. At this point, I only need enough information to change my brother's fate. And everyone else's."

"Is very hard to change the future. The gods do not show us what to do to make change. Knowing what will happen does not mean we know why and how a thing comes," said Mr. Mbele solemnly.

"Do you think we have visions for a reason?" I said.

"I would not be here if I did not think it was my fate to help you."

We rounded a corner and passed through another door. Ivan and Tatiana discussed sources of fruit for their buffet. Mr. Mbele paid them no mind and passed through another door on the other side of the room. In another hallway, he looked both ways. I followed as he poked his astral head through one door and another until he beckoned for me to follow.

We passed into a stairwell which took us down to a corridor lined with cages. In the cages, hissing giant snake bats took no notice of us. We emerged into the pit where I had seen Ilya's possession take place.

"No way to come in here without a fight," said Mr. Mbele. He released my real-world hand and the setting swirled until we stood outside Kibera again between the rotting couch and the freshly tilled ditch we couldn't touch.

"Did you see what you needed to see?" said Jonah.

"You, soldier," said Mr. Mbele to Josh.

"I guess that's me," said Josh, eyeing Mr. Mbele.

"You kill green woman and demon man?" said Mr. Mbele.

"Yes, it's come to that. Give me a diagram of the place and I'll get where I need to go. Once they're dead, I'll walk out with Ilya," said Josh.

"What about Rose and Sage?" said Faith.

"I'll go in too. We'll be better off with a portal exit. Hopefully, I can send Rose and Sage safely back to Sombrio Beach. They'll hate me, but then again, I'm sure they already do," said Melissa.

A sense of dread washed over me. I wrung my hands to calm myself. Something was going to go wrong with this revised approach, but I hadn't seen what. Why? I wanted to reach out to Josh and pray contact would spark another vision. Maybe he needed to plan first for the future to unfold, so I held back.

"I'll take the next shift watching the ditch," said Jonah.

"Me too. If I can't help Ilya, I need to do something other than pace around my tent," said Faith.

"Let's go back to camp. Mbele can draw me the compound layout. And I'll have quiet for planning," said Josh.

Faith lay on the grubby couch, still recovering while Jonah kept a stricter vigil on the tilled ditch. I hugged him quickly. Then, I bolted after Mr. Mbele, Josh, and Melissa who were already well on their way back to camp.

When we arrived, Mr. Mbele took paper and pen from Melissa and drew a basic layout of both levels of Ivan's Kibera compound. Josh nodded and took both pages into his tent.

Gemma and Melissa revised their inventory of our food. I didn't have the patience to participate. I had to try to reach Ilya one more time. If he knew about Josh's rescue attempt, it might stand a higher chance of success. I crept into my tent, sat cross-legged, and gripped Ilya's medallion.

*Ilya, can you hear me? Are you awake?*

The darkness of the tent melted into Ivan's one-room cabin. Ivan and Ilya were in deep conversation.

"I am only telepath. And it was dormant in me when this creature found me. It calls itself Ulu from somewhere called Kad 'aath. Is probably wrong way to say." Ivan's accent was stronger than ever and I had to concentrate to understand him.

"If the creature survived here when it first landed, as Irina showed me, why is it so set to transform the world?" said Ilya.

"Survived, but barely. Had to wear its armor for life support. Is hard for me to know, but I think it was frail here and that's why it was killed the first time. Much stronger if he makes this world like his. Its world is gone, but it talks of others like him. I think it will bring others if it can," said Ivan earnestly.

"Wait, I think Irina's here." Ilya whipped his head to the side. "Sis, you there? Did you call for me?"

*Yes, I'm here. I wanted to warn you that Josh and Melissa are coming to rescue you.*

"No, I need more time!" blurted Ilya.

Ivan stared at him curiously since only Ilya could hear me.

*The other psychic, Mr. Mbele, helped us to see inside that compound. It's not as big as we'd thought, but there are vicious animals in the basement. Ivan's got some kind of force-field-curse-thing on the hedge site, so nobody's getting near it. If they had to wait for your body because Ivan isn't a strong enough vessel, maybe they can't do it at all without you.*

"I doubt they'll wait. Tatiana will just put Ivan on a bed and hunt for Gemma or Camille or some other healer. I think they'd rather have a fresh body, but they'll make it happen without me. I can take control and fight the demon, I know I can," Ilya said confidently.

"Irina, is that you? Can you hear me?" said Ivan.

*Tell him, yes, I can see and hear both of you.*

"She says she can hear and see us," Ilya said to Ivan.

"I am so glad you see the real me, even this dried-up old man I am now."

*Tell him I understand. Tell him I'm sorry. I wish we could save him. If there is any way, we'll do it, but we can't let this transfer happen. We were so stupid to try playing that monster's game.*

"She's trying to talk me out of letting the creature take my body. I want to negotiate. If you'll survive this thing's exit, I can make a deal for it to let you live, maybe even get Gemma to heal you. You can get your life back, or at least what's left of it!"

"Your sister is right. All the power you see in me is from this thing. Telekinesis, energy blasts, all is the creature. Those things will be stronger still in new body. If you can get away from here, go, and don't look back. There is no saving me now. Whatever happens to me after this body dies will be better than the last twenty years of my life. I am ready," said Ivan.

Ilya's broken heart was written in the arches of his eyebrows and his speechless open mouth. My heart ached for both of them.

"This body is weak now. If you and your friends come together, you may defeat him. But if you kill my body, the creature will be dormant again. To kill forever, you must-" Ivan was cut off by a blast of air that shattered the cabin's windows and knocked us all backward.

A deafening roar turned my blood to ice. I dropped Ilya's medallion and lurched back to the tent. Both hands clamped fistfuls of the sleeping bag as I gasped and gulped, shaking with terror.

The notion of trying again flitted through my mind. I jerked my head to this side and that, listening to the air. I couldn't do it. Ilya knew help was coming. I just had to hope and wait.

# Chapter 28

Josh wanted to wait for dark before approaching Ivan's Kibera stronghold. I insisted they go sooner and Melissa reluctantly agreed. After lunch, Josh relented and they left.

The rest of us stayed back at the campsite. We sat around the fire, alternately pacing and subtly practicing our talents. Big displays were out of the question in the middle of the day, but I could hover-shuffle my cards and remotely snap twigs while Cole crushed rocks and Gemma watched us like a tennis spectator.

"They've been gone too long. Mr. Mbele, we should try to see what's happening."

"There is nothing we can do. Seeing is not going to help now," said Mr. Mbele.

I clenched both fists as my stubborn companion stared into the campfire. I watched Kibera helplessly. I closed my eyes and concentrated on Ilya's face. Nothing happened, but I wasn't surprised. I felt a frenzy of adrenaline coursing through me in all directions.

As I examined the patchwork of rooftops ahead, the regular murmur of voices and shuffling changed. A few cries rang out. Then shouts of anger. Pops of broken glass tinkle-cracked in the distance.

Suddenly a stream of people of all ages started pouring out of the nearest street at Kibera's outer border. People were running from something. Had Terra Nova just been released? It couldn't be!

"Guys! Something's wrong! People are running!" I shouted.

I bolted towards the street spewing people. I sensed Cole on my heels. I ran hard until I saw Josh and Melissa among the crowd fleeing. I searched the faces around them for Ilya's skinny frame and shaggy mop of hair. Nothing. No faces but Josh's and Melissa's were recognizable in the stampede.

Cole scooped me up and heaved me onto his shoulder as though I was a child. As he ran with me, I watched flames shoot up through the roof of a nearby shack. Smoke rose from other parts of Kibera. I scanned the crowd again for sickness and blood. Confusion escalated as people continued pouring out, but there were no telltale signs of Terra Nova.

Jonah and Faith cut through the crowd, meeting us at our campsite as Cole dropped me next to Gemma.

"What's happening?" asked Gemma, terrified.

"I have no idea, but Josh and Melissa are on their way back," I said.

"Why didn't she use a portal?" said Cole.

"It must be a riot," said Jonah.

"We were watching the ditch, as directed. There was no change. Whatever this is, it's not Terra Nova," said Faith.

"Can we look now?" I said to Mr. Mbele.

He nodded and crossed the campsite to take my hand. The din of residents swirling around the outskirts of Kibera disappeared and we were back in Ilya's cell. The room was empty.

Mr. Mbele led me back to the courtyard where Cole and I had left Ilya. I heard Tatiana's shouting in the hallway.

"You started a riot, you morons!" yelled Tatiana.

"Boy was begging! He sees your friends come and go, he thinks we have money and should give him!" shouted one of the locals who had been guarding the Krylov's gate.

"And you couldn't have just given him money?" screamed Tatiana.

"You don't give money! They want more and more! No giving away!" said the guard.

"We say no. He gets angry, his friends come and it goes from there," said the other guard who watched the corridor to the entrance. Animated voices behind the smashes and crashes of intentional destruction rose and fell outside.

Mr. Mbele and I entered the courtyard to find Ivan reclined in his cabana chair, drained. Tatiana held her stomach where blood seeped into her shirt. Ilya was bound, gagged, and propped up against the wall.

Another familiar man stood over my brother. I knew I'd seen the stranger before, but I couldn't place him. It was like recognizing someone in a television show, but not being able to place where you'd seen them.

"Stop yelling! You need doctor!" shouted the second guard.

"I need that little brat, Gemma. We need to find the whole lot of them. You said they're camped in the woods. Go get them!" yelled Tatiana.

Mr. Mbele nodded at me and let go of my hand. We were

back at the campfire. My friends stood around us, dazed and confused by the mob.

"Their guards got into it with some boys who were begging and it somehow started the riot. People are trying to get into that compound because they think the Krylovs are rich," I said hurriedly.

"Well they're not wrong," said Cole.

"There's no getting in there for Ilya now," said Josh.

"Also, Tatiana's been hurt and she wants her thugs to find Gemma," I said.

"We can't stay here anyway," said Jonah.

"Pack only what you need. We'll have to try again for Ilya later," said Josh.

"We'll go Ngong Hills. My friend there will take us," said Mr. Mbele.

"Wait. Let me tell Ilya we're not coming. Maybe he can get out on his own if he tries," I said.

"Do it! Tell him to fight those fuckers and run for his life!" said Faith.

I ran deeper into the trash forest until the noise faded enough that I could concentrate.

I pressed Ilya's medallion between my thumb and forefinger. *Ilya, you have to try to get out on your own. Josh and Melissa couldn't get to you. A fucking riot is happening, but I'm sure you know that. I know you're tied up, but please, try to find a way out. Use an illusion. Do something! We know they're after Gemma now. We're going to run and come back for you later.* I paused, willing my brother to answer me. I didn't have to wait long.

*There's a new guy here. He's a variant, but I'm not sure what he does. He's Ivan's friend. I can't hear him. And he's watching me like a hawk.* Ilya sounded fearful.

*Think of something to distract them. Give them an illusion. And do it fast. If you can make it out the front door, you're home-free. Don't come back to the forest. Mr. Mbele is taking us somewhere called the Ngong Hills. I think it's nearby. Get out of Kibera and ask someone how to get to the Ngong Hills. We'll reconnect in person. I know you wanted to save Ivan, but you have to run. Please!* I pinched Ilya's medallion tightly, praying for my thoughts to affect my brother.

*Okay, okay, I'll try. But Tatiana's not in any shape to do her part for the hedge. Both she and Ivan are too weak. This riot bought us some time. Don't worry about-.* Ilya's voice cut out abruptly.

I let go of the medallion and ran to Cole.

"You won't believe this, but Josh found the van. It was right where we left it. Come on, we're going now," said Cole.

We got to the campsite just as Josh pulled up in our Karibu Kab van.

"I guess the Nairobi police are going to be occupied with this incident here rather than hunting for stolen vehicles." I climbed in next to Gemma and Jonah.

We crept along the rough ground, moving even more slowly because of the throngs of people. It was an alarming blend of human emotion. Outraged young men hollered Swahili curses at the air. Young mothers guarded their children, holding them close to their bodies. Elderly people kept as far out of the way as they could, standing against buildings or sitting on debris.

We broke free of the crowd and turned back onto a main road. Josh picked up speed and we wove through traffic.

Emergency vehicles and confused Nairobians caused congestion around Kibera, but we finally emerged onto a free-flowing highway. Mr. Mbele directed Josh southwards and we were soon coasting along the pavement with dry grass plains stretching out around us.

"This road, here," said Mr. Mbele when a turn-off with a sign for the NGONG HILLS COUNTRY CLUB came into view.

"What's a country club doing in the middle of nowhere?" said Jonah.

"Family picnics come here," said Mr. Mbele.

"Should we be here if there are a bunch of families around?" said Josh.

"Is slow on weeknights. Only many families on weekends," said Mr. Mbele.

Our van groaned and creaked as Josh pushed it farther and farther up the winding road to the hilltop establishment.

"This is a great idea. I'm starving. I could use some barbecue," said Cole.

"Are we going to get fed?" said Faith.

"We don't have any money," I added.

"Yes, we do. Sort of," said Melissa as she lifted her clinking duffle bag. I hadn't looked inside, but I assumed she had items of value.

"Good enough. You give to my friend and he will help us," said Mr. Mbele.

The most amazing smell I had ever encountered blew down the hill on a gentle breeze and in through our open van windows.

"Oh my god, what is that smell?" said Gemma. She grinned from ear to ear.

"Who cares if we're safe here, as long as we get to eat whatever that smell is! I've been so freaked out I don't think I've eaten in two days." Faith leaned forward trying to see ahead.

"Is Nyama Choma. We'll have with Ugali and Sukuma Wiki." Mr. Mbele smiled, making it all the more surreal that we escaped a riot to find some kind of traditional East African feast.

"What is Nyama Choma?" said Jonah.

"Roasted goat." Mr. Mbele smiled again.

"I don't care, I'm starving," said Cole.

"I've never had goat meat." I would have tried anything that smelled that good, but like Cole and Faith, I was also ravenous.

Josh parked in the lot we found at the top of the hill. I could see from the manicured green lawn, rock garden, and freshly stained wood cabanas that we were at a tourist destination. A large single-story cabin stood at the center of the property. On the far side, the terrain dropped into a ravine.

Mercifully, Mr. Mbele had been right about the lack of weeknight visitors. We appeared to have the place to ourselves.

"So this is what a Kenyan country club looks like," I said.

"Is a place for weddings, birthdays, parties, that sort of thing," said Mr. Mbele.

"No wonder it smells so wonderful," said Jonah, fascination spreading across his face.

"You wait here. I go find my friend," said Mr. Mbele.

We got out of the van and stretched our legs. All signs of Nairobi were gone. All around us hazy sage hills and patches of green trees rested comfortably under the bright blue African sky. I took in all the scenic beauty, soothing and recharging myself, hoping to share with Ilya later. For now, I knew I had to leave him alone and let him concentrate on whatever he contrived to distract the Krylovs.

Jonah took my hand and led me down a dirt path to a giant cliff-side dining deck. The sheer drop made it a perfect viewpoint for the valley around us. We leaned our elbows onto the thick wood patio railing and breathed in the warm clean air. I glanced back to see my friends wandering the property aimlessly, all decompressing.

"Every time we have a moment like this, I feel surges of bitterness and guilt," I said.

"Because we're getting a nice hot meal?" said Jonah.

"That, and because this place is amazing," I swept my arm out gesturing at the landscape. "We're surrounded by beautiful countryside. We're relaxing and eating. But Ilya's still tied up for all we know. And Kibera is a mess. We haven't fixed anything."

"I feel crappy too. I'm sorry we're not finished yet. We can't walk away, but we can only do our best," said Jonah.

"True. But then there's the other side of it. Why did this become *our* problem to solve? Why aren't we backpacking around the world like other kids our age? I've seen six countries in the last month and I got to enjoy practically zero of it! I should be getting ready for university, but no, I'm trying to save the fucking world!" I said.

Jonah put his arm around me and hugged my shoulder. He rested his head on mine and let the anger flow out of me.

"We have beers now, my friends!" Mr. Mbele came to us, his hands filled with clinking dark brown glass bottles.

Another two men in white collared shirts followed, each with a tray of beer. Melissa trailed behind carrying her black duffle bag which no longer made any noise.

I helped myself to a cold bottle of Kenyan beer. The earthy taste of hops complemented the summer sun nicely. I let the alcohol numb me gently with every sip.

Our two servers quickly returned with food on great huge planks of wood. A messy pile of barbecued meat preceded a platter with flat white balls of cornmeal surrounded by a generous garnish of cooked greens.

I watched Mr. Mbele. He picked up a small steel plate and added a heap of meat, picking it up with his fingers. There were no utensils of any sort. He took a pinch of salt from the corner of the board and added it to the meat. He picked up a handful of the white cornmeal and then another serving of greens. Mr. Mbele thoughtfully took a pinch of everything on his plate, one by one, and took a bite. He smiled and beckoned me to eat.

More plates with more meat, cornmeal, and greens appeared. Soon we were all digging in with greasy fingers. I finished two silver plates and got up to search for another bottle of beer when I felt my legs turn to gelatin under me. I grabbed the edge of the table and eyed my friends.

The shaking came in another violent wave and I heard a shout from the main building.

"Earthquake! Take shelter! Earthquake!"

# Chapter 29

"What the hell?" Faith gripped the table. She released the wood tabletop and left charred black handprints.

"That can't be a coincidence," I said.

"Probably not. But I thought you said Ivan and Tatiana were weak," said Jonah.

"They are. Or they were. Maybe it was Rose and Sage," I said.

"Those two couldn't send an email without help. You think they calibrated and engaged a fracking drill?" said Cole.

"Well, somebody did!" I glared at him. "Or did Kenya coincidentally happen to experience an earthquake the day after we tried to break Ilya away from Ivan?"

The floor rumbled beneath my feet again. The cliff-side patio creaked under its weight.

"This thing could go over any minute," said Josh.

We stood up carefully. A loud creak groaned. Popping snaps crackled up from the wood. My friends bolted. I stopped to grab my backpack and Faith's.

Jonah yanked hard on my arm. "Now!" he yelled.

I ran hard and fast following my friends up the path to the main building. I turned back to see our dinner table drop out of sight as the deck slid off the cliff.

"Oh my God!" I blurted.

Several club staff ran past us out of the main building in a hurry to assess the damage to their central outdoor dining patio. Voices shouted when they saw it had gone down into the ravine. People crowded around the bar, craning their necks up to the television.

"This is the largest earthquake ever recorded in East Africa," said a woman in a purple pantsuit standing near the edge of the Rift Valley. A roadside stand much like the Samburu Curio Shop lay collapsed beside her. Plumes of smoke rose from inside the heart of the valley.

"But the damage at the epicenter here in the Rift Valley is not comparable to the damage back in Nairobi. George, can you update us on what's happening in the city?" said the reporter.

A young man in a white collared shirt stood next to an unrecognizable collapsed structure.

"I'm standing next to the Kenya National Theatre where some five hundred people are missing and presumed dead in the building's collapse. Authorities are still assessing damage across the city, all while Kenyans are reeling from the news of the disastrous tanker crash in Mombasa. Locals are asking how an earthquake of this magnitude could have happened in East Africa. Meanwhile, two other large earthquakes in Peru and Indonesia are diverting some of the world's most preeminent seismic experts. Disasters have been on the rise around the world in the last twenty-four hours leaving first responders frightened and bewildered as they attempt to cope with the tasks at hand in their communities."

"What happened in Mombasa?" I asked one of the waiters at the bar.

"The crash? You did not hear?" said the man.

"An oil tanker tried to dock at a passenger terminal. There is crude oil in the ocean from Mombasa to Malindi. They say it will take years to clean. The coastline may never recover," said a young waitress behind the bar.

"Three major earthquakes in one day. Disasters are on the rise everywhere. This smells like *The Compendium*," I said.

"They're ready to release Terra Nova if they've escalated the rest of their plans," said Cole.

"How are they pulling this off?" said Faith.

"We still don't know what other Compendium factions are working out there," said Melissa.

"If we can stop Terra Nova, it's not too late," said Gemma.

"I'll try to reconnect to Ilya." I didn't wait for permission. I walked outside and found a covered loveseat with a view of the valley and hills. I sat down and tried to picture my brother's face. My whole body shook.

*Irina? Can you hear me?* Ilya's voice came through suddenly loud and clear.

I jolted in my seat. *Yes! I tried to find you. Are you okay? Are you still in Kibera? I thought the whole thing might have caved in after the earthquake.*

*I'm okay. This place fared surprisingly well, at least Ivan's compound did. I tried an illusion – won't bore you with the details. You're not going to believe this. They have an invisible man here. None other than Evonatura CEO, Claude Mueller. I guess my illusions don't work on him when he's invisible.* Ilya sounded lucid. Gratitude washed over me, but his mention of Mueller flooded me with outrage.

*Sonofabitch! Claude Mueller is there? The new variant! I guess that answers who's been coordinating everything with Ivan and Tatiana out of commission. Are they still both too weak to be dangerous?*

*As far as I can tell Ivan is sick, but Aunt Tat is recovering quickly, even without a healer. I can hear her thoughts. She's getting ready to transfer that creature from Ivan to me.* Ilya's calm surprised me.

*No! We still don't know how to kill it! I think that's why the thing kicked us out of Ivan's mind. He knows a way to kill the parasite itself and end the creature forever. We have to get back in!* I shouted in my mental voice.

*Where's your other psychic?* asked Ilya.

*He's still here with me. Hang on, I'm going to get him.* I hopped off the outdoor sofa and ran back into the club. Mr. Mbele frowned at me from the bar.

"We have to connect to my brother," I pleaded. "To get back into my father's mind. That demon camped out in my father can be killed. We have to find out how."

Mr. Mbele nodded and came with me. We went back to the sofa and I reclaimed my seat. I clutched Ilya's medallion and took a deep breath. I grabbed Mr. Mbele's hand with my free one. *Ilya, I have Mr. Mbele here. We're coming to you. Try to get back into Ivan's head.*

"Focus on Ilya's cell in Kibera," I said to Mr. Mbele. I closed my eyes and tried to picture my brother sitting on his cot. The blackness behind my eyes faded and Mr. Mbele and I were in Ilya's cell. I could hear the faint wail of distant sirens.

*Ilya, we're in, can you get to Ivan without standing next to his body?*

"Let's find out. Grab onto me if you can see me because I can't see you," Ilya said out loud.

Ilya closed his eyes to concentrate while Mr. Mbele and I reached out each touching one of Ilya's shoulders.

We snapped into Ivan's cabin, but the room was full of a smoky haze. The once pristine forest outside the cabin's bay window was in the throes of a major fire. The real Ivan had his back to us, tending something on the kitchen stove.

"Dad, you need to finish your story, fast! How do we kill this thing, Ulu?" said Ilya.

Ivan turned around and my heart stopped. His eyes were a cloudy pale blue. He looked at us, but he couldn't see us. His wiry hair was matted with grease. Ivan opened his mouth, but whatever words he spoke were drowned out by an ear-piercing shriek.

The creature's giant red eye stared in on us again. Smoke wafted between the eye and the glass window, but masked none of its ferocity. I saw the wildest rage I had ever seen in another animal's eyes. I froze with fear, but suddenly an idea struck me. I was at a country club far outside the city. This creature was trapped inside Ivan's body. It couldn't hurt my physical body.

I stepped forward with my astral body and took a chance. I lifted my arms to focus my attention, but I knew it wasn't my hands doing the work. I held the creature still. I concentrated on keeping the glass together, glass that had been restored after our last visit, which I knew wasn't really there at all.

"I can't hold it for long!" I felt the demon's resistance, but I held firm. It felt like gripping a giant fish that fought me with every ounce of its life force. The ground rumbled.

"Mbele, you have to get into Ivan's past. Help him remember," said Ilya.

Out of the corner of my eye, I saw Mr. Mbele place his palm on Ivan's forehead. Ivan dropped his spoon and red sauce splattered on the floor. Mr. Mbele murmured something in another language. The cabin's walls caught fire around us. The rumbling became shaking.

Ilya reached out and held Ivan's hand, comforting him.

"It's a dagger! It's buried with Ulu's body in Chester!" shouted Ilya. Mr. Mbele let go of Ivan and the creature's rage overcame my power.

The window exploded and sound blasted in, knocking us with the force of a hurricane. A blow landed in my gut, knocking me back onto the outdoor sofa outside the Ngong Hills Country Club.

Blood dripped down Mr. Mbele's face from cuts on his forehead. Feeling moisture, I touched my cheek. My hand came away sticky with blood. So much for the safety of a vision space.

My heart pounded in my chest. I closed my eyes and focused on my brother's face.

*Ilya, are you there? What happened?* I said desperately.

*Irina, he's gone. Dad's gone. It's only Ulu now.* Ilya sounded utterly defeated.

*Where are you now? Are you safe? Can you get away?* I asked in rapid fire.

*Aunt Tat and Claude are dragging me down a stairwell. I think it's going to happen now. I'm scared, Irina.* Ilya's words cut me. I crushed his medallion in my fist.

*Fight it! Fight the change! If you can, keep him out. I know you can do it! You can stop it all!* I shouted helplessly.

*I'm in the same corridor as the snake bats.* Ilya went silent and couldn't breathe until he spoke again. *Now I'm outside. Ivan's there, but he's a zombie. He's brain-dead.*

*Concentrate, Ilya! You can do this! If you keep that thing out, it has nowhere to go.* I yelled with my thoughts.

*Aunt Tat is sitting down. Claude disappeared. Wait, no, someone is holding me from behind! Ivan opened his mouth. No, something is forcing its way out of him.* Ilya stopped, but I saw what he saw. *It's a tongue. It's longer than a tongue. It's slimy with veins covering its skin. Oh God, it's jumping! It's got my neck. I can't breathe. Can't think. So tight. Let go! GET OFF ME! IT'S IN ME! ULLLLLLGHH* ... Ilya's voice stopped again.

*Ilya? Ilya! Come back!*

Nothing happened. I waited, panic swelling my chest.

*Ilya! Answer me!*

Silence ensued for a long moment. I clung to my mental image of Ilya, picturing the horrid scene with that tentacle of red flesh wrapped around my brother's throat.

A low growl, almost imperceptible at first answered back.

*You've lost, child. My world is coming,* grumbled a deep chilling voice.

The creature's words filled my bones with acid and I leaped off the sofa. I buried my face in my hands. "It has Ilya. It has my brother. What are we going to do?"

"We go back and kill the red-eyed boy and the green woman," said Mr. Mbele.

# Chapter 30

My mouth felt full of cotton and my shoes were full of lead as I walked back to the country club's main hall. My friends watched the news. The television showed Nairobi from a helicopter. The city had pockmarks of damage, but many of the major structures and green fields endured. I willed the camera to show us the rooftops of Kibera that I couldn't focus well enough to see in my mind.

"We've got to go. The demon got Ilya," I said, forcing each word.

My friends regarded me with wet eyes full of empathy and remorse.

"We find a weapon to kill the creature," said Mr. Mbele.

"Kibera might not even be there anymore," said Jonah.

"I'll open a portal and check," said Melissa.

"You will not!" blurted Josh.

"There's got to be a way to check and see if it's safe," said Gemma.

"I look now." Mr. Mbele sat down at a nearby table and folded his hands in his lap.

"I'm trying, but I can't see anything. My mind is a mess," I said, wringing my hands.

"You want to go to Kibera?" said one of the waiters, bewildered at the thought.

"We were volunteering there. One of our friends was left behind," I said.

"I've still got Nellie's tablet and my laptop." Faith pulled one after the other out of her bag. She handed the tablet to Cole.

"What's your WiFi password?" Cole asked the waiter.

The man frowned with confusion, but when Cole pointed at the tablet and the laptop, the man understood. He pointed to a tent card on the bar. Cole and Faith had their devices connected while Jonah and I watched the news.

"Wait, look!" said Gemma.

We watched intently as the aerial view on television passed over the patches of Kibera that survived. Not all the homes had fallen, but we didn't get a glimpse of our precious woods or the dreaded hedge site.

"Guys, I can't find anything specific to our campsite," said Faith as she clicked on her keyboard.

"Me either. People are talking about building collapses and casualties. Nobody's making lists of what's safe. I'm on BBC World, and they're covering the disasters together. People are freaking out everywhere," said Cole.

"These conditions could make transmission of Terra Nova even more rapid," said Jonah.

"Campsite has been looted. The tents are gone. But woods are there," said Mr. Mbele.

"Let's go." Melissa rose and we all followed, knowing

instinctively that she meant to find a spot away from the club staff to open a portal back to the woods outside Kibera.

We followed Melissa to the other side of the club's parking lot where a cluster of shrubs formed a wall next to an acacia tree.

She swooped open a silver portal and stepped through fearlessly. A few seconds later she came back. "Mbele's right. Our gear is gone, but the woods are fine. You can see fire smoke in the air around the city. But Kibera still stands. The part we were near anyway."

"I don't know if this is good or bad." Cole scratched the top of his head.

"We need to destroy the seeds laced with Terra Nova. We can't afford to walk away until we know that's done," said Jonah earnestly.

A blend of grief and resolve filled Faith's face. "I'm not walking away from Ilya."

"Neither am I." I took a supportive step closer to Faith.

"Then let's go." Melissa stepped back through the portal. Josh followed directly, then Cole, Faith, and Gemma.

Jonah moved to go and I grabbed his arm. "I love you."

He held my gaze with hopeful eyes. I wished I had Ilya's gift to pry into Jonah's brain and hear his thoughts. I'd have to settle for the words he chose.

"I love you too. We're going to survive this. And …" Jonah stopped short of adding what I wanted to hear, that we would get Ilya back alive. Instead, he pulled me by my waist and kissed me.

I let my fear and panic fall to the ground, losing myself for just a moment in the kiss, hoping the sensation of Jonah holding me would stretch into infinity. Then he pulled away and stepped into the portal, pulling me in by my hand.

The woods outside Kibera were still as trash-strewn as we'd left them. Residents wandered with armloads of possessions.

The only trace of our campsite was Faith's makeshift rock fire pit. There was no trace of our tents and sleeping bags. We retreated into the trees away from pedestrian traffic.

"Before anyone makes a move towards the compound, we need a dagger. There's something buried with the creature's original body. It's a blade that can kill the parasitic demon's essence permanently. I'm hoping we can use it on Ilya, get rid of the creature, and get Gemma to heal him." I said gesturing at points on an invisible line.

Everyone stared at me in stunned silence for a moment.

"So you plan to do what *this* guy wants." Faith cocked her thumb at Mr. Mbele. "And flat-out KILL Ilya?"

"I can heal his body. I know I can." Gemma didn't sound as confident as her words suggested. Her eyes were full of doubt.

"I'll take you back to Chester," said Melissa.

"The rest of us will stay here. We'll take up positions around the hedge," said Josh, pointing to the locations in the distance.

"You better find this thing fast. If Tatiana so much as comes out, I'm going to kill her on sight. I can handle a little nausea," said Cole.

"I know you can." I hadn't told him that in my vision, he thrashed Tatiana to death only minutes too late. I prayed he could get to her faster.

Was Mr. Mbele right? Could the future be changed? We tried to rescue Ilya and a riot broke out. Would it have happened if we'd hung back? I felt like I was trying to divert a river without knowing where to dig.

"With Ivan dead, maybe that curse thing he had going is dead too. Who knows? It's not like we ever knew how that hex-y whatever-the-hell thing worked," said Faith.

"I'll take a small miracle for a change. Let's go test that theory." Josh and Faith bounded off eagerly.

Melissa swooped a fresh silver oval in the air, concealed by my remaining friends standing shoulder to shoulder. The sky had grown dim overhead, the sun having just dropped behind the horizon.

"Tomorrow morning could be the time from Mr. Mbele's vision. If we don't make it back…" I stopped. I didn't have the heart to finish my sentence.

"You'll be back in time," said Gemma sternly.

"Wish us luck." Melissa stepped into the portal.

I contemplated my friends' earnest faces. I broke eye contact and forced myself to step through the portal.

Melissa had chosen her location well. We were back in the red brick ruins where no one could see us from the church windows or the nearby road. The sun hadn't quite set in Chester, but an overcast sky made the world dark enough. Mist chilled the air, but I was too full of adrenaline to feel the cold.

"There's an archaeological site down the road. Excavated Roman ruins. That's where we'll find the dagger. I'm not sure how deep or exactly where to dig. I'm hoping I can figure that out when we get there," I heard the fear in my voice.

"Great. Lead the way." She stepped aside to let me go first.

The mist turned to a drizzly rain. I pulled my hood over my head and leaned forward. We reached the excavation and I marched down the wood stairs into the muddy gravel pit.

I squinted through the rain to see if I could make sense of

the hollows cut into the other side of the site. It looked more like the beginning of a building's foundation than a remnant of the ancient world.

I found a square brick mound that might have been a table or a seat. I put my hand on the stone and felt it cold and wet under my hand. Nothing happened. Anger swelled in my belly. Why had my psychic abilities started to fail when I needed them more than ever?

"Calm down, honey." Melissa put a hand on my shoulder, squeezed, and let go.

I noticed the tension in my muscles and my quick labored breathing. A wave of nausea rose, but I pushed it aside. I took a deep breath and tried to center myself. I put my hand on the brick and pictured the ancient village from my vision, surrounded by golden wheat.

A bright flash transported me to a small dry hut where I had my hand on a smooth wood table top. I was alone in the hut, although embers smoldered in a fire pit.

I left the hut and found the village in the aftermath of the purple-clad priestess's successful assassination of the alien demon that had taken her people prisoner. How long had that creature dominated the people it found when it crashed to earth? If only they had known how weak it was, how much it relied on its precious armor.

A metallic vibration sounded overhead and I whipped up to see a slim pod with strips of lights all over it descend to us. The priestess marched down the stairs leaving the bloody throne and the dead demon behind her. She crossed the field and headed to me. She pitched the bloody dagger into the pit as she passed the town's well. As though unzipping a suit, the woman moved her hand through the air in front of her, from her forehead down to her navel. Her purple robe disappeared and a luminescent white being took her place.

The brightly-lit pod landed between my viewpoint and the alien priestess. A door must have opened for her. When the pod's base re-ignited and the vessel took off, the creature was gone. Had I witnessed interstellar justice?

The town bustled with villagers running to see the slain demon. I peered over the edge of the well. The bloody dagger protruded from the bucket hanging mid-air.

I lifted my hand to release my grip on the ruined brick and I flashed back to the rainy twilight at Chester's Roman ruins. I turned around to find Melissa examining one of the nearby pits.

"It's in a well," I shouted through the rain. "Is there anything around here like a well?"

"Yeah. I'm standing right in front of it. There's a little sign that says so," said Melissa. She pointed at a small plaque mounted on a new cement pedestal.

I ran to her. Where she stood, only a ring of stone showed through the earth. The original well had been deep. I kicked the dirt inside the well. My foot slipped into the shallow pool of muddy water.

"Can you pull it out ... you know, mentally," said Melissa, waving her hands back and forth over the brick ring.

I paused for a moment. I placed my hands over the well and willed the dirt to come out. The puddle quivered and belched mud. Earth flowed up and out of the well like a clogged toilet.

The sky darkened overhead, but I squinted focusing on watching the mud for a sign of the precious dagger. Wet earth pulsed out of the well in waves until a glint of metal caught my eye. The dagger! I plunged my hand into the freezing mud and dug it out.

"I've got it!" I shouted.

"Is that it? Is that the right one? Do we need anything else?" said Melissa.

"No. Let's get back." I said. "Now!"

Melissa swept her arm through the air. The silver oval opened and we jumped.

"We got it!" I thrust my arm over my head brandishing the dagger. I quickly retracted it when I noticed how much attention I drew from Kibera residents milling around the edges of our one-time campsite.

All my friends were clustered around Faith's old fire pit, which she had re-ignited after sunset. The night sky blotted the rest of the world.

I handed the dagger to Josh. He tucked it in his belt. It went without saying that Josh was the only one with enough skill to stab Ilya without killing him.

"Are we ready to go?" said Cole.

"Gemma should stay behind," said Josh.

"Will someone stay with her?" I asked.

"I can take care of myself," said Gemma through her signature pout.

"Your sister is right. You're our only healer. We need you safe and sound, not just for Ilya. More of us are likely to get hurt before this is over," said Josh.

"I will stay," said Mr. Mbele.

"Okay, final checks. Anyone hurt? Anyone have any questions?" said Josh.

Everyone shook their heads.

"Wait, give me a minute to see if I can still connect to Ilya," I said.

"You told us the demon got him," said Cole.

"But when Ivan was possessed, a part of him hung on, his consciousness. If I can connect to Ilya and warn him, maybe there's something he can do to help. Or at least be ready to fight for his life when the creature inside him is killed," I said.

"Do it." Faith's dark eyeliner had mostly worn off, but I could see where tears had streaked a hint of black down her cheeks.

"As fast as you can. If you can't reach him, we still have to go," said Josh. He checked his weapons one last time.

I ran into the trees, treading on bits of plastic and paper until I found a large acacia. I sat cross-legged against the tree, clasped the medallion around my neck, and closed my eyes.

*Ilya, can you hear me? Tell me you're still in there somewhere. Please say something.*

The fire cracked and snapped in the distance. I heard the chatter of indistinct Swahili outside the trees.

I opened my eyes to see Innoviro's old Victoria office, gutted as it had been when Melissa and I popped back in weeks ago. I took a step forward, listening. Only daylight from the windows lit the empty office.

Urgency pushed me ahead and suddenly the office came to life. Fluorescent lights popped on. Computers, cabinets, and chairs all slipped back into existence exactly where they had been. But the space remained unoccupied.

I walked back to my old desk. A pang of regret stabbed my chest. I had once thought I had the best job in the world. I had a beautiful apartment. I had a future. I swallowed hard and carried on to Ivan's office.

Ilya sat at his father's desk, clicking away on a keyboard.

"Ilya, is that you?"

Ilya looked at me, but there was no flicker of recognition in his amber irises. "Who are you? This is a private office."

"It's me, Irina, your sister. Your twin sister," I said as I held eye contact.

"I don't have a sister. Don't be ridiculous," said Ilya.

"Yes, you do. Listen, we don't have time. You're not safe here. You're trapped in your mind. You've lost your memory. We're going to try to help you, but you have to be ready to fight."

"Fight who? What are you talking about? Listen, if you don't get out of here, I'm going to call security. By the time he's done with you, you'll be the one with no memory. Get lost!"

I could see he was getting angry, but I had to try.

"Your father, Ivan, wasn't who you thought he was. He'd been possessed by an alien parasite as long as you've been alive. The demonic thing that had control of your father's body now has you. This isn't Innoviro. You have to wake up! You have to remember!" I shouted emphatically.

Ilya stood up with a surge of rage. "Get the fuck out of here you creepy little brat! I don't know where you get the nerve to come in here making up stories about my father, but I'm not going to sit here and take it." He stormed at me.

I backed out of the office. Ilya slammed the door in my face.

I felt my limbs shaking. Time grew short, but I had to try once more. I couldn't leave him like that.

I opened the office door and Innoviro disappeared. I was back in the urban sewer below the building. The dark wet catacomb was silent except for the plink-plink-plink of dripping water down a distant pipe.

A single hooded figure sat on a patch of cardboard, hunched over a book.

"Ilya? Is that you?" My voice echoed.

"Irina?"

"Yes, yes it's me! Can you remember what happened?"

"Not really. How did we get back to Victoria?" Ilya's voice quivered with confused fear.

"This isn't Victoria. We're in your mind. Do you remember giving yourself up to Ivan and Tatiana? You were going to try to fight the demon. It took your body, but I think you can still fight it. I'm not sure how it works. Maybe you have to stand up, call it out, and confront it. I don't know. Even if it won't fight you in your mind, we've got the weapon Ivan mentioned. We found the dagger used to kill Ulu's body however many thousands of years ago. We're going to use it now-" My speech was cut off by a swift yank to the back of my collar.

Something picked me up and flung me across the room into a puddle of grime. Ilya sat weak and confused on the ground. I scrambled to see the creature Ulu in his original battle glory, standing between me and my brother. His helm was gone and his glistening black head loomed, ready to strike.

*This one is mine. And you will die!* It snapped at me with it's mind. *Leave here now, interfere no further, and I will give you a quick death. Fight again and you will writhe in agony for years.* The creature's mouth did not move. His forked tongue flicked at me as he spoke. His glowing red eyes bore into me.

"No, *you're* going to die. We're going to send you back to nothingness where you belong. You can't have our world," I said shakily.

He moved towards me. I held out my astral arm, praying my telekinesis would keep him at bay. The creature marched effortlessly. I panicked and let go of Ilya's medallion.

Back in the urban Nairobi woods outside Kibera, I was alone. How long had I been gone? I squinted into the night searching for Faith's fire. I leaped to my feet and ran back to the campsite.

"Ilya's mind is there, but he's a mess," I said to Faith in a rush.

Her face crumpled with grief. She put her hand over her mouth. Cole put his arm around her.

"Then, we don't have any time to lose," said Josh.

Melissa swooped her arm through the air and a portal appeared just as a familiar sound beat the air over our heads. A giant snake bat dove down at Cole.

I lifted my hands to focus my telekinetic energy trying to grip it mid-air. The creature slowed until I felt a thick muscular tube knock the wind out of me sending me to the ground face-first. I saw a massive tail slip back off the dirt and into the air.

"Melissa! Use a portal!" shouted Josh as a snake bat dove at him.

"To where? You want to unleash these things somewhere else?" said Melissa.

"Faith, nuke 'em!" shouted Cole.

Jonah shot a high-pressure stream of water at one, but his target dodged. I scanned the sky. Over a dozen giant flying monsters were circling us.

Faith's stream of fire connected with one and the animal let out a cry of pain. It crumpled and fell to the ground burning.

"There are too many!" said Jonah as his stream of water sent one animal somersaulting backward.

"We need to retreat!" said Cole.

"I'll take us to Cairo!" said Melissa.

She swooped her arm through the air and her silver oval reappeared. Gemma ran through and the rest bolted behind her. Jonah grabbed my hand as a bat dove right for me. He yanked and I ran, tripping over my feet as I fell last through the portal.

Back in the alley in front of Tarak's house, rain fell hard. The once-dusty ground was wet and muddy.

Within moments I could tell there was something wrong with the rain. My eyes burned. My skin stung. Cole pounded on the door. "Tarak! It's the variants from Innoviro. From America. Are you home?"

Tarak's door promptly opened. Giorgio stood in the entryway. "My friends, what are you doing here?"

"May we come in? There's something in the rain. It burns," said Jonah.

"Acid rain is from the explosion. A refinery on the edge of the city had a large accident. News tells us all stay inside until rain stops. I have not been able to go home," said Giorgio.

"Another disaster. We should assume everything is part of *The Compendium* now," I said.

"We should tell Tarak you are here." Giorgio escorted us into Tarak's living room. "Tarak? You awake?"

"We won't stay for long. We can't. We've got to get back. We just needed an out," said Josh.

"We also need your help. You and whoever else we can convince to come with us," said Melissa.

"Hello," said Tarak as he entered the living room.

"Ivan is proving to be much trouble, yes?" said Giorgio.

"Ivan is dead. The alien parasite that had control of him has Ilya now," I said.

"That's terrible news. Of course, we'll come with you," said Tarak.

"Thank you. We could use those laser-beam eyes of yours," said Josh.

"Oh, and there is one more gift I hadn't thought to demonstrate." Tarak placed his hand on the mosaic tile at the center of his coffee table. His hand disappeared. He checked to make sure we were watching. He lifted his hand off the table and the mosaic pattern came with it.

"You're a chameleon too?" said Jonah.

"Dude, wow. Just like Max, back in the States," said Faith.

"Speaking of offense and defense, that reminds me, we've only got one handgun and two tranquilizer guns with three darts left. Can you help with weapons?" Josh asked Tarak.

"Unfortunately I don't own a firearm. It's too late to purchase anything in Cairo," said Tarak.

"If you wanted more guns, why didn't you just say so?" Melissa opened a portal and left us.

"I feel bad that we're asking you both to risk your lives, but if you'd seen what Terra Nova can do to non-variant life, you wouldn't hesitate," I said.

"Don't be silly, we should have come with you the first time," said Tarak.

Melissa reappeared holding a large wood box with a latch. She placed the box on Tarak's coffee table and opened it.

Three large black handguns and several rectangular bullet clips challenged us.

"These are all nine-millimeter semi-automatic pistols. If you don't know how to use one, don't try. These three were the only weapons left at Innoviro's Mojave station. Josh and I can both use a gun. Who else?" Melissa chose a gun and loaded it with a clip. Josh did the same.

"I'd probably crush one in the heat of the moment," said Cole.

"Giorgio and I will use fire. Tarak, you've got natural ammo. Irina can use telekinesis – and probably can't fire a gun. So, Jonah, what do you say?" said Faith.

"I've fired a gun before, but I don't think I'm a great shot." Jonah eyed the weapons warily.

"Don't shoot anyone who isn't possessed or trying to end the world." Josh passed a nine millimeter to Jonah who took it reluctantly.

# Chapter 32

"This portal will take us back to the woods outside Kibera. We should assume those flying monsters are still there. Everyone, be ready to fight," said Melissa. We all studied the floating silver oval reluctantly. Cole left first. Everyone followed until I was alone. I took one last imprint of Tarak's living room as though the image might help before I stepped into the portal.

Tarak's cozy living room was replaced by an onslaught of shrieking, shouting, and flapping bat wings.

"Burn in hell, bitch!" Faith shot a dart of hot orange flame at a flurry of black wings and scales. The thing crumpled and fell.

Another bat dove at me, its bared fangs and red eyes ready to draw blood. A purple-blue streak of fire came out of nowhere and struck the bat out of the sky. I looked over to see Giorgio with his arm outstretched, glaring at the fallen bat. He glanced at me, nodded, and found another target in the sky above. He shot another streak of indigo flame but missed.

I heard a gunshot behind me. A whooshing sound followed and a limp bat landed on the dusty earth before me. I whipped around to see Josh eyeing another bat.

Jonah knocked bats too with jets of water while Tarak's laser beams sliced into the melee. Cole plucked one animal off his back and ripped the thing's head off with a quick jerk.

I couldn't count how many animals were swirling above us, but it seemed too many to fight. A huge bat darted out of the fray and made eye contact with me. It opened its mouth and hissed as venom dripped from its fangs. The monster flexed its legs, two talon-tipped appendages that could rend flesh from bone. It dove at me, I dodged and fell to the ground.

The animal made a second pass as I scrambled. Two sharp clawed hands gripped my hair and pulled. I screamed in pain as I felt my scalp lifting. Something crashed into the bat and we tumbled together until a loud snap ended the grip on me. I flailed at my head detangling my hair from crumpled talons. I wriggled free in time to see Cole pull another bat off Faith.

The torrent of wings overhead dwindled and more shots rang out. I searched the night sky and singled out a bat for myself. The rage of vengeance was fresh in my heart. I raised my arms to focus my energy and I caught one.

The animal's body writhed against the force of my telekinetic grip, but I held it. I moved my arms apart slowly, visualizing the stretch in the animal's midsection. I concentrated on the joints where the wings attached to the body. I pictured a ball joint popping out of a socket.

I pulled harder and the bat wings separated from the snakelike body. The animal hissed and snapped as it fell to the ground. Its tiny little bat legs clawed at the dirt while its tail flipped and flopped.

"Harsh, honey." Melissa fired a single close-range shot into the still-biting head.

I felt my cheeks flush. I had killed one snake bat to a handful for each of my friends. A single bat swooped back up to the stars and Josh brought it down with three quick shots.

"Irina, are you all right?" Jonah had a horrified grimace on his face. I searched the sky. I listened to the night for those horrific wings. The bats were gone. Dead creatures lay in twisted lumps around us.

My adrenaline started to subside. The stinging in my scalp took on a more stabbing sensation. I felt wetness in my hair and I looked down to see my hoodie and T-shirt soaked with blood.

Gemma popped out from behind the nearby tree where she and Mr. Mbele had taken shelter. She ran to me and put her hands on my head. Her hands blinded me with golden light and I felt a tingling pulse all over my body. Without a word, Gemma ran to Cole next whose massive arms were both swollen and purple. Even in the dark of night, I saw giant black puncture marks all over his biceps. Thick yellow mucus oozed back out of the wounds as Gemma's light flowed into Cole.

Tarak lay still on the ground. Giorgio stood guarding him. Gemma moved on to them. Before I could see his wounds, Tarak stood up again. He took a step and dropped to his knees, weak, but recovering. I could only guess what the innocent bystanders thought as they watched a handful of people fight mutant snake bats and recover with what appeared to be magic. I caught my breath and turned to see if we had an audience.

Dozens of terrified men, women, and children were frozen

with fear and awe. My friends perused the small crowd that had watched our bizarre fight. Nobody spoke. Nobody moved.

"Listen!" Josh didn't have to fight to keep the crowd's attention. "There's a man and a woman inside Kibera who did terrible experiments. They made these animals. We're going to fight them, but they're planning to release a virus. It's much, much worse than what you just saw."

Jonah stepped forward, pointing to Ivan's compound. "The white man and woman in there are trying to make everyone very, very sick. Everyone will die. Take your families and go. Don't wait, just go now. Go as far from here as you can."

Not one person moved. I knew a language barrier was likely. Many of Kibera's residents would only speak Swahili. Their array of frowns, wide eyes, and gaping mouths communicated their confusion and shock.

"Can't you tell them?" Josh barked at Mr. Mbele.

He considered the onlookers gravely.

"Perhaps panic is what gives red boy and green woman their chance. We cannot have chaos underfoot now," said Mr. Mbele.

"We don't have time for this. It's already too close to morning," said Cole.

"Follow me." Josh marched to the nearest entrance to Kibera.

"Whatever you two do, stay back and stay out of trouble," I said to Gemma and Mr. Mbele.

"I will keep her safe," said Mr. Mbele as the rest of our group followed Josh.

I hugged Gemma and ran, not daring to look back.

The street leading to Ivan's gate was deserted. Between the

riot and the battle with the snake bats, I hoped the missing residents chose to flee rather than hide. As we neared the gate, four figures blocked it, armed and waiting for us. They raised huge automatic rifles, yelling something I couldn't understand.

"We don't speak Swahili!" said Cole as we approached.

"Lower your weapons or we'll have to attack!" said Josh. He stopped and held his arm out to restrain the rest of us.

Tarak, now fully recovered, pushed through and stepped around Josh. He shouted something back at the men.

"What are they saying?" I asked.

"They work for Ivan. They say we will be shot if we come closer," said Tarak.

"Obviously, but what did you say back?" said Josh.

"I told them their master is the devil and we've come to send him back to hell. I told him to help the people of Kibera and get them out," said Tarak.

The armed guards shouted something in Swahili again.

"They're saying that we have to leave Kibera and Nairobi immediately, or they will kill us all. If we tell people to leave, they will kill us," said Tarak.

"Irina, can you stop their bullets?" said Melissa.

"Those are automatic rifles. They're going to fire countless bullets faster than I can see them. I can't stop them all," I said decisively.

"Maybe you don't have to stop bullets. Can you hold them still, just as they are?" said Jonah.

"If they can't move, they can't fire," said Faith

"I can probably hold them for a few minutes. Long enough for someone to get past and go inside," I said.

"Hold them. I'll handle the rest," said Cole.

"Wait, we'll both go. I'm the only one they can't wound," said Josh.

I stepped to the front of our group. I lifted my arms and concentrated. I focused on their hands, picturing them made of stone, not able to move a fraction of an inch.

"Okay guys, go," I said.

Josh and Cole walked single file at first. When no shots came, Cole closed the distance quickly and folded each rifle in half one after another. The guards stood frozen by my will. I let go. They remained unmoving with terror in their eyes.

Tarak shouted something in Swahili and the men took off, running into the depths of Kibera as fast as they could go.

"What was that?" said Melissa.

"I told them flesh was easier to bend than metal," said Tarak.

"Let's hope Ilya, Tatiana, Rose, and Sage didn't hear any of this," said Josh.

"Remember, Ilya isn't himself. When we find him, nothing that comes out of his mouth is from him. It's the demon," I said.

Josh adjusted the dagger on his belt, reassuring himself it was secure. Faith's features crumpled briefly, then she turned towards Kibera with a glower of hatred.

"Okay everyone, before we go in, we need to get on the same page. We're going in there to kill Tatiana. I will wound Ilya to kill the demon inside him," said Josh.

"We shouldn't leave the hedge site unguarded," said Faith.

"Our two fire-starters should stand guard. And they'll need muscle." Cole eyed Faith and Giorgio. The latter nodded.

"The rest of us will go into the compound. We stick together. And no talking. I'm going to use hand gestures. I'll keep it simple. Watch for my signals when there's a door or a turn.

Irina, stay close to me. You're the only one that's seen this place top to bottom," said Josh.

Cole gripped the sliding metal gate and pulled. The frame creaked and snapped open. He lifted the metal door off the ground and threw it into the street, and then he, Faith and Giorgio ran back out of Kibera.

Josh led the way with his finger to his lips. My heart thudded in my ears. My lips were parched. I reached for Jonah's hand with my left. With my right hand, I picked up Ilya's medallion from where it hung on my chest and rubbed the tiny coin between my thumb and forefinger. In a last desperate attempt to coordinate with my brother, I focused on his face and tried to hear his voice.

*Ilya, if you're awake and if you know where you are, tell me now.*

We tiptoed down the corridor to the open room at the heart of the compound's upper level.

*Ilya, please help me. Help us to help you.* I begged the universe to let my brother answer me.

*I'm so glad you're here, child. I have so many lovely things to show you*, said the demonic voice I had come to loathe.

# Chapter 33

The compound's circular courtyard appeared empty as we approached the archway, barely lit by urban ambient light. Nothing in the dark space moved. As promised, Josh lifted his hand in a silent gesture to halt. He peered around the corner and stepped inside evaluating the rest of the space we couldn't see.

"How many exits?" he whispered in my ear.

"Two. One leads to a hallway of rooms where Ilya was held. The second is a short corridor that ends in a stairwell down to the lower level," I said quietly.

"Is he still in the same room?" said Josh.

"I tried reaching out. The demon was the one who answered," I said.

"Try a vision," said Josh.

I looked around the dark hall hoping to find an object or something I could grip to draw on for a vision. A rustling in the dark courtyard ahead startled us. Josh's hand shot out again.

"It's okay, traitors. It's just me." Ilya's voice was the same, but different. His words slid out like pearls on silk.

He stepped into view and I made eye contact with the red irises that had stalked me since the Capital City Motel. Ilya shot a tiny ball of crackling energy from his hand to my head.

The compound hallway disappeared and I stood in a forest under a bright purple sky. The trees around me were the carnivorous fly-trap pines from Innoviro's research farm. I saw floating orange lights like fireflies through the tree line. I walked to the clearing ahead. The fireflies were floating embers from a fire at the center of the clearing.

As the trees thinned, I saw a pickup truck behind the fire. It towed a flat-fenced trailer with a heap of cargo, like a harvest of something. The closer I got, the more detail I could see. The pile had hands, sleeves, and clumps of hair. Blood stains were dark on their clothes.

A glossy black-headed cobra man came out from behind the truck, hauling a captive by a chain and collar. It was Josh! A chain ran from Josh to another captive. Cole! How was it possible? What material or power did the creature have that could restrain these two? More lengths of chain led to more variants I didn't recognize.

Another cobra man dropped a basket of neon pink pods adjacent to the fire. The first cobra forced the chained variants to their knees and dropped handfuls of pods in front of each of them. Josh, Cole, and the others began to shuck the pods piling husks on one side and shining black spheres on the other.

One of the cobra men picked a body up off the pile on the trailer. He heaved it onto the fire which seemed far too small for the purpose. The fire flared up like a gaping mouth and vaporized the body mid-air. The other cobra man tossed a body at the fire with the same result. The first cobra threw another body and on it went, vaporizing bodies while the variant slaves stared at the ground, shucking pods.

I took an astral step back, trying to pull myself out of the vision. Where was I? Had my friends been abducted and taken to another planet? I turned around in the forest and saw the lights of a far-off city. I ran to another gap in the trees. Where the ground ended I had a view of a bay and an expansive stretch of coastline.

In the distance, I saw a vast ocean that stretched to the bright purple horizon. Between the water line and where I stood in the variant forest were the unmistakable lights of the Las Vegas strip. I had wanted to see Vegas at night and there it was, presumably with the Pacific Ocean on its doorstep.

The vision ended abruptly. I felt as though my mind had been released. I was back in the Krylovs' Kibera compound, observing the hallway ceiling. Jonah and Melissa's faces hovered over me.

"She's coming around!" said Jonah.

"Then it's time for me to move along," said demon-possessed Ilya.

I sat up in time to see the image of Ilya evaporate into thin air. "It's using Ilya's illusions."

"Then where is he?" said Tarak.

"They must be on the lower level, where the bats were kept."

"Was there anything else down there?" said Josh.

"Other than that open-air pit, nothing I saw, but I might have missed something. Visions aren't perfect informers." I sat up and nausea filled me.

"Let's go," said Jonah, supporting me as I stood.

Josh led the way. I sensed his unease. His military training had never extended to illusions and mutant beasts. I admired his attempt to lead confidently, but as we crossed the courtyard, I knew none of us were ready.

We crept along the corridor and down the stairwell to the lower level. We passed empty cages and reached the door to the outdoor pit. Josh pushed the door open and we found the bare dirt floor empty. We filed out into the pit, scanning in every direction. There were no windows or additional doors. The walls were simply a concrete cylinder leading up to the courtyard, the roof, and the sky. I knocked on the wall and it clanged like metal.

"Good thing we left Faith and Giorgio to torch the hedge. It's almost dawn." Jonah craned his neck up, searching and listening.

"Let's get back up to the upper level. We'll do a sweep before we meet up at the hedge," said Josh.

"Sorry to be the bearer of bad news, kids, but you'll be sitting this one out," said a disembodied voice I didn't recognize.

The door back to the compound's lower level closed by itself. From inside, the pit door had no latch or handle.

A man materialized in front of the door and a glimmer of familiarity struck me. He was older now, but still similar enough to his portrait for me to recognize Claude Mueller. He lifted his gaze to a point above the pit.

"Girls!" called out Mueller.

A flapping sound flickered overhead, not the frantic thumps of the snake-bats, but the more elegant swooshes of the harpy twins. Rose and Sage flew into view and spiraled down to us.

"It's not too late to stop this. You can still do the right thing! They're not creating the world you think they are. You're going to be slaves!" I called out to them.

Rose and Sage smiled at me, said nothing, and each took one of Mueller's arms. They hoisted him up carrying him out of the pit in seconds.

"You evil bitches!" Josh shouted after them.

"Forget them, let's get back up to the hedge." Melissa swooped her arm in an oval. No portal appeared. Her brow wrinkled. "What the …?" She tried again. Nothing.

"Try the door," said Jonah.

Tarak and Melissa each took a turn, grabbing the bottom of the door in the gap between it and the dirt. They pulled in unison, but the door didn't budge.

"Let me try." Josh's armored skin made him strong, but for this, we needed our strong man. The image of Cole thrashing Tatiana flickered back to my mind as I regretted letting him go with Faith and Giorgio. Josh pulled on the door and he too failed to open it. My pulse quickened. My vision would come true. Those bees were coming!

"Irina, try forcing it." Jonah tapped his temple to allude to my ability. "Concentrate, you can do it."

I held my arms out, focusing my mental energy. The increasingly familiar sensation of telekinetic force was gone, just as though it had never been there. "It's not working. It's like the ability isn't there anymore," I said.

"Maybe none of our gifts work here." Tarak put his hand on the smooth rounded wall, testing his chameleon skin. His olive-toned hand remained the same.

"My power is working. I can feel a water main underground. If I break it, I might be able to force the doors open with a pressurized stream." Jonah pointed a vertical hand as though mentally slicing the doors.

"And if it doesn't work we'll all drown," said Josh.

"I can tread water," said Tarak.

"What if you don't have enough control? Screw it, I can tread water too." The urge to get out of the pit took over. Faith, Giorgio, and Cole were outnumbered facing an alien-inhabited Ilya combined with the powers of Tatiana, Mueller, and the harpy sisters. With Terra Nova unleashed as a result. I'd take my chances with drowning.

"If whatever Ivan set up down here works on me once the water rises to this room, I won't be able to feel the water, much less control it. But I can't think of anything else," said Jonah.

Josh threw up his hands.

I looked down at the ground with raw fear churning inside my belly. If Tatiana and her lot killed my three friends left above, would they move on to find Gemma and Mr. Mbele afterward? Or simply let the chaos of Terra Nova consume them along with the rest of Kibera.

"Do it," said Tarak.

"Get back against the wall, all of you." Jonah reached to the ground, willing the water under the earth to come to him. The protesting howl of a metal pipe filled me with dread. A moment later, a geyser exploded out of the ground between us.

Jonah tried to control the water, but it sprayed unchecked. The geyser cut its opening in the ground wider as water fell back to earth. In minutes, the water was up to my knees.

"Looks like we're treading water after all," said Melissa.

We waited as the cold murky water got deeper.

"Shit! There's something in the water!" shouted Jonah.

"I felt that!" Melissa blurted. She shrieked as something pulled her across the surface of the water.

I screamed too as I watched Jonah yanked under.

"Something has my leg!" yelled Josh.

We locked eyes as Josh made a snap decision. He tossed the demon-killing dagger at me. The blade turned end over end in a flat spin. As I caught the handle, Josh was dragged underwater.

I shoved the side of the dagger handle in my mouth and tried not to gag, treading water as I prayed that my legs stayed free of whatever tentacles grabbed my friends.

A thick tendril of wet muscle shot out of the water a few feet away. I couldn't scream with a dagger in my mouth. I whimpered as I watched the appendage search for me. Finally, the water flowed up to the inner edge of the compound's courtyard.

I rolled onto the courtyard floor, pulled the dagger out of my mouth, and ran for the exit without looking back.

# Chapter 34

I pounded the ground as hard as I could, as fast as I could, running to the outer border of Kibera. I ran with the dagger in my fist, tucked upside down against my forearm. I raced to the tilled earth, praying the ditch remained empty. I rounded the corner and saw the abandoned sofa. The battle was underway. Faith shot a blast of fire at Tatiana but missed. Giorgio shot at one of the harpy twins and missed. Cole leaped to tackle Ilya and took a blast of electric energy to the chest. Cole flew back and landed on his ass, skidding into a pile of trash.

"Ilya! Fight back against the demon!" I watched as the harpies circled the fight. Sage caught sight of me and dove. I skidded to a halt and concentrated on stopping her in mid-air. It worked! Sage froze, wings outstretched, unable to flap or move a limb.

"Hello, little girl," said a disembodied voice.

Mueller materialized in front of me and punched me in the stomach. I lost my grip on Sage and collapsed in pain. I saw streaks of orange and indigo fire ahead. Cole darted back to the ditch as Mueller's fist rammed into my cheek.

A bolt of pain tore through my cheekbone and jaw as I fell flat on my back. I looked up at Mueller's face to see a bolt of cold flame engulf him. He screamed as he burned, dropping to his knees. He rolled back and forth belting an inhuman wail as he uselessly tried to blot the inferno around him. A moment later he stopped moving.

I got to my feet in time to see a blast of orange connect with Rose, dropping her from the sky as she too screamed and burned. Sage shrieked into the night feeling her sister's agony.

Demon-Ilya knocked Cole back again and Tatiana plunged her hands into the ground just as Giorgio took a shot at Sage and missed.

Sprouts shot out of the ground and grew rapidly as the hedge sprang to life. Ilya threw balls of energy at Faith and Giorgio, knocking them both to the ground.

Sage dove at me with wild rage in her eyes, but I held her again long enough for Giorgio to regain his footing and torch her with a huge blast of fire.

I watched her fall, thinking of Melissa's plan to send the sisters safely to Sombrio Beach. I hoped she and the others freed themselves from those tentacles, escaped the water, and were moments behind me. *Jonah can breathe underwater. He's fine. He'll save them.*

I ran to Ilya and stopped, flipping the dagger hilt in my hand.

Faith and Giorgio both shot blasts of fire at Tatiana while Cole charged Ilya once more. Ilya jumped to dodge Cole and block the flames, sending them back at the fire starters, and allowing Tatiana to finish her work. The hedge was grown.

Cole collided with Tatiana. Just as I'd seen in my vision, he picked her up by her ankles and beat the ground with her body. He whipped her back and forth muffling her helpless cries until he dropped her limp lifeless body.

Ilya turned his attention to the hedge and lifted his arms. I seized my moment. I jumped into him, knocking his body down to the ground. I landed on top of him. In one smooth movement, I plunged the dagger into his belly.

Ilya stared back at me with a crumpled expression of pain and confusion. For a moment, his features bore none of the malice of Ulu and I thought, *What have I done?*

"Nooooooo!" Faith ran to us. "Ilya!" she screamed.

Ilya's eyes flashed red and he grabbed his stomach. He heaved and the fleshy red tentacle erupted from his mouth. I darted sideways. The thing missed me by an inch.

I scrambled to the patch of dirt where the alien parasite, all that remained of the demon Ulu, lay writhing and twisting. I raised my dagger, aimed, and drove it into the flesh below the thing's tooth-ringed mouth.

Hot pink liquid seeped from the slimy red worm, but it stopped moving. I caught my breath. It was done.

A pool of blood grew underneath my brother. "Gemma! Where are you? Gemma, we need you now!" Faith cradled Ilya, hugging him hard. Cole and Giorgio watched, both recovering.

"You're all right. It's fine now. Gemma's coming. It's over," said Faith.

I heard footfalls pounding towards us but I couldn't see my sister. The world went blurry. Tears streamed down my cheeks.

"Gemma, hurry!" Faith screamed between body-shaking

sobs. "He's dying!"

Gemma's face broke out of the darkness and found us. "Out of the way!"

She pushed between me and Faith to reach Ilya's belly. Golden light shot out of her hands and illuminated the sticky pool of blood before it blinded all of us. I glanced away until the light died down again. It took a moment for my eyes to adjust back to the dark of night.

Faith released Ilya and let Gemma examine him. Ilya lay still on the ground, covered in blood, not moving. His eyes glazed over, fixed on the sky above.

"Did it work?" Desperation filled Faith's voice. She smoothed his hair back and kissed his forehead, weeping. She knelt beside him, bouncing with frustration, humming with anguish.

"He's fine, right? Please. God, just tell me he's fine. Tell me I didn't just kill my brother!" I paced back and forth.

"I don't know. I've never healed an injury this bad before." Urgent uncertainty slid across Gemma's soft features.

"You were too rough! You fucking killed him!" Faith rose, bearing down on me. "You dumb bitch!"

"You think I wanted to stab him?" I fired back defensively.

Jonah, Josh, Melissa, and Tarak ran to us all dripping wet.

"What happened? Is it over?" said Jonah.

"Did the healing work?" said Melissa.

"Not yet," said Cole.

"Shut up! It's going to work!" I shouted.

Gemma surveyed the rest of us. "We should give it a minute. Is anyone else hurt?"

"See if you can heal Rose and Sage. They were burned, but they might still be alive," said Cole.

"Don't move an inch!" Faith rammed her finger through the air at my sister. "You stay here and try Ilya again!"

"I'll come back for him. Don't worry." Gemma moved off and another flare of bright light ballooned beside us.

I didn't take my eyes off Ilya. I wiped my eyes and my nose with my sleeve.

"What about Mueller? Or Tatiana?" said Jonah.

"Fuck them. If they're not dead already, leave them," said Josh.

"Before we do anything else, Faith, Giorgio, you need to torch that hedge. I don't know if it's still a liability without Ivan's energy to bring those bees to life, but we can't take any chances," I said.

Faith got up and Giorgio followed her. She unleashed a rage-fuelled stream of fire that blasted the hedge into an instant inferno.

Another ball of bright light bloomed beside us. I heard wings flapping and I knew the harpy sisters had just left. Gemma rejoined us.

"All right, you healed the harpies. Now do Ilya again! Please, just try!" Faith's frantic insistence gave way to more weeping.

"I healed his wound. I don't know why he's not awake," said Gemma, quietly.

"Fucking do it again!" Faith angrily smeared tears off her face.

"Do it one more time," I said.

Gemma looked back and forth between Faith and me. Jonah put his hand on my shoulder. Gemma knelt over Ilya and placed her hands on his belly again. She closed her eyes to focus. Her hands hovered but the golden light didn't appear.

"If there's nothing for me to heal, there's nothing more I can do," said Gemma.

Faith took Ilya's head in her hands and kissed him. She closed his eyes, laid him back down, and began sobbing again.

279

# Chapter 35

I backed away to let Faith grieve. Jonah reached out to me, but I shoved his arm away. I pushed past Cole. I felt all their eyes on me as I walked out into the dark, away from Kibera, away from my dead twin brother. We won, but I lost Ilya. My nightmare came true. I'd killed him.

I dropped into the worn flat cushions of the dirt-coated abandoned sofa. I put my head in my hands and let the tears come again. Misery consumed me. I hugged myself and buried my face into the stinking upholstery.

The crackling of the hedge fire and the murmur of the city faded away to nothingness. I sat up and opened my eyes to re-orient myself, but I was not outside Kibera anymore.

The sky glowed light blue on the horizon. Color spread above me turning navy to soft gray. A golden glow rose with a fiery red-orange ball at the center.

I was back in the grassy meadow where I met Mom; her visiting room between worlds. And there on the patchwork quilt sat both my parents - my mother and real father - and my brother.

I walked across lush grass feeling it tickle my bare feet. I wore a sleeveless, blue and white striped cotton sundress that I recognized from my childhood, only now it fit my grown body.

"Ilya? Mom? Ivan?" I called out as I hurried to them.

"Irina!" Ilya stood and hugged me. He was clean, strong, and healthy. He wore a black Ramones T-shirt and his gray denim jeans. His amber eyes were full of life and his cinnamon hair shone in the sun as he grinned. He felt real, as real as everything else around me. This place had a tactile quality that my visions didn't.

"Where is this? Is this heaven? Am I dead, Mom?"

"You're back in the visiting room. I told you you'd find a way to see me again, Irina."

I hugged my mother leaning in and breathing deeply. I tried to drink in her essence. I didn't trust the idea that I could pop out to another plane of existence and see my dead mother any time I felt like it. I wanted to pull away to enjoy her smile, but I didn't want to stop feeling her arms around me. I felt safe and content, but at the same time, angry that it couldn't last.

"What about you? Did you die?" I asked Ilya.

"I think so. But they told me I have a choice," said Ilya.

"They who?" I said.

"We told him because we know." The ravages of age had reversed and Ivan was the father I'd never had. His complexion was sun-kissed again and his eyes sparkled as he took Mom's hand.

"The demon that infected your brother pierced a hole in his soul. Gemma didn't have the skill to heal him. But I do. I can heal his soul and send him back if he wants to go," said Mom.

"Of course he wants to go!" I blurted.

"I'm still thinking about it," said Ilya.

"What do you *mean* you're thinking about it? You have to come back. Faith is tearing herself apart over you," I said.

"Calm down. It's a great adventure, being dead, going with Mom and Dad. Finally the *'real'* Dad and the Mom I never knew - to see what happens to the dead. I've always wanted to know," said Ilya.

"Everyone wants to know! You're not staying dead, and that's final!" I planted my feet and crossed my arms.

"You could always visit me, here, the way you found Mom," said Ilya.

"I can't get back here on purpose. It just happened. Both times," I said.

"Sweetie, you could train yourself. Even if Ilya goes back with you, I hope you'll still come to us from time to time." Mom kissed the back of Ivan's hand. I wondered briefly where Darryl was, but it seemed irrelevant.

"Darryl can't move between worlds. He crossed months ago," said Ilya.

"Another plane of existence and you can still hear my thoughts. I can't handle this right now. Faith is losing her mind. If I have to go back and tell her you stayed dead on purpose, she'll never forgive me for stabbing you." I felt a flash of shame.

"My boy, go with your sister. You have a long life to live." Ilya considered Ivan. He gazed at Mom and then at me.

*Please, please, come with me. Come home. The dead will wait.*

"Do we have to go now?" Ilya answered me out loud.

"Time isn't standing still on Earth. If you're going back to your body, you shouldn't linger here," said Mom.

Ilya hugged Ivan, taking in as much as he could as I'd done with Mom. Ilya gave Mom a quick hug too.

"Okay. I'm ready," said Ilya.

I stole one more hug from Mom. I stepped to Ivan and took in the presence of my real father. It was as close as I would ever come to knowing him. His eyes had a twinkling energy I had never seen in the haze of my visions. He was full of love. I blinked hard to keep tears at bay. I hugged him briskly and pulled away.

"I'm ready too. Send us back," I said.

Mom reached out and placed her hand over Ilya's head. Golden light flowed from her and she moved it over my brother's body, stopping at his heart. The golden light got brighter until it was white hot. Light exploded from my twin and blinded me.

I fumbled in pure white light, trying to grasp at something, anything tangible. I woke up back on the couch outside Kibera.

"He's awake! He's waking up!" shouted Faith at the top of her lungs.

Hoots and howls of delight went up from my friends in the distance. I knew Ilya made it back too.

* * *

It was the perfect time of year for Sombrio Beach. Summer travelers had returned to school or work. Warm sunlight kept a cool ocean breeze from chilling us. A few of the canvas pergolas from Ilya's original camp survived the summer. We added a few more new tents.

Mr. Mbele had left us almost immediately in Nairobi,

departing as gruffly as he had joined us. Melissa returned Tarak to Cairo and Giorgio to Santorini, leaving the rest of us exhausted from the worldwide chase of *The Compendium*. We sat around another of Faith's roaring bonfires, protected again from onlookers by Ilya's illusory wall.

"We could leave the blame on that demon, Ulu, but that doesn't cover it. *The Compendium* was like any other group of evil shits. It takes more than one lunatic to navigate a fleet," said Ilya.

"Destroying Terra Nova was always the priority, but we knew it wouldn't be the end. Think of all the disasters they're still cleaning up out there," said Jonah.

"There could be more dangerous variant animals, more diseases, even, heaven forbid, more Terra Nova, hiding somewhere in a lab behind nothing more than a flimsy cupboard door," I said.

"I still can't believe we all came out of that." Josh sat behind Melissa with his arms firmly folded around her. Neither of them was the type to make declarations about being a couple. This gesture was as much of an announcement as we would get.

I was happy for them anyway. "Do any of you ever get the sense that it was meant to be? I mean, it all happened so quickly. Sometimes I think we won by chance, not because we were stronger or smarter."

"We won because you did something incredibly hard, and brave," Ilya said to me. He sounded grateful, backed by his intent stare.

"I don't ever want to see my man hurt again, but I'm glad you tried to kill him." Faith smiled at me.

Faith and Ilya were connected at the hip too. Faith had very little of her former rigid disposition. Since Ilya came back to life in Nairobi, she took every opportunity to hold his hand, kiss his cheek, or his lips.

And I knew that feeling. I hadn't stopped stealing glances at Jonah's electric blue eyes and wondering if he would ever slip away from me again.

Only Gemma and Cole sat apart, but that pairing was in the mail too. I'd learned to read Cole's face and I saw him eyeing Gemma the way he used to look at me. She blushed every time she caught him. One of them would give in sooner or later.

"When are we back on the road?" said Cole.

"Back on the road?" said Gemma.

"Irina's probably right. Worst case scenario, there are Compendium factions out there still executing orders for more disasters or just more gradual ecological damage. Best case scenario, there are leftovers from biological weapons and genetic development that could cause serious damage if they ever get loose," said Cole.

"I'll always regret that we weren't able to unravel *The Compendium's* agenda more efficiently. Maybe we could have stopped more than Terra Nova. All those spills and storms and earthquakes. The outbreak in Chester alone was horrific. So many people died that shouldn't have," said Jonah.

"We can focus on where we succeeded or where we failed. Either way, we are where we are. All we can do is keep going forward, ideally in the right direction," I said.

"I'll dig back into Compendium docs tomorrow," said Faith.

"We'll do it together," said Melissa.

I leaned in and gave Jonah a quick, soft kiss. I nuzzled into his neck and looked out at the ocean. The sun crept towards the horizon where the sea and the sky blended into a hazy strip. Jonah's body felt powerful and comfortable at the same time. I was too content to move. Now that we had our lives ahead of us, I could relax and enjoy the moment.

"Are you still feeling sick?" Jonah contemplated me with concern.

"Now that I'm not fighting to stop the end of the world, I think I'll bounce back fast enough." I smiled at him confidently.

# Epilogue

S hanghai's glass towers pierced the sky as we approached the downtown core. On a crowded city bus headed onto a river bridge, I saw a shore shrouded by bushy evergreens and fluffy deciduous trees. It hardly seemed possible that only a few months earlier this city had been the site of an enormous chemical disaster.

I felt through the front pocket of my purse for my pack of tarot cards. I wouldn't touch them directly anytime soon, but I kept them on me for luck.

"Do you think we should have made the trip right away after Sombrio Beach?" I asked Jonah who was seated next to me. His crisp white collared shirt and bright eyes struck a dashing figure.

"A lot of *The Compendium's* worst initiatives were unleashed ramping up to Terra Nova. I think the urgency died down once Ivan, Tatiana, and Claude weren't snapping their proverbial whips."

"This Jinhua guy, Harold Yu, might be telling the truth or

he might be covering up, you never know." Ilya piped in from the seats behind us. His new short combed haircut revealed a different, almost professional, version of my twin.

"I think he's full of shit." Faith had cut her hair too and now sported a blue pixie cut.

"He said he was being blackmailed to sabotage Jinhua's facilities and develop malicious technologies." Ilya pointed out.

"I'm curious to know why he wanted us to come to him," I said.

"I'll figure him out fast enough," said Ilya.

The bus pulled up in front of a modest square building of gray concrete and large windows. As we hopped off the bus I saw signs for an airline company and a health care office. A café occupied the corner of the bottom level. It was an ordinary building. I hadn't expected a sign. Evonatura hadn't posted one either.

"Are you sure this is the place?" said Jonah.

"What would that say? Jinhua Enterprises: A Compendium Company?" Faith smirked with bright pink lips and eyes black as ever with makeup.

"This is the place. They've got the top floor," said Ilya.

"You heard him up there?" I asked.

"He told me over the phone." Ilya walked into the building with purpose and we followed.

"Can you even pick one mind out here?" said Jonah.

"There's a lot of mental chatter in this building. But I'm used to it. And everyone's thinking in Mandarin. Once we're in the same room and he's talking to us, thinking in English, it won't be a problem," said Ilya.

We stepped off the elevator and found the top floor of the

plain little building surrounded by walls of glass. A faint harp and piano melody filtered in from an unseen source. A young girl sat at a large glass desk along the far wall. Rows of plush microfiber armchairs lined either side of the wall. Guests here obviously waited in comfort.

Harold Yu had been expecting the four of us. The young girl greeted us shyly, disappeared briefly, and reappeared with a platter of teacups. Jonah smiled and took one. The rest of us hesitated. Faith and Ilya eyed the cups with caution. I had an extra reason to be careful about what I ate and drank.

Ilya's frown suddenly turned into a smile and he picked up a cup, so Faith and I did too. If Ilya knew the drink was safe, I wondered if he already knew my secret. Probably. We took four seats together along the wall not bathed in bright sunlight.

"Mister Yu is finishing a conference call at the moment. He thanks you for your patience," said the girl.

"We're happy to wait," said Jonah.

The girl returned to her desk, followed by a soft tapping of keyboard keys.

"Is he really on a call, or are we just being fashionably delayed?" I whispered to Ilya.

"Whoever he's talking to, it's in Mandarin," said Ilya quietly.

"Can you pick out how many people are in this office?" Jonah whispered, leaning towards Ilya.

"On this floor? I can pick out six, but they're all thinking and talking in Mandarin. It's hard to say what each of them is doing. I don't see any mental pictures of hands-on science. If I had to guess, I'd say this is strictly an administrative headquarters," said Ilya.

The clip-clucking of dress shoes drew our attention. The

sound grew louder in the hallway.

"Good afternoon, respected Innoviro guests," said a small slim man in a metallic charcoal suit. "I am Harold Yu. Thank you for accepting my invitation. Won't you join me in my office?"

"Thank you for having us." Jonah extended his hand to Yu, who took it happily.

Yu led us down a long hall clear across the top floor of the building. We entered his office which had a view of the Yangtze River.

"Please, sit." Yu reclined in his leather executive chair.

"I don't mean to be blunt, but why did you ask us to come here?" said Faith.

"You haven't seen my endeavor underway?" said Yu, eyeing me thoughtfully.

I felt heat in my cheeks. "No, but that's not shocking. My abilities have cooled off recently. I'm sort of burnt out."

"I wanted to see you in person, to assure you that my association with Ivan Krylov and Claude Mueller was not a voluntary arrangement."

Ilya eyed Yu for a moment. "He's telling the truth."

"You had us travel across the Pacific Ocean for assurances?" said Jonah.

"How about an apology?" said Faith.

"You do have my apologies. And more," said Yu.

"More?" I said.

"I would like to hire you. All four of you, and your other friends as well if they are willing," said Yu.

"Hire us to do what?" said Jonah.

"He wants us to clean everything up, properly, with real funding," said Ilya.

"Are you kidding? You want us to clean up *your* mess?" said Faith.

I knew she saw the value in his proposal, but took offense merely to be difficult. I opened my mouth, contemplating telling Yu that we were all on the same page. My friends and I already wanted to take on this mission. We would make similar plans regardless.

"I want you to help me make amends for evils we all had a hand setting in motion. How long were the four of you Innoviro employees?" Yu gave Faith a cold hard stare.

"This would be paid work?" said Jonah.

"You will be very well paid. More than you'll be able to fetch in Canada," said Yu.

"What *exactly* do you want us to do?" said Jonah.

"I want you to share your Compendium documents with me and cross reference everything you have against our database of worldwide geographical events and ecological threats."

"So we identify Compendium damage, flag outstanding malicious projects, and restore balance?" I said.

"Essentially, this is my offer," said Yu.

"Why do you even care?" said Faith.

"He's worried about the bad fortune coming for him and his descendants if he doesn't make this right." Ilya eyed Yu curiously.

"It's not like we're working on anything else." Jonah leaned back in his chair.

"Guys, we were already considering doing this on our own." I had to share the concession.

"Sign contracts for one year and we can re-evaluate your progress and your interest in continuing after that." Yu leaned forward with an earnest expression, hoping to emphasize his sincerity.

"I'll do it." Ilya appeared pleased.

"Sure, why not?" Faith gave a small frown but stopped short of rolling her eyes.

"Can we have a day to think about it?" I said.

"I will have my assistant prepare the contracts. You can sign when you return tomorrow. In the meantime, I have arranged for you to enjoy a cruise on my private yacht along the river and to the ocean for a proper view of Shanghai," said Yu.

"That sounds pretty awesome," said Jonah. Yu had won over my boyfriend.

"Hang on, if you've got all this money, why did you let Ivan and Claude push you around? What did they have on you that made you do so much evil crap that you didn't want to do?" said Faith, her eyes narrowing at Yu.

"If I was willing to bend my company to their will to keep my secrets, what makes you think I would confide in you?" Yu sounded polite, but firm.

"That cruise sounds lovely. We'll see you tomorrow." I stood and put my hand on Faith's shoulder.

We followed Harold Yu's assistant's instructions to a nearby riverside marina. Yu's private yacht was nothing short of opulent. His boat sat moored alongside dozens of others, all slick and bright white.

We were escorted on board by two men in pale gray uniforms. The men seated us at a table with a crescent sofa at the bow of the boat. He told us a gourmet meal would be served very soon. We had the best seat in the house as the boat pulled away from the dock.

Shanghai slid past as the boat glided through the water.

"Did you ever think we would be here, living like this?" Ilya's cleaned-up new look suited the atmosphere. He took a beer from the cooler next to us, stared at the Chinese characters briefly, and cracked the cap.

"We're not living like anything. This is Yu's boat. I don't think we'll ever see it again after tonight." Faith accepted a beer from Ilya.

"Ever the optimist. Maybe this is the start of a great relationship. What if Yu turns out to be the leader Ivan wasn't?" Jonah gazed up at the Shanghai skyline, reaching his arms out along the back of the sofa in a relaxed pose.

"I'm going to take a little walk while we wait for that food." I smiled and left everyone, making my way along the deck to the back of the boat. I peeked in through the tinted windows at the boat's main quarters. I refocused on my reflection, my eyes traveling from my carefully straightened cinnamon hair to my fitted jersey-cotton dress.

Clothes like this would not last much longer. I turned my attention to the city gliding by. I had a lot on my mind. Where would I live? How would I make my living in the long run? What would my life become?

I sensed Jonah standing behind me.

"There's something I need to tell you." I turned to face his vibrant eyes. "I'm happy to get on board and work for Jinhua, but I'll need a break in about six months. May tenth specifically."

"What do you mean? What's happening on May tenth?" Jonah's furrowed brow suddenly softened and his eyebrows arched. There it was. He understood. He gripped the boat's railing to steady himself.

"How long have you known?"

"Since we got settled in your apartment back in Victoria.

When we got home after Sombrio Beach, I noticed I still felt sick the way I had in London, Cairo, and Nairobi. I thought it was stress, or something horrible, like a secondary Compendium virus. I went to a clinic and the doctor gave me a pregnancy test," I glanced behind me to see if we were alone.

"Wow, I just … it never occurred to me."

"It never occurred to me either." I'd already decided to have the baby. I hoped for a bit more excitement from Jonah. "So, what do you think?"

"I think it's amazing!" Jonah's face lit up and he lifted me into a crushing hug. "Oh no, sorry. I'll be careful." He gently put me back down. He put his hand on my belly. "Do you know what it is?"

"Not yet, but I know it'll be a variant. That much is pretty certain." I placed my hand over his.

"Can we tell Ilya and Faith?" he asked.

"I was just waiting to tell you first." I caught Ilya and Faith staring at us from a few yards down the boat deck. I could see from their faces that the announcement wasn't necessary. I smiled at my brother and he grinned back. "But keeping secrets from a mind-reading twin doesn't always work perfectly."

Jonah followed my line of sight and waved at Ilya, smiling.

# About the Author

Christine Hart is a metalsmith and mother who writes speculative fiction. Her backlist includes The Electric Girl (MG) and The Variant Conspiracy (NA) trilogy. Her debut Watching July (YA) won a gold medal from the Moonbeam Children's Book Awards.

She holds a BA in English and Professional Writing, as well as current membership with the Federation of BC Writers. When not writing, she creates wearable art from raw stones, vintage glass, and unique gems. She shares her eclectic home with her husband and two children.

## The Compendium (The Variant Conspiracy)

Irina and friends are scrambling to pick up the trail of Ivan and Innoviro. They race from Vancouver to Seattle and south to San Franciscio, hoping to recruit more variants - and stop an engineered earthquake.

All while Irina fights to keep her lover's unstable genetic degradation in check.

When the group reaches a secret facility in the Mojave Desert, they uncover a shocking new horror.

## In Irina's Cards (The Variant Conspiracy)

Irina leaves small-town life behind after a strange deck of tarot cards propels her into a supernatural mystery and a world of fringe genetic science.

Working for Innoviro Industries, she falls in love while uncovering the dangerous nature of the company's business. Meeting other 'variants' brings Irina closer and closer to a frightening plot that could threaten all life on Earth.

**The Electric Girl (Middle Grade Novel)**
Polly is trying to forget that her mom has cancer. Until a freak electrical storm and a unicorn arrive.

Sy'kai wakes on an orchard floor. She doesn't know where she is-or what she is-but she knows something is hunting her.

Polly and her friends find Sy'kai (Psyche) and two questions hang over their heads. Can an alien deliver a miracle for a human mother? Can a group of teens defeat an interdimensional demon?

**Her Experience Connection (Short Story)**
Anna is a stay-at-home mother, nearing her fortieth birthday. She is considering a transition either back into the workforce, or on to a slower phase of motherhood.

Until she is offered a third option. Another restless mother recruits her into a world of virtual escapes and customized fantasies.

Has she discovered an exciting new lifestyle? Or will she fall head-first into a bottomless digital hole?

### A Charmed Woman (Short Story)

Barb is a weary divorcée running a thriving vintage boutique on Vancouver Island. She uses her work to help her heal while she rebuilds her life.

Until a friend of her son comes to visit with an unbelievable story and a strange gift for her to pass along.

Can Barb take the opportunity to reconnect with her reclusive son? Or has his retreat into the wilderness reached a point of no return?

### The Crystal Miners (Short Story)

Paige and Randy are on their second round of pandemic-era vacationing. The first time, they toured filming locations around BC's Lower Mainland.

Now that they can travel within the entire province, they're touring weird properties for sale. They started with a former rural school and then moved on to a northern lake island.

Their last stop is an abandoned mining community. Paige is apprehensive. Are they in for one more eccentric outing … or something truly bizarre?

**Stalked (Sidestreets Novel)**

It's the summer before her final year of high school, and Amy and her best friend Elise are stoked about their summer job. Two months, no parents, a dreamy twenty-something boss, and a remote Vancouver Island resort. It sounds like the perfect opportunity for shy, artistic Amy to reinvent herself. But when her dream boss turns creepy, Amy has to decide how far she's willing to go to get the recommendations she needs for her future.

**Best Laid Plans (Sidestreets Novel)**

Robyn's family has always struggled to make enough money to survive. When Robyn's grandmother leaves them an apple orchard in British Columbia, Robyn thinks things will be different, but Robyn's father still can't pay the bills. He asks Robyn for her own hard-earned money and encourages her to drop out of school to work in the orchard. Robyn desperately wants to go to university, but to make a better life for herself, she'll have to leave her family behind.

**Watching July (Young Adult Novel)**

16-year-old July has been through hell. Her mom was killed in a hit-and-run. Her other mom packed up and moved them to the middle of nowhere. And then July meets the boy down the road.

Surprised to find herself falling in love and making friends at school, she starts to see the possibility of building a new life. But when it is revealed that her mom's death was not what it seemed, July finds herself in a world of danger.